THE CATCH!

The Catch!

by Paul Sargia

MILL CITY PRESS

Mill City Press, Inc.
2301 Lucien Way #415
Maitland, FL 32751
407.339.4217
www.millcitypress.net

MiLLCiTy
PRESS

© 2022 by Paul Sargia

All rights reserved solely by the author. The author guarantees all contents are original and do not infringe upon the legal rights of any other person or work. No part of this book may be reproduced in any form without the permission of the author.

Due to the changing nature of the Internet, if there are any web addresses, links, or URLs included in this manuscript, these may have been altered and may no longer be accessible. The views and opinions shared in this book belong solely to the author and do not necessarily reflect those of the publisher. The publisher therefore disclaims responsibility for the views or opinions expressed within the work.

Library of Congress Control Number: 2022922566

Paperback ISBN-13: 978-1-6628-6669-2
Ebook ISBN-13: 978-1-6628-6670-8

TABLE OF CONTENTS

PROLOGUE ix
CHAPTER 1 – The Catch 1
CHAPTER 2 – At the Park Tavern 15
CHAPTER 3 – The Next Day 25
CHAPTER 4 – The Big Splash 37
CHAPTER 5 – Uncle Gene and the Missing
    Heirloom 51
CHAPTER 6 – Recruiting Sir Steve 63
CHAPTER 7 – Out on the Intercept 67
CHAPTER 8 – Tailing Dr. Wilson 85
CHAPTER 9 – Waiting for Robin's Call 103
CHAPTER 10 – Robin's Ordeal 109
CHAPTER 11 – Michael's Prescient Advice 121
CHAPTER 12 – The House on State Street 127
CHAPTER 13 – Surprise 145
CHAPTER 14 – Romantic Interlude 155
CHAPTER 15 – The Sound at Carnegie Hall 169
CHAPTER 16 – The Heirloom on Display 175
CHAPTER 17 – Standing by with the Light 179
CHAPTER 18 – Dr. Wilson Again 197
CHAPTER 19 – More Irritation 205
CHAPTER 20 – The Dirty Blue Car 219
CHAPTER 21 – Dr. Wilson Takes Over 227
CHAPTER 22 – Under Watch at Home 239
CHAPTER 23 – All Through the Night 253
CHAPTER 24 – The Catch 269
EPILOGUE 283
ACKNOWLEDGEMENTS 287

Bayonne & the New York Metro Area

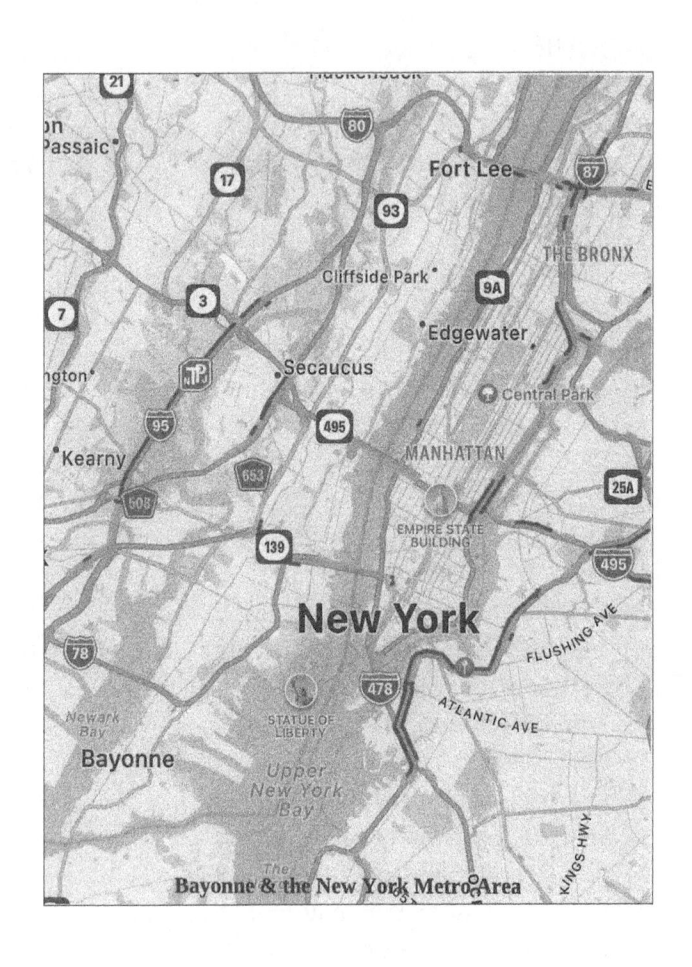

Prologue

October 1978

"Everybody shut up and listen up!"

Dr. James Wilson, in his fifties with dirty blonde hair streaked with gray, stands inside a living room in front of about twenty men who have been milling about restlessly.

He's of good size, fleshy enough to indicate indulgence in the good life, but not enough to diminish a devilish handsomeness. Most prominent is his air of authority, accentuated by his impeccable attire.

"I'll be brief. It's to inform you that it's almost time to move out of New York. We've done well here, but, at this point, it's getting chancy. The Feds need to be kept guessing. So, I've put together a plan for moving all our product and ourselves – yes, that means the *whole* operation – for when that time is right."

Chapter 1

The Catch

August 1978

Whoa, I'm awake! What the—? Crazy dreams again!... But the sun! It feels good.

Johnny Sloper, thirty-nine years old, breathes a sigh of relief as he opens his eyes to the light, the sun casting its warm rays across his sheets and a body, wet with perspiration.

Slowly he gets out of bed in his well-tended, modest Bayonne, New Jersey home not far from the bay and makes his way over to a window to bask. *Today's what?... Right, Sunday. Great! No need to rush. Softball in the park day!*

The expression on his face then turns serious as he shakes off his restless night in bed. *What's wrong with me? What's with the empty feeling I can't seem to get past? How did I get to this place? Did I bring it on myself? Maybe... I must have! I may be fit for a guy my age, but a feeling of worthlessness won't go away. One thing I know is true. Yes, that thing! I'm often pretending to be something I'm not. Can I stop doing that and just be me? Gotta think so.*

The Catch!

At the same time, not far away, in New York City's Grand Central Terminal, a slender black woman is belting out Amazing Grace as she strolls across the floor of the main concourse. The pure, soulful sound of her powerful voice rises to the cavernous vaulted ceiling and echoes all about as many of the early morning commuters pause in awe of its ethereality.

Nearby, within the same structure, an arriving train swooshes to a halt at the end of its track. Inside it, an aging man, with piercing blue eyes in a Navy captain's uniform, protectively holds a good-sized, steel case by its handle close to his body. When the train doors open, he steps out onto the platform and proceeds 100 yards to and through an archway entering the main concourse, still resounding with the celestial singing.

High above, sunlight streams through Seventy-five-foot-tall windows on the Vanderbilt Street side of the building and down across the floor he strides on. On the east balcony hangs the giant Kodak Colorama photograph, depicting a spectacular tiger baring its fangs. And, directly above, the constellations of the zodiac with its twinkling stars, decorate the smoke-marred massive ceiling. However, nothing seems to make an impression on him or take his attention as he continues to move briskly past the information booth in the center of the space, by the ticket booths lining the far wall, and then up to and through the terminal waiting area. Finally, he steps outside through the main doors and disappears down a sidewalk.

It's a beautiful, late summer day at Bayonne Park on the city's west side. The ball fields here are bordered by Newark Bay. For Johnny and his fellow weekend athletes, they are oases for working off the staidness of a week pent up on the job

Johnny arrives at the park by car, gets out in its parking lot, and takes in the sunlight. *Ah, this is great! Rejuvenating really. Fills me with a current of energy ready to... who knows what!*

Rabbit is already there. Just out of trade school, he's skinny, fast on his feet, and quick with a drink. No sooner do these two begin to toss a ball around than they engage in that old standby, mocking humor. When Johnny throws a ball that smacks into Rabbit's glove, jerking his hand and body backward, followed closely by a pained yelping sound, a bit of verbal repartee is now in order.

Rabbit looks scornfully at Johnny. "You've got to watch yourself, Slopes." He wears a headband to keep his shoulder-length hair out of his face. "You've got to be an example to us younger fellas. A real ballplayer doesn't have to show off like that."

"What's the matter?" Johnny counters. "Did they have to scrape you off the barroom floor last night that you can't catch a ball without screaming like a wounded animal?"

"Oh, no. Nothing like that," Rabbits says with a touch of sportsmanlike sarcasm. "I can take the pain. I'm just looking after your reputation as honorable old man around here. Geez, you've got to be close to forty. You've got some life left...."

Rabbit shakes his wounded hand to make the point.

"... but if you keep abusing it, nature will dump on you with one big lump. And nobody flocks to a disabled old shithead."

Johnny shakes his head amicably. "Who wants flocks, anyway?"

The Catch!

"Who wants to be a shithead?" Rabbit says matter-of-factly. "And what a loser, rooting for those decrepit Yankees!" he adds with a snicker.

"You watch! They'll make an enormous comeback and fool everybody," Johnny replies, overconfidently. It's mid-August and the Yankees are way behind the Red Sox in the standings.

"Fat chance!" is the laughing retort.

"Thanks for the critical analysis," Johnny says, faking being amused.

Johnny grimaces to himself, but only momentarily to prevent it from being noticed. *Okay, what Rabbit's saying might just be true. That's one for him. Maybe I'll even the score later. Or is that my pretend self-talking?*

Elsewhere, in the vicinity, a stubbly-faced, overweight man, in his twenties, trudges onto the field. Another young man, stretching to get ready to play, takes notice.

"Hey, Sir Steve! Saw you with Virtuous Vera last night."

The overweight young man identified as Sir Steve shouts back, "Took you by surprise, eh, that I took virtue in hand?"

"We could see you were holding hands, sir. Did you rub noses, too?"

Stopping in his tracks, Steve responds, "What are you talking about, you snickering loon? We had a virtuosic time of it, last night. She couldn't get enough."

Suddenly a voice booms out with a humorous edge. It's Johnny's and it's directed at the one stretching. "Why don't you leave him alone before we ask what you did that was so virtuosic last night?"

Steve, Steve. We're not exactly buddies. And I wouldn't recommend the way he takes care of himself to anyone. But the imaginative way he enjoys life with a disregard for what others think is something I've gotta respect.

Steve smiles, thankful for the support, then focuses his attention on an adjacent field where two uniformed league teams are playing.

Then, looking about at the motley assortment around him, including Hispanics and various other nationalities from different economic levels, he shouts, "Hey, we've got some great guys today, the perfect time to take on the Iron Keg boys. What do ya all say?"

The Iron Keg Marauders, sponsored by a local brewery, their uniform logo an overflowing mug of beer, is perennially one of the best teams in the Hudson County Softball League. Johnny and the others, who usually comprise their ragtag pick-up team, have played them previously with disastrous results.

Then with the antithesis of a winning spirit, someone says sharply, "And get our asses whipped again? I don't think so."

C'mon, I've gotta say something. That's ridiculous!

"Hey, don't fall for that dead dog mumbo gumbo, guys!" Johnny is quick to reprimand. "This could be our day. On any given occasion those Maroooodies can be mashed. We've got the muscle and the balls. If we forced ourselves to hunker down, damn it, there'd be no problem."

Instantly, the consensus is to face off against the Marauders one more time.

It's amazing. Except for that rascal, Rabbit, I'm like their revered, elder statesman. Whatever I say motivates them.

Johnny turns his back away from the others who don't see him frown. *It's getting old, though. The game is obviously a hopeless cause. But, now that I've got them charged*

The Catch!

up, I've gotta follow through. I'll just have to take the bluff down to the wire, then play the "martyr" when we lose.... Maybe the Marauders won't even play us.

Unfortunately for Johnny's surfacing conscience, an agreement is made to play the Marauders after they finish their league game.

In the meantime, two teenage girls hang around the field, checking out the goings-on while Johnny hits fungo fly balls to Rabbit in the outfield.

"Johnny," one of the girls, shouts.

Johnny turns, and suddenly it's as if there wasn't an encounter with a conscience. *Those sweetie-pie teenyboppers again. I can't help it. Gotta do some teasing.* "Eh, you're back," he shouts, acknowledging them.

"Of course! We want to see you dazzle us again. You were so fun to watch last week."

"Dazzled you? Are you kidding?" Johnny responds, turning on the charm and feeling his verbal mojo come to the fore. "I was playing with a headache last week. I really had to take it easy, but this week you're in for a treat. I feel so good, don't be surprised if I step up to the plate with a tree trunk for a bat."

The two girls seem to go into a swoon, having gotten Johnny's attention.

"And this morning I woke up with this spring problem in my legs. I'll have to make sure when I jump up to catch a ball that I make it down in time for the next play."

Rabbit, who's standing aimlessly in the outfield, sees his opportunity. "Don't let this old guy fool you, girls. Don't let him impress you with that spring problem bull. Mr. Shortstop's real problem is that spastic arm of his. I don't care if he bounces from here to the Brendan Byrne

The Catch

Arena, I just wish to God he could throw a ball to first base without it taking a permanent detour into the bay."

After Rabbit finishes his spiel, Johnny turns back to the girls and, after pausing with cool assurance, asks, "What's your name, sweetheart?"

"Darlene."

"Well, Darlene and friend of Darlene, I apologize for the negative attitude you just had to endure. My friend, Fast Cheeks...."

The girls begin to giggle.

"... err, Rabbit... who the hell remembers what his real name is?... is kind of on the serious side. Well, I'm serious, too. Perhaps I do throw the ball into the bay on occasion, but we're in a beautiful park, after all, and that's one way to appreciate its waterfront."

The girls just stand, gawking in silent admiration. Johnny, having evened his score with Rabbit, winks cutely at the teenagers, then turns back to the outfield and exhales. *Geez, I better watch it! I really don't need teenyboppers with puppy love crushes on me, do I?*

It's then that two other young men arrive on the field. One is the manager of a local bank. His broad shoulders which suggest a once athletic body, now indicate a deteriorating one as they slump down toward a molehill of a gut. He explains something to his Black, younger companion, who's lean of build and, at first sight, hard to gauge as he listens intently.

"Johnny, over there, is the center of attention here," the bank manager says gleefully. "He's a great guy. I'm sure you'll like him."

In the meantime, a naughty grin appears on Johnny's face, while watching Rabbit chase down every fly ball he's

The Catch!

hit him with the speed and grace of the creature he's nicknamed for. *The guy's too good. Need to take him out of his comfort zone.*

He then swats the next ball in Rabbit's direction, but, deliberately, not quite in his range, and bellows, "Better blister, Fast Cheeks!"

Rabbit fruitlessly attempts a diving catch, but the ball bounds by him as he lands sprawled out on the field with a thud. Johnny smirks to himself at having made him look foolish.

"Hey Johnny," a male voice, shouts.

Shoot! Did someone see that?

Feeling embarrassed, Johnny turns to find out it's his bank manager friend calling, whom he hadn't yet noticed.

"Thunderfoot! How are you?" he shouts back.

"Just great!" an upbeat Thunderfoot tells him as he approaches, along with the Black man. Both are in their late twenties. "How are you?"

"Couldn't be better," Johnny says, looking perplexed. *Why does he look so out of character? Thunderfoot, cheerful?*

"Who's your friend?"

"He's Michael. Michael, this is Johnny." *Those bright eyes. The serenity on that face. So uncommonly collected.*

Michael extends his hand to shake. Johnny seems to stiffen up, then shakes it. *Not very cool on my part! What do I say? This is unnerving! Why? I'm NOT a racist, after all.*

Michael speaks first, "My pleasure. Fred... uh, Thunderfoot has been telling me about you."

Say something! "I'm sure Fred has painted an impressive picture. Can you hit?" Johnny says in an unnatural, clipped way.

"It's been a while. Might be a bit rusty, but I think I can do okay," Michael says.

"Good. What position do you play?"

"Anywhere in the outfield is fine."

"Terrific, we can use you."

"Great."

"Well, that takes care of that," Johnny concludes, abruptly turning his attention to the adjacent ballfield where the league game was being played. *Why am I trembling?... You didn't handle that very well, that's why!*

Sir Steve hurriedly meets up with them. "We ought to get this thing going, Slopes. The Maroooodies are done over there."

A short time later, the ragtag pick-up team gets their wish, the Marauders making good on their agreement to play them.

The game starts off fair enough. Playing in anticlimactic fashion after another victory, the Marauders seem unmotivated and, amazingly, Johnny and his crew are looking good. Sir Steve's been pitching, and, so far, he's been unhittable while his team has scored twice after two innings.

Curious about Michael, Johnny watches him closely during his first at-bat. *What is it about this guy?*

True to his self-evaluation of being a bit rusty, Michael fouls off several pitches before finding his groove and connecting for a line-drive double to right-center field. A vibrant Thunderfoot yells out enthusiastically, "Way to smack that thing, Michael!"

Thunderfoot is ecstatic. When was the last time I saw that?

By mid-game things have gotten pretty dull, though. *Nothing's happening. We're not scoring and who would have thought the Marauders wouldn't be? They're bound to wake up. Gotta keep the charade going and revive the ole psyche-out routine. Keep the guys' hopes up. If the ship goes down, I'm not going down with it.*

Johnny starts off the next inning with a tactical approach to taunting.

"All right, you showboating Marooodies," he shouts from his position at shortstop, "what makes you think you're worthy of those fancy uniforms? I haven't seen one get dirty yet. You're obviously a bunch of momma's boys afraid to bust loose."

"What are you talking about?" comes a reply from a barrel-chested Marauder. "We always end up kicking your asses all over the field."

Then a warning comes from Rabbit, shouting from right field, "Don't get these guys riled up, Slopes. We're the ones who need incentive, not them."

Johnny raises a forefinger to Rabbit, signaling him to be patient, that he has things in hand. Then he turns his gaze back to the Marauder bench, a confident smile masking his foreboding.

"You kicked our... what? Now let's watch our language, boys. There are ladies here.... Well, I do recall losing a few games, but I also recall my clothes getting plenty dirty from playing fair and hard."

"You mean the same dashing look you're got on now, Mr. Sloper?" comes a witty Marauder quip.

Johnny, who wears a pair of old cutoff shorts and a faded tank top, broadens his smile. "Oh, yeah, it's the same all right. It's called style... and I wear it everywhere I go—to work, to play, and yep, even to bed."

This draws laughter from his teammates and the girls in the stands. The Marauders, though, are stony silent until one of them yells, "Give us a break, Sloper, will ya!"

"And that's why the ladies root for us. Right, ladies?" Johnny concludes, looking in their direction.

Over in the weather-beaten, green grandstand, which runs the length between home plate and third base, the two teenage girls look quite pleased. "Right... Right," they say in succession.

As expected, the Marauders remain undaunted. They are a talented and disciplined group and soon their lackluster play reverts back to high caliber. It's becoming an exciting, well-played game.

I feel elated, but something's buggin' me. It's my act, of course. Hard to control. So far, so good, as far as the game goes, but there's this Michael. Every time I see him – at-bat, making a play in the outfield, or shouting encouragement – he makes me feel uneasy.

As the game goes on, Johnny keeps up his teasing. After a Marauder, who is a personal friend of his, slides into third base with a triple, he shouts, "You coulda had a round-tripper on that ball, you buffooning Marooodie. You gotta bust it around the bases!"

And when Thunderfoot makes an error in the outfield, he coos, "Don't worry about it. Brother Slopes loves ya!

Then late in the game, after some seesaw scoring by both sides, Sir Steve comes racing around the bases and makes a dramatic headfirst, belly-whopping slide across home plate, sending up a huge cloud of dust which puts the ragtag team ahead.

Johnny turns to the stands, "Style, eh girls?"

Suddenly, it's the last half-inning of play. The Marauders, being the home team, are coming up to bat. Still, one run in the lead, Johnny's motley crew is precipitously close to pulling off an upset. He watches in near disbelief as his hyped-up team takes the field for the last time. *Holy crap, we may win this thing! My heart's pounding.*

In particular, he observes Michael as he calmly lopes out to left field. *What is it about him?*

Within moments, things get scary. In between two outs being made, the steady Marauders bang out a base hit and a double, leaving men on second and third. Another base hit will undoubtedly score both runners and the game will be lost. This is excitement of the utmost in their normally undramatic lives.

Out in right field, Thunderfoot appears edgy, almost terrified. In his desperation, he glances across the outfield at Michael in left who is already crouched down in position, relaxed and ready for the next play. Thunderfoot then follows suit.

Back at shortstop, Johnny is pacing his position. *We're going to lose. I know it, but can't let it show.*

"Okay, you showboat leaguers," he begins between batters, "Show us how dead you are! We've sucked everything out of you. You've got nothing left."

A tall and lean, tough-hitting Marauder steps up to the plate. *This one's a real threat! Gotta fake it some more.*

"Here we go. It's the lanky again. You're gonna hit it right to me this time. Right here!"

Johnny holds his glove up head high. "Right to me! This is it. Zingo! Out number three!"

"Don't listen to that crap, big guy," comes a voice from the Marauder bench. "You're our savior. A little base hit wins it against these no-goods."

"No, it's coming right here," Johnny reiterates, aggressively, again holding his glove up for the batter to see where he wants the ball to head. This elicits an angry stare from the batter. *Don't know what to think now. Is he rattled... or have I psyched him up instead!*

Momentarily, Sir Steve readies himself to let a pitch fly. All is quiet as he goes into motion and releases the ball. The toss arches through the air headed toward the meat of the plate. The powerful batter waits, ready to take full advantage of it. Then he swings fluidly, level to the ground, hitting it square and sending it off on a mean line drive in Johnny's direction. *I don't believe it! It's coming right to... damn!*

Within an instant, it's clear fate has intervened—the ball is rising. What, at first appears to be a ball coming at him about head high, is now spinning and speeding on an undetermined path upward. Johnny lets his instincts set his body, then leaps straight up into the air as he follows the spheroid with intent. But, as his frame lifts off the turf, it's soon apparent that his attempt will be in vain. Despite being stretched upward to his max, well into the air, the ball passes several inches above his glove.

Well, we've lost. It's over, and I put on a good show. All that's left is for Johnny to watch the outcome. And to that end, he twists his body toward the outfield to get a decent view as he tumbles to the ground.

Maybe it's how he hits the hard clay of the infield. Maybe it's a sudden dizzy spell from turning in the air. Maybe, whatever. Johnny is on his hands and knees

The Catch!

looking into a blinding sun and he isn't hearing right, none of the usual sounds around the ballfield—nothing from the grandstands, no birds chirping, no leaves rustling in the breeze. But he does hear something—beautiful, tension-filled sounds, repeated over and over. *High-pitched singing? Yes, singing as if they're voices of sirens from out of nowhere.*

As Johnny's eyes gradually adjust, he notices something in the outfield and makes out a figure running as if in slow motion through the brightness toward the gap in left-center field.

Soon he realizes it's Michael, and he has a beat on the ball. His body exudes calm and carelessness as, at the last possible moment, he gracefully dives and reaches full extension just as the ball lands into the furthest part of his glove.

It's the most incredible catch and, at first, Johnny wonders if it was for real.

However, when the sound of Thunderfoot's scampering feet, making their way over to the day's hero, and the words out of his mouth, "Way to go, Michael! Unbelievable!" reaches Johnny's ears, he realizes his senses are back to normal and what he has witnessed in such an unearthly way, really did happen.

Chapter 2

At the Park Tavern

———⊰⋅⇌|⇋⋅⊱———

The custom this summer has been for the players to go over to the Park Tavern after games, where the most important thing in the world is to analyze the game, followed closely by getting inebriated. Johnny joins them as they head there. *I'm not eager to do this today but to not lose face, I'm going anyway.*

On the walk over many players congratulate Michael. He modestly thanks them with an easy smile. Several others congregate around Johnny, still the kingpin of the group, and share their disbelief at the unexpected win. He doesn't say much, mostly nodding and making hand gestures in response to their comments. *I can't get over the weird way the game ended.*

One boisterous Marauder sidles up to Michael and says aloud in true jock fashion, especially so Johnny can overhear, "Here's the son of a bitch! He ruined the day for us and even showed up the Great Sloper."

Momentarily, Michael spots a Latina woman standing in the parking lot between the ballfields and the tavern. He then weaves through the crowd to get to her. Attractive, nicely dressed, and with an air of sophistication about her, she appears out of place among this sports-minded group.

Wow, he's kissing her—only on the cheek, but I'm jealous already!

Michael appears to tell this woman something and she nods agreeably. Then he walks her to a nearby car.

I'll be damned—they're hugging! If that's his girlfriend, lucky guy!

Once inside the tavern, it's dark—very dark compared to the brilliant day outside. *Adjusting to this doesn't help the strange feeling I have after that catch. There's too much chaos here—the noise is deafening!... Gotta take a pee. Great—a momentary chance to escape from this.*

Swarms of people are all about—at the bar, by the pool tables, and around the pinball machines. The only places less crowded are the tables and booths, soon to be overtaken with unrestrained activity as the newly arriving ballplayers make their way over from the bar.

Sir Steve raises a mug in the middle of the throng and with a sleepy grin exclaims, "To Michael, for making a bunch of badasses like us look good!" The other pick-up team players respond with some whooping as they hoist their beers.

When Johnny comes out of the men's room sometime later, getting a beer at the bar is a much easier task. A foamy mug is put down in front of him and he picks it up. *Ah, this is more like it—a brew to numb what bothers me.*

He brings the mug to his lips and surveys the scene. *Where is he?*

Noise and bodies are everywhere. Michael is easy to spot, though, sitting alone at the end of one of the tables.

Just as I imagined—by himself. Practically the only body in the place not moving—in a chair, or otherwise, still looking super-composed, like when he was going after that ball.... Okay, get a grip. Time to face what's got me unnerved.

Johnny approaches Michael's table nonchalantly. *Can't let him catch on to what I'm feeling.*

When he's a few feet away, Michael looks up. *Closer, so he hears you.*

"Michael, you're something of a mystery man."

"If I am, it's only because you don't know me," he says in a friendly voice. He gestures to a chair. "Want to sit?"

"All right, let's get to know you."

Johnny sits down maintaining eye contact. "That was quite a play you made."

"Thanks, I'm glad we had a chance to warm up before the game. Would have hated to embarrass myself out there."

Johnny just looks at him. *A very down-to-earth admission, not what I expected from someone who's just stunned me half an hour, or so, ago. But his presence, and the sound of his words, still make me feel there's something different about him.*

"It was quite a play," Johnny reiterates. *Already said that!*

"Thank you."

Do I mention how surreal it was—the blinding sun, the high-pitched singing sounds, all while seeing him carefreely make that winning catch? No, not yet. That was just too weird. Better yet, something else without sounding full of myself.

"I'm sorry I was so short with you before the game. I don't know what came over me."

"Forget it. It's not easy to adjust to someone new."

"I was being rude."

"You aren't now."

He's being downright agreeable, yet it's unsettling being focused on him. There's something about his voice, his manner. I can't put my finger on it. And I can't dismiss it, either.

"Say, why do all of you call Fred, Thunderfoot?"

I'm the one looking for answers. But, wait, I'd better shift gears. Answer him!

"That's right, you wouldn't have heard that before. It's our nickname for him in our little circle. Why? Back a few years, when we'd have pick-up, touch football games, he used to be able to punt the ball a mile. He always came through in the clutch!"

Johnny can't help but smile as he remembers.

"Fourth down, we'd give the ball to Fred and he'd boom that thing so high and deep, we'd practically be downfield before it came down."

"I assume he can't boom them like that anymore?"

Johnny pauses and frowns. "No," he explains, "not quite like that. Sad—he seems weighed down by life of late. I guess you noticed. Family, career, getting ahead, and all that. I'm surprised he even plays nowadays."

"Keeping his hand in, probably," Michael says. "Nobody wants to feel the exploits of their youth passing them by."

"I suppose," Johnny says, pausing again, "but he was altogether different today."

"Oh, in what way?"

"Alive... excited. Haven't seen him that way in years. And, he was super proud of you making that catch."

"I'm glad it did some good," Michael says with a grin. "Could have hurt myself big time on that play."

Odd how down-to-earth he sounds, considering there seems to be much more to him than just what he says.

"How did you meet, by the way?"

"I work for a firm auditing Fred's bank. We'd see each other in the bank's kitchen and got to talking about life in general and connected. Eventually, he told me about your Sunday games. Said it was an interesting group of guys. I used to play a lot, so I came."

"Glad you did. Never thought we'd be able to beat those guys."

Michael smiles not saying anything.

His eyes still on him, Johnny continues searching Michael for a clue.

Shoot, don't know what to say now!

Finally, Michael breaks the silence. "You know, I don't know much about you. What do you do?"

"Me?" Johnny sounds surprised.

That's good! We'll talk some more.

"I have a marina business here in Bayonne, renting boats and space, providing maintenance and storage—that sort of thing. We're open six days a week. Closed on Sundays."

"Sounds great. Been here a while?"

"About fifteen years."

"Married? Kids?"

"Neither. How about you? Was that your wife in the parking lot?"

"No. Close friend."

"Mmm, I'd get closer."

Michael nods and says, "Robin's a beauty all right."

"Why was she here?"

"The plan was to meet up at the park, then decide what to do. We get together fairly often. But I told her I was interested in joining everybody at the tavern."

"And she was okay with that?"

"Yep. We have a bond that leaves room for flexibility. We'll meet a little later, in about an hour."

"From the looks of her, I would have gone off with her, instead of coming here."

"There's a time for everything. I felt I'd rather stay here."

Johnny scratches his head, obviously intrigued.

"Why?"

"Intuition. Never go against it." Michael says, then adds honestly, "Well, almost never. When I don't, I always regret it. It's something Robin understands about me because she's the same way."

I've heard things talked about like this before, but never firsthand from someone who sounds so genuine.

A waitress then enters their space. "Are you doing okay here?"

Caught off-guard, Johnny realizes he hasn't taken his eyes off of Michael the whole time.

"I'm good," Johnny says. He hasn't touched his beer since the initial sip. Looking down at Michael's glass, he notices it's practically empty. "It looks like you're almost ready. What are you drinking?"

"Seltzer."

"Seltzer? You don't like beer?"

"Actually, I do, but it's mid-afternoon. I don't want to be sacked out the rest of the day." Michael says. He turns to the waitress. "Another seltzer would be fine."

When she leaves, Johnny says, "You're an interesting guy. Getting back to that other subject...."

"Which one?"

"The one piqued by the memory of your lady friend, Robin."

"You mean women?"

"Yeah. Women, women," he says with a certain amount of exasperation.

"Sounds like you've made them quite an issue."

"Oh, yeah. They come. They go. They're strange. They're wonderful. I love them. Then I can't stand them. I find them satisfying, then I don't. Yes, it's an issue, probably man's oldest. And it's very frustrating to me… I suppose because I'm getting older and haven't settled down yet."

"Maybe you're not meant for a serious relationship, or you're not ready for one. Have you thought about that?"

Johnny shrugs his shoulders. "I just don't know anymore."

"Perhaps you just need to take a closer look at where you're at."

"Just maybe you're right," Johnny responds, half-amused by his dilemma. "I know this much, though. They're great to have around, especially when the pressure of the grind hits. Then I just go, find a willing lady and relax. How about you?"

Michael subtly shakes his head. "No, not necessarily."

"What do you do, smoke wacky tobaccy?"

Michael shakes his head again without saying a word.

That's interesting. Figuring him out isn't easy.

"No, you wouldn't. You're not into drugs. You're not even into drinking beer after a game," Johnny says, doing his best not to sound judgmental.

Michael looks at Johnny, momentarily, as if he's carefully considering what he's about to say, then responds, "First of all, to tell you the truth, I'm more attracted to men."

Wow, never would have thought that!

Michael continues, "But don't worry, I'm not scouting around to find someone to quote, 'relax with.' I have more respect for men... and women than to view anyone as a plaything."

Whoa, that stings! And I'm probably not hiding it very well. Johnny looks down momentarily in thought. *Gotta stick with this, though! It didn't sound personal and he's still piquing my interest.*

"You're different, all right," Johnny says, looking up at Michael again. "That's pretty brave to admit being gay in this day and age, especially being Black in the middle of a rowdy bunch of jocks."

"For some reason, I feel safe telling you."

"Hmm," Johnny responds, looking unsure, "I'm not, you know?"

"No doubt about that!" Michael confirms, with an amused grin.

As Johnny grins awkwardly back at him, Sir Steve barges over. "Hey, Johnny!"

The intrusion visibly startles him.

"Sorry! Didn't know you were busy."

"It's all right. What's up?"

"Beer relays in back. Wanna join us?"

"Later, maybe."

"All right, I'll keep tabs on ya," Sir Steve utters as he scoots away. Johnny watches him go, taking in the tavern's boisterous surroundings. Then he turns back to the contrasting serenity before him, pauses, and says, "You should play with us more often."

"I don't know about that."

"Why not?"

Michael shifts forward in his seat and looks directly at Johnny. "I love softball and physical activity, but when it becomes a battle of egos and bravado, I find that atmosphere not worth getting caught up in."

I can feel the sweat rolling down my sides under my shirt. This is probably what I need to hear.

"I'm not sure I understand."

"What I'm saying is no one has to put on a show of bravado or flash a colorful personality to prove anything. There's a natural presence that people have and yours is evident without having to do any of those things."

"How do you know that?"

"Just one look at you shows you're brimming with life. You may not be happy with yourself, but something seems to be churning inside—as if you want to make yourself a better human being."

How did he know that?

"Johnny Sloper, just what are you up to?" comes a purring, female voice piercing the moment.

Johnny gazes in its direction and instantly mellows, shifting into flirtatiousness. Standing not far from him is a woman, and she looks every bit as alluring as her skin-tight clothing suggests.

Keeping his eyes fixed on her, Johnny confesses to Michael, who has already leaned back in his chair, "I'd like to finish this, but... a little later, a little later."

The Catch!

With that he gets up from his seat and dances over to the woman, a respite from Michael's stunning, yet welcome perceptions.

Sharon, Sharon—so, so sexy! Hard to ignore. Could the void since her separation need filling again? That wouldn't be so bad, would it?

In another part of the tavern, Sir Steve stands over a table with four young men on each side. Each is poised with a mug of beer in hand. "On your mark, get set... down 'em!"

One at a time, on each side of the table, beers are downed until the quickest side finishes first and the last man stands up, raising his mug in victory.

Minutes later, Johnny moves away from the bar with Sharon. Michael is still at the same table not far away.

"Sharon, I'd like you to meet someone I just met," he says with a touch of uncertainty.

Before he can take another step, however, Sir Steve approaches them excitedly. "Slopes, baby, the guys are placing bets on a beer relay. Four Marooodies versus four of us. Want in?"

"Only if Rabbit is drinking."

"He's our anchor. That means you're in, right?"

Johnny raises his hands in surrender and digs into a pocket for his wallet. "How much?"

"Two bucks. By the way, we need a number three man."

"How about you?"

"Not me, Slopes. I've had a continuous buzz since last night. Time to slow it down."

Johnny turns to Sharon. "The guys need me."

His eyes then meet Michael's and signals that he's headed to the beer relay table. "Be right back after this."

Chapter 3

The Next Day

Another morning. The sun has risen, but this time clouds hide it from view. Johnny is on his stomach as he opens his eyes in bed. He immediately closes them. *My head is throbbing! Another bad night!* Then he says aloud, "What did I do to myself?"

"Are you okay?" comes a female voice from somewhere overhead.

Wha…? Everything's foggy. Wait...

"Is that you, Sharon?"

"Of course, it's me. Don't you remember anything?

"Not much," he responds with a groan and slowly begins to turn over. *My head—dizzy!*

Upon completing the task, he sees a blurry Sharon hovering over him, barely covered by a sheet. A smile comes to his lips.

My! What a blessed sight!

"Mmmmm," Johnny murmurs, followed by "Oooooooo!" evidently experiencing a pounding wave of pain. He then closes his eyes.

Damn, wait for it to pass. I want to enjoy this.

The Catch!

Johnny reopens his eyes after a few seconds, the pain, evidently, receding some. "Did we..."

"Not really. You had a lot of trouble, Johnny."

At the same time, inside a New York City museum, the aging man in the Navy captain's uniform is looking at something. He's in a room full of exhibits. Next to him is the suave Dr. James Wilson, a good fifteen years his junior. He, too, looks with interest at what's on a recessed shelf behind glass. It's a spotlighted, sculptured figurine, standing erect, mouth open, either shouting or singing something with evident intensity. Despite being only 14 inches in height, the intricacy of the work to form the facial features and body posture can't help but elicit awe within the viewer. Besides that, its gold-plated surface, with encrusted jewels, glitter magnificently in the light.

"Yes, it's quite a piece," the younger man observes with understatement and leans in closer. "Oh, it's a Granville, a J.D. Granville. Must be worth a fortune."

"I have no idea how much, doctor," says his companion, Captain Eugene Sloper.

Still, at his Bayonne home, Johnny, now dressed for the day, combs his wet hair in front of a bathroom mirror. Sharon waits outside the open door wearing a man's over-size dress shirt down to her thighs.

"Thank God for Alka-Seltzer," he says. "At least I can go to work."

Sharon looks at her watch. "Aren't you going to be late?"

"You forget. I'm my own boss. Besides, you know I have Ralph, my dependable college kid, to back me up. He knows to get to the marina early in case I'm late."

He finishes combing and steps out of the bathroom and gracefully slips his arms around Sharon's waist.

She reciprocates by putting hers around his neck. Then, holding her close, he begins kissing her neck and right ear.

"Mmmm," he murmurs. "Too bad I have other responsibilities."

"Yeah," Sharon sighs, breathily.

Johnny continues kissing her, moving on to a cheek, nose, and forehead—short, soft little nibbles of lustfulness.

"You sure wanted to finish your conver-.... Oh, that feels good!"

"Conversation?"

"Yeahhhh," Sharon says, obviously aroused.

"What conversation?" Johnny asks, continuing to nibble.

"With the guy at the tavern yesterday."

"Oh… that's just a vague memory now."

"He won't be a memory when he shows up at the marina for lunch."

Johnny stops kissing. "What?"

Wham! It feels like a wave of locked-away guilt just knocked me on my butt!

Sharon steps back. "More memory loss?"

"Tell me!"

"You insisted he come for lunch today. You could barely walk after those beer games, but you made sure he didn't leave until you set something up."

"Yeah…, I think…"

"Have you forgotten? Your friends were practically carrying you out of the tavern when you broke away from them. Then you put your arm around this guy saying," Sharon imitates a drunken Johnny. "'I'm sorry, buddy. Ole Slopes didn't mean to break his word. Let me rectify this, okay babe?' I ended up driving you home in your car."

Johnny stares out into space.

How could I forget all that? Disturbing, really disturbing!

"Yeah... it's coming back, slowly."

Minutes later, the sun is no longer behind clouds as Johnny steps out of his home for the drive to the marina. Sharon, noting the change in him and the weather, decides to leave on her own. "A walk in the sunshine will do me good," is how she puts it.

The marina is just a mile away. Located on the Upper New York Bay, just south of the Statue of Liberty and the southern tip of Manhattan, it's an ideal spot for boaters. Besides its closeness to the Lady of the Harbor, it makes for easy passage to all points around the Big Apple, which is surrounded by the Hudson, Harlem, and East Rivers. It also provides easy access to the Atlantic Ocean, which borders the southern part of Long Island and the coast of New Jersey.

When Johnny arrives, he pulls his well-kept, '64, steel blue, Ford *Falcon* convertible into the sandy marina parking lot. To him, getting the lot paved would spoil the impression of water and adventure beyond the marina's tiny office building, dock, and accompanying boathouse.

He gets out and walks past the large, hand-painted sign, announcing "Johnny's Bayonne Marina" and to the office's front entrance.

Once inside, he crosses the office to its bayside back-door and goes out onto a deck and over to its railing. There, he further clears the last vestiges of his hangover by taking a deep breath of fresh air. Then he surveys the bay, looking resplendent as it reflects the bright morning sun. To one side, accessible from the deck, is a wooden walkway that zigzags down to the dock, and the boats moored below.

The Next Day

Johnny then looks over toward the large boathouse just down from the dock and set back from a sandy part of the shore. He notices that the doors are open and smiles.

Dutiful Ralph is already on the job, just as I figured.

From there he returns to the office—slightly more than a one-room shack with a bathroom, and observes how neat and well-maintained it is.

Great, everything's in order. Just the way it should be.

After making coffee in his reliable Mr. Coffee machine, with Joe DiMaggio's stamp of approval, he settles down at his desk. In front of him is a large picture window giving him a great view of the bay beyond the marina. The panorama is an aesthetic pleasure he only has to look up to enjoy, which he does whenever he feels too bogged down with paperwork.

Not long after, Ralph comes in for a short visit and is thanked for being on time. As for Johnny, "I got a little hung up this morning," he explains, without mentioning that he was hung over.

Ralph is twenty and Johnny's sole help. "The Empire's in fine shape," he reports. "Just the usual cleaning to take care of."

The Empire is their term for the marina, an example of the relaxed, yet proud attitude they have toward the object of their efforts.

After Ralph leaves, Johnny checks the time on his nautically-themed wall clock. It's just after eleven a.m.

Michael coming soon makes me edgy, especially considering all that went on after Sharon showed up yesterday. But I've got this yearning to meet something unknown face to face. His coming could be it. Nothing to do with him being gay. I'm comfortable with my own heterosexuality.

The Catch!

It's what's behind the calm demeanor he exudes. It seems to run very deep in him, something I've never quite experienced before in someone. I'm nervous but eager to get the most out of the visit. Is this me talking?

At one point Johnny's interrupted by a staticky voice calling his name. He snatches the walkie-talkie on his desk. "Go ahead, Ralph."

"The *Harbor Mist* is all set. What's next?"

"How about doing a number on the *Intercept*?"

"My favorite chore on the empire!" Ralph replies with gleeful sarcasm. The *Intercept*, a good-sized cabin cruiser, is Johnny's prized possession among his fleet of vessels. It also takes longer than any other boat to get shipshape between trips out to sea.

Johnny grins to himself and puts down the walkie-talkie.

The kid's always a nice break from the routine.

As the noon hour approaches, he gets up repeatedly and glances out the window on the front door. Finally, he sees Michael getting out of a car in the parking lot wearing a suit. It's a good opportunity to observe him without being noticed.

That he's a fit-looking, young Black man isn't so unusual. That there's no clue that he's gay is unusual, at least compared to how I've seen gays in movies and on TV. But, more importantly, there it is again—that contentment in his eyes! I've gotta know what that's about. Back to my desk, though! Don't need to be seen watching him!

Across the Hudson in Manhattan, it's a swank place. It's here that the scent of an exceptional cologne leaves a trail behind the maître d' as he escorts two men to a spot near a potted Ficus tree. A rose in a narrow crystal vase is centered on their table which is covered with a fine linen cloth. And the place settings all have silver cutlery with linen napkins folded into designs with a flourish.

After being seated and receiving coffee from a silver pot, Captain Sloper raises his cup of fine white porcelain and says, "Ah, a step up from the officer's club. Imagine... lunch in a place like this! You are a man of fine taste, doctor."

Dr. Wilson looks with indulgent pride at the fineness of the cup he holds in his hand. "Yes, my medical research affords me the luxury of being in the city." His words are fringed with icy self-absorption. "It's an opportunity I take full advantage of."

"Tell me more about your medical research."

"I'm afraid it's under wraps. You know how it is. If you reveal too much too soon, the public gets excited and the media makes a big to-do about it. That can be quite a blow to a project if what you've been working on doesn't meet people's expectations soon enough."

"I perfectly understand."

"Why don't we talk about your heirloom, instead."

Back at the marina, Johnny springs up from his desk as his guest enters his office. "Ah-ha, Michael! Glad you could make it. Nice suit!"

"Thank you! My usual work attire. How are you feeling today?"

Johnny cringes. "Fine... Alka-Seltzer came to the rescue."

"Good ole Alka-Seltzer."

"I guess I looked pretty foolish when you last saw me."

"No worries. I never judge people on first impressions."

"You say that as if you mean it."

"I do."

The Catch!

Another surprise. Didn't expect indulgence! What do I say now?

Michael fills the gap by gesturing out the window over Johnny's desk, "It's really beautiful out there today!"

"Let's eat outside then."

A few minutes later, the two men are out on the deck. Ralph is in sight, scrubbing the bow of the *Intercept*.

"Ralph," Johnny shouts.

Ralph stops what he's doing and looks their way.

"I ordered a pizza at Dominick's. Can you pick it up?"

Ralph looks relieved to have his favorite job on the empire interrupted. "You got it, boss."

"That's impressive," Michael observes.

"What do you mean?"

"You didn't have to order him."

"Oh, that. He's a good kid. The respect is mutual."

Michael nods approvingly.

Moments later, the two men sit at a small, weather-beaten table with its umbrella up, facing the bay.

"What a beautiful place," Michael begins. "I live nearby in Jersey City, but rarely get a chance to see the water like this. Is this all yours?"

"No, not everything. I own several boats—some are being paid off. Most are rented by the hour, except the cabin cruiser, which Ralph's been cleaning. That's at a day rate. The rest of the boats belong to people who have leased slip space. The office is mine. I had it built and even pitched in during its construction. The space on the pier is leased, though. Uncle Sam owns it. It used to be Navy property, but my Uncle Gene, the captain, was able to negotiate a generous deal for me to set up here. He was also my guardian after my parents died in a car accident when I was a teenager."

"Sorry to hear that about your parents.... Your Uncle Gene must be pretty special, being there for you."

Johnny grimaces. "What he did was the best kick-in-the-pants I ever got. Got me into gear with a career when I was floundering, but I wouldn't call him pretty special."

"How come?"

"I don't think he's ever cared about anything other than the almighty flag and the dignity of the family name. I think it's more important to him to be able to tell his cronies that all his relations are successful—a matter of misplaced pride if you ask me."

There's a considered pause before Michael says anything. "Well, you're here and doing well, I assume?"

Right there—he did it again! Steering the conversation in a more positive direction.

Johnny swallows hard. "True. Business has been good," he concurs. "You're a glass-half-full type of guy," he goes on to acknowledge. "A straight shooter, too."

"Huh?"

"For example: what you said just before my friend Sharon stopped by yesterday."

A modest, baffled grin appears on Michael's face. "What the heck did I say?"

This briefly relaxes Johnny and he forces a laugh. "It's what made the biggest impression on me! Something about there being no need for bravado. Just be natural. It sounded correct, but..." he shrugs his shoulders.

"Oh, right. Why bring extra attention to yourself? It can come across as ego inflation and anything inflated is subject to bursting is how I look at it. Know what I mean?"

"You don't like that I'm a bit of a showboat?"

"Whether I like, or dislike anyone's behavior is beside the point. It's for you to decide whether it's good for you or not. I can't be the judge of that."

Now I'm the one who's impressed. Need to hear more like this.

However, just then two tanned and attractive young women come out the back door onto the deck. Michael sees that something has caught Johnny's attention and looks in that direction.

My newly-awakened conscience tells me to be careful, but, God, are they ever beautiful!

"I'll be right back, Michael," Johnny says. "Business." Then he greets the ladies with a smile and an extra abundance of charm, "Hi Melinda! Hi Janice!"

Michael waits while he escorts them back inside the office. After a minute or so, they all come back out with a set of keys. Johnny leads the women out to the dock and helps them into a speedboat. He continues his assistance until Melinda and Janice are wearing life jackets and ready to go. Finally, he unties the boat from its moorings and pushes them off just before the engine sputters to life and they speed out into the bay.

Johnny is grinning from ear to ear when he returns to Michael. "Good-looking bait, huh?" he says with too much of a swaggering air and sits back down.

"Attractive," Michael says, aloofly.

I get his drift, but I can justify my enthusiasm. "Sorry, it just seems to be part of human nature to be looking."

"But why think of them as bait?" Michael questions. "I'm sure they have more going for them than good looks."

The Next Day

Johnny frowns. "Hmm, covered this yesterday, didn't we?"

"It's my turn to be sorry," Michael says, backing off. "We can talk about something else…heard you're a big Yankee fan."

"I am!" Johnny says, sounding pleased. *I'm dumbfounded at the way he can make a jarring point without pressing the issue.*

It's not long before Ralph is back with the pizza and the three of them eat and chat amicably among themselves. Ralph in particular is engaging as he drives the talk due to his fresh perspective on life at his age. When lunch is finished all three have responsibilities to return to and Michael leaves, but not before they all wish each other well and express their desires to keep in touch.

An hour or so later, Melinda and Janice return, their tanned skin freshly adorned with a radiant glow from the afternoon's activity in the sun. As they settle up with Johnny in the office, he can't help but silently appreciate their beauty, their young bodies exuding raw sensuality.

As Melinda hands back the speedboat's keys, Johnny inquires, doing his best to hold back on the charm, "How was your excursion today, ladies?"

"Just beautiful," Melinda says as if the words are being exhaled sexily, rather than spoken.

"It was great! The bay is so gorgeous today," Janice concurs with a delicious smile.

Their allure is too much for Johnny to not remark on. "Ah, but the bay takes second place compared to the two of you."

Janice's smile gets more enticingly delicious as she shifts her body into an I've-just-been-flattered pose. "You're so sweet!"

Melinda doesn't shift. She twinkles her baby blues and adds to the scintillating conversation, "You're too much, Johnny!"

Johnny holds out a receipt for their payment, but Janice waves it away, "We don't need that, but come think of it, we could use you. How would you like to be a splash at our pool party Friday night?" The smiles on both ladies enhance the already beguiling offer.

The somewhat purifying effect of being around Michael seems counter to the sensual impulses I'm feeling. Gotta be cautious here.

"Sounds great... but I'm not sure. I'll have to let you know. Okay?"

The two women echo their okays as they sashay out the door still oozing their sexiness, seeming to say, 'you'll come because we've irresistible.'

That night Johnny is home by himself. In the semi-darkness of his den, he pours cognac into a glass. *Why am I feeling so somber? I can't remember the last time I wanted to be alone.* He moves over to a window and takes a sip of his cognac, then stares out at nothing. *Don't be stupid. Of course, you know why. It's because of Michael and the things he's saying that are stirring me up.*

Chapter 4

The Big Splash

*G*reat, *another sunny day!*
It's the next morning. Johnny has just awoken and sits at the edge of his bed. *That uneasy feeling I had last night—it seems like it occurred to someone else.*

He stands up and stretches.

The pool party! The pool party! What am I going to do about that? Gotta decide. Oh yeah, the thought of Melinda and Janice in their bathing suits—mm, mm, mm! Not the best reason to go, though, is it?

On the other hand, it's good to relax once in a while, especially after a week's work. Whatever gave me the idea that going to a pool party would be a bad thing in the first place? Am I not already on the road to some sort of new life, just by noting a need for change? A smile breaks out on his face and gets bigger and bigger.

Later at the office, after taking care of the day's preliminaries, Johnny picks up the phone and calls Janice, "I'll be there Friday," he says with definiteness.

When Friday arrives, the air is heavier. The sun still beats down but through a dense, hazy smog. Johnny had begun his work day feeling upbeat and full of anticipation for the party ahead. Now, as he's about to leave the marina, the air is reaching its apex of weightiness and foulness and again he feels an unidentified nagging sensation.

Is the bad air a sign? Have I covered up something that needs to be looked at? All right, it's good to question these things, but I don't know. Don't be so analytical! You never know—tonight could hold a lot of promise. Why get all guilty? Just go with it. Who knows what thrill might be in store? Actually, what I'm feeling is like a yellow blinking light. That's right—you may slow down at one, but rarely is there a need to stop.

Johnny needs a bathing suit, so he stops at a department store on his way home. There, he scans the aisles and makes his way to menswear. As he walks, he can't help but notice the admiring glances of a couple of women. They do double-takes at his well-put-together physique.

Cool! For someone almost forty I've still got it going on. But let's get this straight. Staying in shape is no longer just to please the ladies, or to stay competitive in sports. It goes deeper than that, right? Total well-being, which gets bandied about in those self-help circles these days, is more like it!

Once in menswear, he notices that long johns and heavy wool socks are beginning to dominate rack space for the coming onset of fall and winter.

Ah, another sign that things are meant to change, not stay the same.

Then he begins going through what's left on the bathing suit rack for men, checking them out one at a time, dismissing the real conservative and the very splashy ones.

At one point, he pulls out an outrageous Speedo-type emblazoned with the same slogan of a popular fast-food chain, "HOME OF THE COLOSSUS," on its front. He quickly puts it back, though, when he notices a matronly woman not pleased with the short-lived look on his face at the thought of owning it.

"I'm as outraged as you, ma'am. No way would I buy one of these!"

C'mon, lady, do I look like a sleazeball?... Well, maybe I just did.

She gives him a scrutinizing look and moves on.

At the checkout, Johnny is more than a little satisfied with his final choice of a modest, Hawaiian-patterned, boxer style. This prompts the checker to say, "Boy, you look happy today."

Good sign! Maybe life IS changing for me.

The evening is as welcoming as any evening following a hot, sticky day would. With the coming darkness, the air has cooled, allowing the moisture in it to feel refreshing against one's skin. The harshness of the overbearing sunlight, glaring through the haze, is now softened by developing shadows, creating a more relaxed atmosphere.

Due to the combination of buying the suit before heading home, talking business over the phone with Ralph, who stayed to shut down the marina for the day, and getting ready to go out, Johnny is late for the start of the party. Now, as he finally approaches the house shared by Melinda and Janice, he's ready to have a good time. Music and chatter can be heard and light can be seen above the roof, permeating the blackened sky from out back where the pool is. The interior of the house seems mostly dark with a yellow porch light outside. Under his breath, he says out loud, "I can't believe it's yellow. It's not blinking, but it is yellow!"

The Catch!

He rings the doorbell and to his surprise, Melinda immediately swings the door open. She's wearing a deep-plunging, Lycra bathing suit. *What do you know, all lights suddenly look green.*

This is confirmed when, without saying a word, she wraps her arms around his neck and puts her lips to his long enough, as if to say, 'That ought to keep you longin', mister.'

When she pulls back, Johnny says, "I know I'm a great guy, but I didn't expect—"

"You deserve it, Johnny."

"And you just happened to be by the door?" he responds, a slight tremor in his voice, betraying being turned on.

"Well, I noticed you were late. I didn't want you to have to go around back and miss out on an official welcome." Then Melinda grabs hold of one of his hands and squeezes it. "Glad you're here. You know, I do like you a lot."

On the Upper West Side of Manhattan, the museum, which just ended its Heirloom Exhibit, is normally closed at this hour. However, tonight the banquet room, used only for special occasions, is in full operation, having employed a catering team and extra security.

A dinner, complete with live chamber music, is well underway. Elegantly appointed tables are set up to accommodate eight guests each and are spaced to allow easy mingling between them. It isn't a huge room, but then again, this is a selective group and the atmosphere is cozy.

Captain Sloper, in full regalia, sits at one table. Dr. Wilson is just returning to his seat next to him, looking slightly disturbed.

"Did you find it all right?" The captain asks.

The Big Splash

"Oh, no problem there. Something else on my mind. It was just where you said it was," the doctor assured, forcing pleasantness. "I can take my mind off my painting, now that it's locked in your car.

"Good. Care to discuss the other thing on your mind?"

"No—involves work. And, as you know, all that's top secret."

"Of course," the captain says, dismissing his concern.

Back at the pool party, Johnny leaves Melinda, who wants to stay inside to freshen up, and steps out onto the back patio to survey the scene.

There are lots of lights, decorative colors, and active bodies, none of whom he recognizes as of yet. There's a bar set up, along with a table filled with various salads, fruits, snacks, and, of course, an assortment of meats, which are being cooked on a barbecue grill behind it. Both are staffed by a local caterer. The rest of the patio is made up of small round tables and chairs, which are mostly occupied, and an open area filled with those dancing to the current disco craze, played by a DJ operating a cassette deck with giant speakers.

On the outskirts of the patio is the built-in pool, sporting its below-surface lighting and custom, curvy design. Despite glowing invitingly, there's hardly a soul in it and understandably so. What better way for guests to start the evening than by exposing their terrific bare-it-for-summer physiques in designer clothes and swimwear? Janice, apparently taking a breather from hosting, is one of the exceptions, and doesn't go unnoticed by Johnny as she bobs in the refreshing splendor of the pool.

Taking all this in, Johnny's immediately sucked into the pleasing atmosphere.

The Catch!

Love the vibrancy of this! Only, nobody knows me, nor that I'm here. Should I do something about that?

He steps through the crowd of unfamiliar, high-spirited faces to a deserted part of the sitting area and takes a seat. On the table next to him is a forgotten half-filled cup of beer. *Hmm, got an idea. Can't resist. This should be fun!*

He picks up the beer and looks at it, then, when a disco song ends, he shouts into the night air, "There's something terribly wrong with this party!"

Within seconds all human sounds hush and the DJ hesitates to play the next song. All that can be heard are the pool jets circulating water and the pulsating of electric current powering the lighting.

Finally, there are a few nervous giggles as eyes make their way to Johnny, still sitting and examining the cup of beer. Then a male voice braves, "So, what's so *terribly* wrong with it?"

Uh oh, on the spot now! I'll have to follow through with this.

Keeping his cool, Johnny raises the cup higher, toasting the scene, and smiles, "Nothing, now that you know I'm here."

Everyone just gawks at him. *Now, I'm really on the spot! Do or die time!*

He puts the cup down, and as the bewildered onlookers watch, he bounds out of his chair, screams with delight, and does a somersault fully clothed into the pool. The resultant splash sends water everywhere.

As planned, he surfaces a few feet from Janice. Caught up in the eccentricity of the bizarre moment, she exclaims, "You're too much, Johnny!"

"Well, you did ask me to be a splash at your pool party."

"So, I did," she says, giving him a short, emphatic kiss on the lips. "This we'll remember."

The still attentive partygoers let loose with a smattering of applause, boos, whistles, and comments, including, "Showoff!" and "Very cool, man!" before returning to what they were doing, including the DJ who restarts the music.

Johnny and Janice are alone in the pool now, treading water to stay afloat. She can see the extra effort it takes him due to the weight of his clothes.

"You're sinking," she says cutely. "Would you like to lessen the burden and remove your clothes?" she inquires, laughing.

"At least my shoes. I'd like to rinse the insides, too."

The two of them then swim to the shallow end of the pool and begin to ascend the mostly submerged concrete steps. Janice leads the way while Johnny, a bit winded, can't help but admire her from behind in the artificial light. *Wow, she looks like a shimmering goddess coming out of the water!*

When they reach the patio, she stops and turns back to him, and says with exaggerated demureness, "You can free yourself of your apparel in the john, John-nee! It's off the hallway. I hope you brought swim trunks."

He gazes back at her appreciatively. "If you freed yourself of your apparel right now... I don't want to think about it."

"Liar!... You think about it all the time! Maybe later, you, gorgeous hunk," she intones, oozing sex while walking away. "By the way, there's a clothes dryer behind a door down that same hallway."

After stripping down to his swim trunks underneath his clothes, Johnny returns to the patio.

I don't know what I'm doing. I've gotten all jazzed-up, but I'm also feeling kinda empty.

Now the disco music is blaring full throttle and almost everyone is dancing. Johnny meanders over to the barely occupied tables. When he spots an older, out-of-place-looking man, he takes a seat next to him.

The gentleman glances up from a paper plate he's eating from and says unexpectedly, "You're something of a hotshot for someone who's not a kid anymore."

Johnny grimaces and doesn't say anything aloud. *I'm sure I deserve that.*

And the older man isn't about to show any mercy. "1978, and we're obviously in the throes of a loose era, but no matter, men are supposed to mature and behave like gentlemen eventually. What makes you so insecure?"

The comment makes Johnny cringe. *Great, an extra punch to the gut! Does he have to be so blunt?*

Johnny tries to deflect the verbal putdown by diverting his attention to the unfinished plate of food in front of the man, and asks, "How's the food?"

"Find out yourself!"

"I think I'll do that," Johnny says, getting up abruptly and heading for the bar. *I need a drink... or two. The old man's stick-it-to-you attitude isn't going to stop me from having a good time.*

It turns out, that Bessie, who's a bartender moonlighting for the caterer, is behind the counter. "Bessie," he exclaims, "I didn't know you were here!"

"Well, I noticed you," she says ruefully.

Johnny winces. "Oh, that."

"Yes, that."

"I'm getting the third degree from you, too?"

"You shouldn't be surprised. It didn't appeal to anyone here who isn't a bimbo, or a chauvinistic jock."

"All right… bad move," Johnny admits sincerely.

Bessie softens her tone, "It's nice to hear you say it. I know you're a good guy at heart."

Johnny nods in gratitude.

"So, what will it be, Mr. Sloper? I just can't imagine."

"Anything on tap will do."

Bessie looks confounded. "Don't you want…"

Johnny's face suddenly reveals he knows what she's getting at. "Of course, the Sloper Special," he says perking up for her benefit. "That's exactly what I want."

Bessie fills a mug with beer from an ice-cold keg. After it's full, she places it on the counter in front of him and says, "Okay, here it goes, 'A brew with….'"

As Bessie pauses, she kisses the tip of a finger, then delicately dips it into the beer. Johnny takes her cue as she gives it a little twirl, "… a little bit of you."

"Now don't you ever go ordering an ordinary old brew from me again!" she says in jest.

"Lesson learned, Bessie."

Bessie's caring nature can see the troubled look in Johnny's eyes as she touches his hand. "Everything okay?"

Johnny's only response is to make a face and shrug his shoulders as he steps away from the bar. Bessie laughs uncertainly, still not sure what to make of him.

Back in Manhattan, a big blue, late-model Mercury sedan heads down New York City's Park Avenue. In the front passenger's seat, a pair of hands fidget nervously. The driver, the stately Captain Sloper, takes notice. Then Dr. Wilson, the car's only other occupant, speaks up distressingly,

"Captain, you know, this is ridiculous. I'm taking you well out of your way. Pull over! I'll take a cab."

"No way, my friend. I'm a man of my word. I said I would take you."

"I insist! This is too much to ask."

The doctor now sounds panicky. He looks all about, twisting in his seat. As the car stops for a red light, he notices a taxi slowing to a stop right behind them.

"There's an empty cab behind us," he shouts as he opens his door. "If we hurry, we can do this before the light changes."

Befuddled and with no chance of rebuttal, the captain quickly shifts the car into park and hops out. Both men converge at the rear of the vehicle. While the captain unlocks the trunk, the doctor signals the taxi driver. When the trunk opens, the doctor wastes no time reaching for his large suitcase inside. After transferring it to the cab, he turns to the captain. "Thanks for everything. I enjoyed your company."

Still perplexed about the change in plan, the captain doesn't delay the doctor's departure. "Sure. Take care of yourself."

By now Janice and Melinda's pool party is rocking. Johnny joins the crowd on the dance floor and works his way through a few partners, not to mention more than a few brews. At one point he dances to a slow number with Bessie who's on a break. She still senses that something's bothering Johnny. All she can do is hold him tight to show that she cares.

Many drinks and songs later, he's dancing up a storm with Melinda, who has changed into a blouse and jeans. Still in his swimsuit, he begins to shiver in the cooling night air, his shirt and pants still in the clothes dryer. Melinda reaches over and touches his arm. "You're cold!"

"That's no problem," Johnny says, pulling her to his chest and almost losing his balance in the process.

"You're freezing!" she says pushing him away.

"Sorry, babe."

"Babe, huh? You're coming inside so you can put something on." She then grabs his hand and leads him toward the house like he's a lost child.

As they pass through the sitting area, the older man is still there. He looks at them go by, shaking his head.

"Who is that guy?" Johnny inquires.

"Janice's dad, Bill. He owns the house and rents it to us. He converted the upstairs into an apartment for himself."

Upon stepping inside, Johnny momentarily feels a bit dizzy, but soon adjusts to the warmer household air.

"Your clothes are in the dryer, right?" she asks while leading him down the hall.

"Who can think of clothes when I'm with a beauty like you?"

"Oh, you're thinking about that, huh? Are you sure you're up to it after so much drinking?"

"Sure. I'm still standing, right?"

Melinda halts in place abruptly, obviously savoring the idea. They're in front of a bedroom doorway. "Why don't we stop here, then—my room?"

A half-hour later Melinda is redressing. Johnny is still in her bed, pretending he's not as woozy as he feels.

"The party's probably beginning to break up now, I better get back out there and give Janice a hand."

She then smiles devilishly at him, silently thanking him for the good time.

The Catch!

"Later," he says as she backs out of the room.

Shortly after she's gone, Johnny's feeling nauseous. It doesn't help that the admonitions of Bill come to mind, considering his just completed escapade. "Oh, no, this is getting serious," he mutters to himself before convulsing, as another intense wave of nausea overcomes him.

Knowing he can't stay where he is without braving worse consequences, he gets out of bed naked, his head swimming, and ventures out of the room in the direction of the hall bathroom.

"Damn," he mutters to himself, as he sees its door close, another partygoer beating him to it.

That attempt a failure, he wanders into the closest room. It turns out to be the master bedroom, undoubtedly Janice's. After he spots a bathroom in it, he rushes straight for it, upchucking as he reaches the commode.

When he's through, he steps out of the bathroom still dizzy and feeling exhausted. He knows he'll never make it back to Melinda's room. So, instead, he lies down on Janice's bed and pulls a blanket, folded at its end, over himself. Moments later, he slips into an alcohol-induced sleep.

It's very late when a sensation Johnny feels on his arm wakes him up. It's Janice looking down at him with an amused smile. *Mm-m-m, nice!*

"What a surprise," she says with wicked delight. "I was wondering what happened to you."

"Well, here I am," he says, thinking incorrectly that he must be better now. "Been here a while. Must have dozed off."

"Just as sly as always, my gorgeous Johnny," she says as she shuts her door and begins to undress.

What the heck! I'll just go for it!

The Big Splash

Johnny is too drunk to take into consideration all the previous warnings, including inner ones, and immediately engages in foreplay. The excitement of his arousal has him under its spell, despite the return of a pounding head. Then it happens—intense pain in his gut. With a loud groan, he lies back in the bed, knowing this is going to last a good while.

"What is it?"

"My gut."

Moments later, Melinda is at Janice's door and doesn't hesitate to open it. "What was that sound? Is there a man...? Johnny's in your bed!"

"So what? He was waiting for me. Now he's in pain. I think he had too much to eat and drink."

Melinda is outraged. "He was just with me. That's what!"

"You're kidding!"

"No. We had sex."

"How could you?" Janice screams. "You know I had a thing for him."

"Well, I did, too! I just kept it to myself."

"I just lost respect for him and you, too, you bitch!"

At this juncture, Johnny is sitting incapacitated at the edge of the bed.

The commotion brings Bill down from his upstairs apartment, his feet heard bounding down the steps. When he arrives at Janice's door, he crosses his arms and looks at each of the three, eventually, lingering on Johnny. "What's he still doing here? What did I say about men after hours?"

Later, not feeling much better, and slumped in the passenger seat of his *Falcon*, Johnny is driven home by Bill while Janice follows in another car. When both cars reach

The Catch!

Johnny's house and park, Bill says, "I assume you can get inside on your own."

Johnny nods, affirmatively.

After handing him the keys, Bill grabs hold of Johnny's arm roughly. "I'd rather not see you around again, Sloper, you hear?"

Johnny doesn't answer. The humiliation on his face says it all. Bill then gets out and into the waiting car with his daughter.

The big, blue Mercury sedan is parked in a space near a phone booth. Traffic from the New Jersey Turnpike can be heard nearby. The captain is on the phone. The gas pumps and food facilities of the service area are in the background.

"Operator," he says impatiently, "please put that through for me *collect*. I'm at a pay phone."

"Who should I say is calling?"

"Captain Eugene Sloper."

"Please hold while I put it through, Captain."

"Of course, I'll hold!" he says, impatiently.

Within moments, Captain Sloper hears a phone ring at the other end of the line until an answering machine picks up. The operator comes back on the line and says, "I'm sorry, sir. No one is there to accept a collect call."

"All right!" Captain Sloper says disappointedly, then slams the phone down.

"Damn it, John. Damn it!"

Chapter 5

Uncle Gene and the Missing Heirloom

It's late morning when Johnny opens his eyes. *Disturbing dreams again! Why?*

I can't play stupid. I know why! But now I've got a reprieve. I'm awake! To hell with being helpless in murky dreams. I'm free of them now, but my body feels pretty crappy as if a steam roller is about to finish the job of embedding me deep into molten asphalt…. Okay, that ain't happening. I'm alive! A little, anyway. However, today, work won't be an option. Gotta recoup, think things over and call Ralph.

He gets hold of Ralph at the office, where he's already been wondering where Johnny is, saying he's tried multiple times to reach him.

Oh, that must have been the ringing in my dreams.

Ralph says he has no problem taking on the extra responsibility. In fact, he's downright thrilled. "Just think," he says, "I have the entire empire under my command."

"And just think, there'll be only one peon you'll have sovereignty over in your vast jurisdiction," Johnny teases, despite his condition. "Don't forget that you and your subservient self still have to answer to me when I get back."

Ralph smiles, satisfied with himself on the other end of the line. "Don't worry. I've already rented a few boats out to customers. I'll just have to save the cleaning chores, so dear to my heart, until tomorrow."

After the call, Johnny can't help but smile.

Hiring that kid was the best thing I did for the business—especially now. Affords me time for some reflection. Like, why am I stuck in this muck of my own making?

As Johnny hones in on this, the memory of the pool party seems to move into the background, yet the impetus for change is fueled by it.

Gotta focus on eliminating all unnecessary and offensive things about myself. This can't go on! I don't want the past way I've been living to continue.

Johnny begins to jot down his criteria on a pad. It's not easy and he dozes off periodically while wrestling with this.

At one point, after drifting off, he's awakened by a phone call from his sister, Jane. His only sibling, she wonders why he isn't at work. After telling her, skimming on details, he endures her commentary.

"That's something to be concerned about, Johnny, considering you've always had a cast-iron gut, I'm coming right over."

Living nearby, and a school teacher off for the summer, she'll do anything to keep busy, even if it isn't really necessary.

After she arrives and dutifully prepares soup and toast for him, he gets a call from Fred, a.k.a. Thunderfoot, who

Uncle Gene and the Missing Heirloom

also couldn't reach him at work. "Maybe Rabbit's been right, needling you about slowing down," he tells Johnny.

"Apparently, the kid's jabs were spot-on after all," Johnny confesses. "I need to stop being such an idiot!" *Such a good feeling to admit that.*

Fred knows about Michael's visit to the marina and brings it up.

"Unusual guy. Kinda woke me up to some things, not quite the same way as Rabbit." Johnny comments.

"Kinda woke *the Great Sloper* up to some things?" Fred says in jest.

"Yeah, he gets into your head. Haven't you noticed?"

Fred considers this. "Sure, I know what you mean. He has a way of subtly pointing things out without shaming you, like how sloppy our bank record-keeping has been."

"Unusual guy," Johnny repeats, staring out into space.

On the other end of the line, Fred scratches his head. "You're right. There's always a positive vibe in the air when he's around."

"I think it's rubbed off on you."

"May have," Fred acknowledges.

Now that we're talking about something other than sports... "How about we plan a little excursion around Manhattan next Sunday, instead of playing softball? I can take the *Intercept* out. You, Michael, your wife, and me. He can bring someone, too. Maybe get some fishing in."

"Sounds like an excellent change of pace to me!"

Towards evening, Johnny is sitting up in bed half asleep, his pen and pad still on his lap. When the doorbell rings, he opens his eyes, listens, and hears Jane's footsteps make their way down the hall to the front door. She meekly greets someone there. Then a voice booms out loud and clear, "Jane, what a surprise. It's good to see you. Is John here? We need to talk."

Geez, Uncle Gene!

"Yes, sir! He's in his bedroom," she says, louder than before.

"In bed?"

"Uh-huh— the last time I was in there."

"You're visiting and he's in bed," is the puzzled response. "What's going on?"

"He wasn't feeling well, but he seems better now."

"Don't tell me—a night boozing it up again!"

Hearing no response from Jane, only his alarm clock ticking quietly, Johnny assumes correctly that she's only given the visitor a sheepish look.

Then, with no hesitation to them, strutting footsteps are heard moving through the house toward his room. Johnny sits up straight in anticipation and shakes off his drowsiness. There's a knock on his door.

Before he can answer, the voice booms out again. "John, it's your Uncle Gene. Are you decent?"

"Yes, sir," is the reverent reply. "C'mon in."

The door opens and the very serious-looking Captain Eugene Sloper comes through it. His starched and disciplined manner is quite evident on his fit frame as he steps up to the end of the bed, towering over his nephew.

How disconcerting it is for an otherwise confident, and often cocky, independent, grown man, like me, to still cringe like a frightened recruit at the sight of his uncle?

"How are you feeling, John?"

"Much better. Thank you!" There's a quiver in Johnny's voice, which he's having trouble controlling.

Now, I'm awake! He's never been accused of making anyone sleepy and he's never, ever conjured up anything remotely resembling fun.

"Perhaps you should take better care of yourself."

"You're right. I plan to, sir."

Captain Sloper looks at Johnny as if he's heard that before.

"Of course, you plan to, but there's something more important to worry about than your escapades, which I'm sure have something to do with you being in bed today," Uncle Gene goes on.

Johnny remains silent and tenses at what's coming next.

"Bad news—our valuable family heirloom is missing. The Granville figurine is gone. Probably stolen!"

"You're kidding."

"No, I'm not kidding! Don't ever doubt me, John! The heirloom you're next in line to inherit is gone," he reiterates with a grimace. He turns away from Johnny, accentuating his agitated state.

Johnny is contrite. "Sorry. Why don't you sit down?"

"No, I'll stand!"

"Okay," Johnny says, keeping his tone serious to match his uncle's. "What happened?"

The captain turns back to him. "As you know, the Granville was on display in New York at that heirloom exhibit."

"Yes, I stopped by one day last week to see it after you called me."

"You should have told me. We could have met at a cafe or something."

"I thought of that, but I don't like leaving the marina for long stretches if I can help it. Today I couldn't help it."

The Catch!

"Well, good for you that you saw it," Uncle Gene says with a tone mocking Johnny's obvious sense of duty without genuine interest. The comment is only a momentary diversion from what Uncle Gene is getting to.

"Anyway, I'll tell you what's happened from the beginning… I felt the exhibit was a good opportunity to take some time away from the base in South Carolina. I could visit your Aunt Gladys in New Rochelle and take in New York City, too, by shuttling back and forth from Grand Central Terminal.

"It was quite a time. It was good to see Gladys in one way. She does her best to make me feel at home, but, unfortunately, nothing's changed since our marriage. I got antsy each time to get away from her and head to Manhattan.

"The first time to the city I took a train down. It was last Sunday when I delivered the heirloom to the museum. Everything was already set up for the exhibit. All I had to do was deliver it and have them put it in place."

"They did a nice job of making it look important," Johnny interjects.

"It is important!" Uncle Gene irritably erupts again. "I was pleased to see it proudly exhibited among other great art, doing it justice after being locked in a vault for so long."

He then takes a second to let the irritation pass.

"That's the day I met Wilson, James Wilson, a doctor and medical researcher, supposedly from Vermont on some vague project in New York. Top secret, he said. I say supposedly because of things I'll go on to explain. Anyway, he was volunteering something to exhibit, too, a small renaissance painting.

"He seemed particularly interested in our Granville from the moment he saw it. Knew how valuable it was…."

He also seemed interested in me, although I now think that could have been a ruse. At the time, I thought maybe my being a captain impressed him. All in all, though, I was happy to have a companion to pal around town with."

Nodding to himself, satisfied with his assessment so far, Uncle Gene continues, "Together, we went to a few Broadway shows, visited museums, and ate in fine restaurants. From the beginning, I sensed something odd about him, though. I felt like I never got to know him. He seemed very sophisticated, then he would say something very crude. I couldn't figure him out. I just accepted him as a contemporary with some chinks who has very expensive taste."

Uncle Gene glances with a critical eye around at Johnny's pedestrian, yet ordered, decor.

"Anyway, as you know, the exhibit ended yesterday and was followed by a dinner for all who had volunteered their art. Just before sitting down, I picked up the Granville in the museum's storeroom. It was already bubble wrapped and labeled. I then put it in my steel case and locked it in the trunk of my car."

"You had your car last night?"

Uncle Gene shakes his head. "I said I put it in my car! I had driven it up to Gladys' when I first came north and left the car in New Rochelle until last night's dinner. The plan was to start the trip back to South Carolina afterward. The museum had permitted us to use its garage for the evening."

"Gotcha. Does the steel case have a lock?"

"Good, a pertinent question for once. Yes, it does, but I felt I had no use for it. I figured, if someone was going to steal the heirloom, they'd take the whole case."

The Catch!

"Of course," Johnny concurs. "So, what—?"

"Wilson had packed his heirloom, his painting, which also had been bubble wrapped, in a hard-shelled suitcase.

"So, then Wilson approaches me at the start of dinner and asks about a ride to his apartment when it's over. It won't be far out of my way, so I agree. Then he asks if he can put his suitcase in the trunk of my Mercedes. I say sure and give him the keys. Between courses, he does just that. At the time, I had no qualms about him going out to the car. Then comes the ride home. Wilson is acting fidgety for some reason.

"We're on Park Avenue and all of a sudden, as if in a panic, he tells me to pull over, he'd rather take a cab than inconvenience me. I tell him that's nonsense. I don't mind one bit. But when we stop at the next light, he hops out. An empty cab is right behind us. So, there's a rush to transfer him and his suitcase from the trunk before the light turns green. We say hasty goodbyes, but then, as he gets in the cab, I hear him tell the taxi driver to take him to State Street, Brooklyn."

Uncle Gene pauses a beat, then says dramatically, "The thing was, the plan was to go to his apartment which was on East Seventh street in the East Village. I even remember the street number – fifty-five – because we stopped in there a couple of times."

The impact of reliving that scene on Park Avenue grates on the captain's nerves. "As bewildered as I was," he continues, shaking his head about the discrepancy, "I didn't linger on it too long. I just got back in the car and left directly for South Carolina. Then, somewhere on the New Jersey Turnpike, I had this disturbing urge to check the trunk. At the next rest stop, I pulled in and took the bubble-wrapped package out of my steel case. When I unwrapped it—no Granville! There was a rock of some sort about the same size inside."

"Could the rock have been of some value?"

"I have no idea. It was interesting looking, but to me, it was just a rock."

"Could the museum have given you the wrong bubble-wrapped heirloom?"

"I don't think so. That would mean someone got mine. I've been checking with the museum and no one's come forward saying they have it."

"Hmm."

"Although it's only been a day, I suspect Wilson took it. He could have had the rock in one compartment of his suitcase with his painting in another and switched it with the heirloom when he first went into my trunk."

"It's odd that he told the taxi driver he was going to Brooklyn, too."

"Exactly! So, I headed right back to New York, deciding what to do. I tried calling you collect from another rest area, but I only got your answering machine. I was thinking of staying with you after doing a little investigating, but no, you were probably out gallivanting... as usual!"

Johnny swallows hard, knowing how the previous night went.

"I also tried Wilson's number in the city where he's been staying. No answer. So, I stationed myself across from that apartment on Seventh Street and waited half the night. When he arrived in the wee hours, he got out of a cab not carrying his suitcase. Thinking fast, I realized it wouldn't do any good to confront him then. It's what's inside the suitcase that's of importance."

The Catch!

"Sorry I wasn't available for your call."

"Me, too! Do you know how expensive it is to stay at a Manhattan hotel? And I only got about three hours of sleep."

Johnny shrugs his shoulders with regret.

"At least I'm not destitute.... So, continuing, this morning, with very little rest, I called a law enforcement friend from Carolina. He advised me to keep the authorities out of it for the time being. He said New York is such a media-hungry city that the story would probably leak to one of the tabloids and make things more difficult. We could be dealing with an overzealous amateur who was just taken by the sculpture's worth. Besides if the world knew that we had it, we wouldn't be able to display it in our homes. That's why I didn't allow the museum to post on its placard that it was on loan from me."

"But you've never had it on display in your—"

"That's because I've never felt that my home did it justice," Uncle Gene cuts in to defend himself. "When you're married to the service, you never feel where you live is your home. Maybe in your home someday, if you ever settle down and," he looks around again at his surroundings, "have a wife who'll add some class to your living situation. You're next in line, you know."

"I guess I am," Johnny manages to say.

"You are! And I hope it will mean something to you because it's obvious it doesn't now!"

Damn! I obviously sound apathetic. But, it's true, I really don't want to bear the responsibility for it.

"By the way, I told the museum to get in touch with you if something should come to their attention."

Johnny nods, submissively. "Okay."

"For now, if I could, I'd like to tail Wilson around the city, hoping he would take me to Brooklyn or do something suspicious, but I have to report back to Carolina where duty calls. So, I need your help."

"So, you want me to be a sleuth?" Johnny asks with a sarcastic edge.

I know that sounds callous. So what? I'm already used to him being irritated.

However, Uncle Gene responds with unexpected and controlled low-key aloofness, "You shouldn't be so goddamned obnoxious, John. Your heritage is at stake."

His change of tone is surprising. Now my attention is piqued.

"My theory is," his uncle continues, "assuming Wilson did make the switch, is that he's storing it in Brooklyn. That's in case his apartment in the Village was ever to get searched. Somehow, we need to discover where on State Street in Brooklyn he went and find out if our heirloom is there."

"State Street, huh?"

"You can look it up on a map. You can read a map, right?"

Johnny gives him an *are-you-kidding-me* look.

"I think the best plan of action is to have Wilson followed from his East Seventh Street apartment until he either goes to State Street or some other place where the heirloom might be located. Of course, you have to be careful. If he's not the amateur I think he is, there may be some danger. Under those circumstances, don't hesitate to call the authorities."

"How about hiring a private eye?"

"That would cost an arm and a leg for something you and one or two of your multitudinous friends can do by yourselves. Besides, I think it's important that you be directly involved with something so significant to you and the family."

Geezus! Gotta get this over with, and just accept taking this on so he'll leave.

"Okay, sir, you've done a lot for me, and since it's for family—"

"The challenge is yours then, John."

"Sure, I'll see what I can do."

Uncle Gene hands him a piece of paper. "Good. This is a description of what Wilson looks like, his Village address, and his phone number. I also left the number for a New York detective whom I'm acquainted with, just in case. In the meantime, take better care of yourself!"

"Okay, sir. I will."

"I expect the best from you. I'll be in touch."

Uncle Gene stiffly pats Johnny on the shoulder, turns, and leaves out the bedroom door. His footsteps can again be heard going down the hall.

"Goodbye, Jane," his voice booms out one more time.

When the sound of the front door closing reverberates throughout the house, Johnny slumps back against his pillow.

Relief!

Chapter 6

Recruiting Sir Steve

*U*ncle Gene – the captain – is such an irritation. A necessary pill to swallow, though. Someone I've got to kowtow to because, honestly, I'm afraid of the consequences. Maybe lose the marina and then what? I know I never had any real ambition. He solved that problem and, yes, I've found contentment in working in the peaceful, and, quite frankly, splendid surroundings on the bay. But now this heirloom business! He's making such a big deal about it. Something which means very little to me. Okay, something valuable that's ours – the family's – is missing. Of course, it seems right to go after it. But it's just going to be held onto, creating extra responsibility for the bearer. What's the purpose of passing this thing on, anyway?

Yet, as the sound of Uncle Gene's footsteps becomes a faint echo in my head, the irritation is easing and the idea of solving a mystery is becoming more and more appealing.

Come think of it—kinda relish the notion of being a sleuth with, as the Beatles sang, 'a little help from my friends', a welcome diversion from the marina. And Ralph's dependability makes it possible.

The Catch!

The next day is Sunday and that morning Johnny doesn't have the usual thing on his mind.

I just can't think of playing softball after Uncle Gene's visit. I've gotta do some planning. Hmm, with the boat cruise scheduled for next week, it'll be two Sundays in a row without playing. Gotta follow my gut, though. I guess Michael would call that intuition.

Johnny picks up the phone and calls Sir Steve.

"What, no softball today?' says a groggy Steve after Johnny requests he come see him at his home.

Steve, who's between jobs, who's never really had a steady job, and who may never engage civilization quite in the fashion of the average American, agrees to come over. He arrives an hour later and Johnny explains what he wants.

Steve is his usual unique self as he digests the request in the cozy, casual atmosphere of Johnny's den. "What's goin' on, Slopes? Getting into the private eye biz?"

"It's a family matter. Something important's come up. What we'll do is go out together at first to get things going. If we don't get results, we'll have to try something else. Can you do this for me?"

"Sure, following this Dr. Wilson sounds like fun. How 'bout free use of your speed boats in fair accordance with time spent?"

"In fair accordance,' huh?" Johnny says, cracking a smile. "Watching a lot of cop shows lately?"

"Only Police Woman—Angie Dickenson. Now that there's top shelf!"

"Mm, with you there."

"I figured you'd be," Steve says with a sly grin.

Johnny goes on to explain that it's important when following Wilson to always keep some distance from him because he has no idea how dangerous he might be, or might not be, for that matter.

"When do we start?" Steve says eagerly.

"How about later this afternoon and into the night? We'll go in my car and check out the area where Dr. Wilson lives, see if we can spot him on the street, and go from there."

"You got it! This'll be the most exciting thing I've done since I went out with Vera," Steve joshes.

"Just don't be so virtuosic that you get *us* spotted," Johnny joshes back.

"Don't worry. I know the difference between being virtuosic and virtually invisible. The only time he'll know he has a shadow is when he casts one himself."

They then set a time to meet later and Steve leaves.

Next Johnny calls Ralph at home. He tells him he expects to be coming to the marina late the next day. Can he fill in as he did on Saturday?

"I know I'm a Mr. Do-It-All," Ralph says, "but that was a lot to handle by my lonesome. Can I ask my best friend, Pete, to help out?"

Johnny gives his permission and says he'll be happy to pay Pete cash whenever Ralph requires his assistance.

Shortly later that same morning, his sister is ready to go home and he humbly thanks her for her help. *Acknowledging her is new for me. Interesting! It's suddenly hit home for this dummy how much she deeply cares about me.*

When Steve and Johnny meet up later, they drive into Manhattan directly to East Seventh Street and hang out in

The Catch!

the car near number Fifty-five. A man fitting Dr. Wilson's description perfectly comes out of the building around seven p.m. They follow the taxi he hails to a combination topless club and restaurant in the Chelsea section of town. He doesn't leave until one a.m. They then follow his taxi back to his apartment.

"Let's call it a night," Johnny tells Steve. "Can you come back by yourself late morning and follow him around then?"

"You bet!"

Chapter 7

Out on The Intercept

———⸻✦⊱╟⊰✦⸻———

*N**ice being able to sleep in late after a long night, knowing Ralph is taking care of things.*

Johnny gets out of bed and gets to the marina about noon where Ralph is like a ball of fire, literally running about the wood-planked dock and walkway, to and from the office, managing all the walk-in business.

"How are things going," he asks Ralph, who's just nudged a motorboat being rented away from the dock. They both watch as it takes off with a roar.

"Great. It's just been terrific. Pete's been doing all the cleaning," he says breathing heavily from all the activity. "It's starting to feel like my place."

"That's the way you're supposed to feel, except when I'm here," Johnny responds with exaggerated sternness.

"I guess you're back for good now?" Ralph says, apparently disappointed that his day and a half as ruling authority on the empire might be over.

"We'll see. Let me look around." *I'm just not in the mood for work with all that's going on. Gotta make sure everything is up to snuff around here, though.*

The Catch!

Johnny meanders around the marina. He inspects a few boats. They're all clean and the gas tanks are full. Then the boathouse—it looks as neat as can be. In the office, he glances over Ralph's record-keeping and finds it uniquely done, yet not lacking any necessary details. However, when he pulls out the register's money drawer, several bills spill onto the floor. It's overfull.

He sits down at his desk, pulls out a bank deposit slip, and begins counting money.

A little later, he's outside on the deck by the railing, holding a zippered bank bag. "Guys, come here," he calls out, and Ralph and Pete come scurrying from different directions down below, with an infectious energy that makes Johnny's insides swell with warmth.

"Ralph, I never told you this, but this is something important you need to know, now that I'm relying on you more."

"Okay."

"Never start the day with more than fifty dollars in the draw. It's too dangerous. We need to get this deposited right away."

It's then quickly arranged for Pete to take the bag for deposit at the bank.

As Pete heads for the door, Ralph looks anxiously out the office window. There's a woman patron out on the dock, waiting for assistance with a returned boat. Johnny stops both of them from rushing off.

"Just one more thing. It'll only take a second. Do you guys think you can carry on for the rest of the week?"

Ralph lights up, "C'mon, is the Fonz cool?"

"Sure, this is fun!" Pete says.

"Great! I'll be in and out, taking care of a few things."

"No sweat, boss," Ralph says as he hurries away to help their customer.

"Yep, no problem," Pete reaffirms as he goes out the door.

But before Johnny can leave, the office phone rings. "John, it's Uncle Gene. Have you got things underway?"

"Yes, sir," he says, then tells his uncle about the uneventful previous night with Steve, followed by, "How was your trip back?"

"Routine. Never mind that, though. Your inheritance is the most important thing you should have on your mind. And, of course, I won't be happy until..." *Do I really need to hear the rest? I'm feeling a knot in my gut at the thought of following through on this agreed-upon responsibility.*

While enduring the high humidity all that week, Johnny prepares for the Sunday excursion on the *Intercept*, along with fruitlessly hanging out at night with Steve.

One time in the wee hours, he finds himself in his den with the usual soothing glass of cognac. *Looking forward to this, even with the anticipated challenge of Michael coming. It wouldn't be worth it otherwise.*

Sunday arrives dry and crystal clear with a warm sun bathing all of Bayonne and beyond. After a Saturday storm, all the bad air has been pushed out. Now, a calm breeze, heated to perfection, caresses everyone in its path. It feels wonderful to breathe the enveloping freshness.

When Johnny arrives at the marina, Ralph is already there wearing a colorful tie-dyed t-shirt, which seems to put an exclamation point on the good weather and, perhaps, an upbeat sign for the day's prospects. He's inside the *Intercept's* cabin, stocking the cruiser with fishing tackle and food at his boss' request.

The Catch!

Johnny has just checked things out in the office and now stands on the dock next to the *Intercept*. "Ralph, the office fridge is empty. Did you already bring some beer on board?"

There's dead silence. Then Ralph appears meekly on deck. "No. We're all out."

"We're all out? You guys must have been drinking up a storm while I was gone."

Ralph puts on a guilty college boy smile. "It was a hot week, boss. And you've told me to help myself in the past."

Johnny shakes his head at his stupidity. "I guess I did say that, but you'd think... what am I going to do? No beer!"

Then from up on the walkway comes an unexpected female voice, "No need to worry. Michael and I brought beer."

Johnny turns to see for the second time the elegant beauty of Michael's friend, Robin. *Whoa! She's even more alluring now, especially since she's looking right at me.*

Robin's soft, dark hair eases around a brightly lit, smiling face. She's wearing an immaculate white, halter top over denim clam diggers, both accenting her figure nicely. Michael is at her side, also beaming. Johnny acknowledges him with a glance and a pleased expression on his face, then meets again with her beautiful brown eyes.

"There's no need to worry," she repeats, and points to a good-sized beverage cooler Michael is carrying. "Besides beer, I made a batch of pina colada, rum included."

What challenging afternoon? I'm suddenly feeling relaxed, even light-hearted.

"Beer and pina colada! See that, Ralph? You're saved by a woman. Thank Michael for bringing her along."

"Thank you, Michael," Ralph deadpans.

Johnny goes back up the walkway and greets Michael, who, in turn, formally introduces him to Robin. *God, need to hold it together. Even more in awe seeing her close-up!*

Unable to unlock eyes with her, he says to Michael, "I'm glad you brought Robin with you. I guess I was too preoccupied to invite female company my—"

"You invited me," Robin corrects him. "And who says one has to be paired off?"

Whoa, how do I take that? Is she glad I'm unattached? Or is she just trying to make me feel comfortable? Stop thinking about it and... "Then I hope you don't mind being the only doll with us today."

"As long as you don't mind if I don't act like a doll."

"Oops, wrong choice of words!" Johnny says cringing, "Foot-in-mouth disease. It's not always in remission."

"Don't worry. It sounded like a compliment."

Johnny bows slightly to her, more of a flirtatious gesture than a thank-you-for-forgiving-me.

"Speaking of women," Michael chimes in. "Isn't Fred's wife coming?"

"Unfortunately, Jeanie won't be."

Johnny looks over Michael's shoulder. "Here he is now. Hey, Thunderfoot, good timing!"

Fred bounds down the walkway by himself and high-fives Michael, then Johnny, a break from his formal, banker approach to greeting. "Glad you're feeling better, Slopes! I'll take a cruise over softball any day."

He moseys back over to Michael and shakes his hand and pats his arm. "Super that you're here, Michael!" He turns to Robin, "And it's a pleasure to meet...?"

"Robin," Michael answers.

"It's my pleasure," Robin says.

"Sorry to hear your wife couldn't make it," Michael laments.

Fred shrugs his shoulders. "She took the kids to the new *Superman* movie. Wasn't happy I'm doing this instead."

Michael frowns, "For better, or for worse. You signed up for it."

"I know... the better seems to be getting less and less."

Having overheard the conversation, Ralph yells out from the deck of the *Intercept*. "That means more pina colada and beer to go around."

The others smile uncomfortably. Johnny shoots him a stare and shouts back, "Have you got this bucket ready to go, wise guy?"

"Just about," Ralph answers, and self-consciously slinks away.

Johnny then looks at Michael, "I never asked. Is there anybody in your life?"

"Not now. Maybe never. I'm content just having friends at the moment."

Not long after, the *Intercept* heads out to sea. Ralph is at the helm, perched on the flybridge atop the cabin. He no longer wears his tie-dyed shirt, just the sun's rays. At Johnny's request, he's playing pop songs, heard above the hum of the engine from a boom box next to him. He bobs back and forth to it, his hair blowing in the breeze.

Michael climbs up to join him and holds out an audio cassette. "Hi, Ralph! I was just telling Johnny about this one. Can you put it on?"

"Sure."

Down below, Johnny emerges from the cabin after stripping down to his Hawaiian trunks. He pauses a moment, stretching his arms and shoulders back. *Nice!*

Feels like a new day. A new chapter. No more dark clouds. No more pool party shenanigans. Time to be a better me.

About then Michael's cassette begins to play. It's a song by Gerry Rafferty called *The Ark*. It's about a world living in a dream and a time for all to wake up and set out on a journey, assumably to find change and a more purposeful way of living.

"Interesting lyrics," Ralph shouts out to Michael who steps onto the ladder on his way back down to the main deck. Michael responds with a thumbs-up.

Johnny has been listening and appreciates the song, too, as he finishes his stretching.

As Michael approaches him, on deck again, Johnny comments, "The voice sounds familiar, but never heard this one."

"It's Gerry Rafferty. He has that big hit on the radio now—Baker Street. You've probably heard it. It has that great sax solo. It's on this same cassette."

"Sure. I know it." Johnny nods his head in recognition and keeps listening.

As the song ends and the next one begins, Johnny looks up at the flybridge where Ralph is ready for him. He's cut the speed of the craft to a crawl now that they're out in the middle of the bay. Johnny signals wordlessly, pointing north toward the lower tip of Manhattan. Ralph nods and complies with the command.

The cruiser comes alive again as the throttle is thrust forward for extra power. At the same time, Ralph raises the volume on the boom box as the *Intercept* curves beautifully on the complacent sea, all its chrome shining as the touch of the sun's rays gradually moves along its surface in its arced turn.

A little later, while the cassette still plays, Johnny observes Michael and Robin on deck. They've peeled down to their bathing suits, too, and stand at the boat's railing, taking in the scenery. *A good build for a philosophical guy—something extra to back up his words, I'd say. As for her, that's another matter. She's got the toned figure promised beneath her clothes. No deception there.*

Not wanting to stare, he glances over at Fred, not far away, where he's losing his balance trying to pull off his slacks. It's fruitless. Finally, after waiting for the *Intercept* to level off, he tries again. This time he succeeds and straightens up to reveal his prominent molehill of a belly.

Johnny can't help but make a funny face upon seeing Fred's disclosure beneath his clothes.

"Don't smirk! It's a product of my profession," Fred declares. "Anybody who sits all day gets a gut."

"You mean like accountants," Johnny says, pointing to the svelte Michael who is now coming their way.

"Give him time. He's young yet."

"Sounds like you're skirting the issue," Michael says, having quickly surmised the context of the conversation. "Somebody who has the smarts to be a bank manager has got to know better than that."

"Speaking of an issue not skirted," Johnny intervenes, subtly gesturing with his head in Robin's direction, "how about that for really fine form? She's got more than pina colada going for her."

"Ah, yes!" Fred agrees wholeheartedly.

"I agree," Michael chimes in.

"You find her attractive?" Johnny asks, surprised.

"Being gay doesn't mean you don't appreciate beauty, no matter the gender."

"Whatever," Fred says, "beats what I have at home."

"Maybe, if you set the example, you wouldn't be saying that," Michael ribs him.

"She might be thinking the same about you, Fred," Johnny adds.

"You guys!" Fred exclaims. "I get the message. I'll start doing something about it, but don't expect washboard abs like you have."

Robin looks their way in the middle of their banter and Johnny notices. *She's gotta know the topic of our conversation with that boys-will-be-boys smile.*

Her eyes lock with Johnny's just before she returns her gaze back over the railing. *Control yourself, guy! Those eyes—they're special, as Michael's are. Only hers have an underlying, extra somethingness drawing me in.*

Robin stays put for the time being, and Johnny is able to contain the enthrallment of their brief eye contact, pointing things out to the men about the boat, their prospects for fishing later, and the passing scene. He doesn't have to say a word, though, as the Statue of Liberty comes into sight. All aboard the *Intercept* have their eyes glued on it. No matter how familiar the landmark is, it always seems to draw attention. Where else would a lady towering over a small island, striking such a dramatic, poignant pose, elicit so much feeling about the homeland? Even Ralph is captured by it. He stops bobbing to the music while he gawks.

I've gone by this before, but it feels different this time. No longer just one of ma, pa, and apple pie. More like a serene symbol of an attitude, a standard for what's allowed this country to prosper... although not everyone has! That's unfortunate, and I've got to ask myself how do I, Johnny Sloper, hold up to that?

He looks over at Michael then.

Black and gay—he seems to have made it here, yet so many like him have not and cannot.

Me being philosophical again! Am I becoming an oversensitive wimp?... No! That's my old, stupid way of thinking. It's gotta be okay to have those thoughts, examining why some things don't feel right. How else can there be change, if I don't question myself and, for that matter, the world around us?

Soon, the looming high-rises of Manhattan's financial district dominate the skyline, and the moments of reverence pass. Then it's shattered as remarks about scheming investment bankers are made by Fred, despite being a humble player in that business as the manager of a small bank branch. Robin joins the men at that point and lively conversation ensues about a whole range of topics. Michael, Johnny notes, doesn't indulge in any of the embellished critiques of the world at large, which Fred is so adept at bringing up. Even though Michael has some things to say, there's no bitterness in his observations. Robin, who is up on the issues, speaks more in line with how can we do better at making things better.

As the noon hour approaches, Johnny climbs the ladder to the flybridge. Approaching Ralph from behind, he pauses at the boom box and lowers the volume. Ralph turns and sees him.

"You're doing all right, kid."

Ralph wipes his hand across his wet, beaded forehead. "Thanks. I think it's getting to be pina colada time."

"I think you're becoming a little boozer," Johnny teases.

"Get outta here!"

"I'd better check with Robin. Maybe she made some without rum."

"Thanks, boss. I'd appreciate that. And if there isn't any, don't worry about it. Dying of dehydration on a cabin cruiser on a hot, sunny day, while I'm still young and have a good tan, isn't a bad way to go. It's just too bad I don't have a reputation yet, so they'd play it up big in the papers."

Johnny shakes his head in jest, "You noodlehead!... We've decided to have lunch on one of those abandoned piers over there," he says, pointing toward Manhattan's West Side shoreline. "You can have your pina colada. I'd hate to see you die before earning your reputation."

"All right!" Ralph shouts and immediately begins to maneuver the *Intercept* in that direction. Then when he feels Johnny's hand on his shoulder, he turns, at first, in surprise. Then he realizes the reassurance of the touch, nods his recognition, and carries on.

Johnny bounds back down the ladder and meets Michael, standing alone by the railing and taking in the shoreline they're closing in on. Along the edge of it, for about a quarter-mile or so, is a park. A softball game can be seen being played within it. The familiar sounds of the sport become more audible as they get nearer.

"You picked a perfect day, Johnny," Michael says.

"A perfect day for playing ball, too," Johnny adds.

"Would you rather be playing?"

"Normally, yes, but no. I wouldn't have organized this, otherwise."

Later, it takes but a few minutes to set up deck chairs and a folding table on the abandoned, old pier. There were only four chairs on board, so Ralph is relegated to sitting on a milk carton. He doesn't mind, though. He just relishes being included in the first place.

Robin's pina colada is a big hit as everyone munches on deli sandwiches, watermelon, and chips. And, as rum and beer are absorbed into their systems, the conversation becomes more and more easygoing.

Gotta find more out about Robin. I'm sure she's more than just pleasing to the eye.

Maintaining a matter-of-fact tone, Johnny asks "Are you from around here, Robin?"

"Yes, right here in Manhattan. I have an apartment in the West Seventies."

"Ah, a New York girl... err, woman."

"Thanks for the correction."

Johnny nods humbly and continues, "What do you do?"

"I'm a freelance writer, specializing in fashion."

"Hmm, you do have the look of someone in style," he says, now bordering on flirtatiousness.

Robin smiles subtly without a word as if she doesn't want to fan any possible flames.

"How long have you and Michael known each other?" Fred asks her.

"Five, no six years, I think."

"Right, close to six," Michael clarifies.

"That's a good bit of time. What makes your friendship click? Obviously, it isn't sex."

Johnny shakes his head, annoyed, "Fred!"

"How do you know?" Michael asks with a tinge of humor, "Some of us go both ways."

"Now you're pulling my leg," Fred shoots back.

Robin makes a face. "I love Michael, but for the record, it's only been platonic. Okay?"

"Hey, what I heard," Ralph says from his milk carton to pontificate sophomorically, "was that platonic relationships are more honest and satisfying because they eliminate the sex games people play to entice each other."

"How would you know?" Johnny admonishes with a grin. "You haven't earned that reputation yet!"

"Yeah, but I do a lot of watching and listening. And, more pina colada, please. It helps to enhance learning and reputation development."

"All right, all right," Johnny says with a big grin. "That's enough of that. We're embarrassing our new friends. Like it or not, I'm changing the subject. I have a mystery to tell you about."

"Not one involving sex, I trust," Robin hopes.

"Nothing to do with sex... as far as I know."

"This still ought to be good," Ralph says, pouring himself more pina colada.

"Take it easy with that stuff," Johnny warns him. "You've got to pilot us back."

Ralph stops mid-pour, then says, "Okay boss, you've got a point. But what have you been keeping from me? A mystery? I thought we had no secrets between us on the empire."

"This has to do with my own private empire, beyond the marina of swabbed decks and Dominick's pizza."

"Does this end the discussion about the games people play to have sex?" Fred complains, clearly feeling the effects of the alcohol.

"It looks that way, and thank God!" Robin concludes as all is quiet, waiting for Johnny to go on.

Warm and comfortable with a balmy breeze, the abandoned dock is a perfect spot for hearing about Johnny's mystery. After a few moments, he begins, "While I was home one day, my Uncle Gene paid me a visit..."

He then goes on to describe everything surrounding the disappearance of the heirloom. And, from the expressions on the faces listening, it's evident that each has different thoughts about it, while all maintain an avid interest.

"And so, in the meantime," Johnny concludes, "Steve and I haven't found out a thing by tailing Dr. Wilson all week, which currently leaves me with no results and an uncle on my back."

There's momentary quiet. Then Ralph speaks up. "It sounds too obvious that the doctor would be the true culprit."

"There he goes again," Fred laments.

"It's obvious he's too obvious," Ralph insists.

But Fred will have nothing of it, "You've seen, or read, too many murder mysteries with their deliberate twists and turns to keep people guessing. In real life, it's usually the obvious one whodunit."

Sticking up for Ralph, Johnny chips in, "You may be right, Fred, but there are always exceptions."

Michael and Robin continue to let the story sink in. Finally, Robin speaks up, "Tell us more about the heirloom, the Granville figurine. What did it look like? How did it come into your family?"

"Sure. It first belonged to my great grandfather, a painting contractor, who, at one time as the story goes, did work for the Rockefeller estate in Westchester County. His crew's job was huge, painting the entire interior of their mansion. Every day while supervising, he would admire the Granville, which sat among multitudinous art in their collection. So, when the work was done, they were so pleased, that it was gifted to him. Granville was unknown back then, but his work gained international recognition and value when President Kennedy said he was one of his favorite creative geniuses."

"Sure, everybody in the art world knows of him now," Robin agrees. "What was the figurine of?"

"It's of a man about twelve or so inches high," he says. "It's all gold. I think gold over bronze, with multi-colored gemstones embedded all over it. The man stands erect and very composed with his mouth open as if intensely shouting out a declaration, or vehemently opposing something."

"Sounds interesting!" Robin says.

"Anything else about it?" Michael asks.

"Not really... well, maybe. My uncle told me Granville was a bit of a philosopher."

"That's right. I've read that," Robin adds.

"Then you might be interested to know there's a poem inscribed on its base."

"I am interested! Do you remember any of it?" Robin asks.

Johnny puts a hand to his chin in thought. "I never gave it much attention. Wait, let's see. It starts with *Catch the glory*, I think, and something about sound and *the catch being all*.... That's all I can come up with."

"Oh!" Robin blurts out. "You've got to find it! I think it's very important that you find it!

"What?" Johnny says perplexed. "What makes you say that?"

"I just know."

"I intend to," he says, very surprised by her enthusiasm.

"I'd like to help you, too."

"What?"

"Help you. Help you find it."

"You're kidding," he says, trying to hide the delight in his voice. "We've only just met. Why?"

"Let's call it intuition. I just follow what I'm feeling."

Johnny casts an eye toward Michael while he responds to Robin, "You, too, huh?"

"What?" she asks.

"We're both on the same wavelength," Michael explains, answering for her.

Johnny manages a skeptical, "Uh-huh," then, "That's a nice offer, but I don't know." *Women and their enthusiasm—I've seen how that zealousness can disappear very quickly. But maybe hers is the real thing. It does look it. Those eyes—so clear!*

"Michael, you'd like to help, too, right?" Robin asks.

"Of course. As long as it's okay with him."

Johnny looks over at Michael, "You, too?"

Michael nods, affirmatively.

Everyone waits for his response. Finally, speaking slowly, he says, "Sure, I'm blown away. Your help would really be appreciated! Steve and I don't seem to be getting anywhere by just following Dr. Wilson."

"I could find time to help, too," Fred ventures.

Johnny turns to Fred, grateful for the chance to take everyone's attention off his surprised demeanor. "I appreciate the offer, Fred, but your family... the bank... those are big responsibilities you have. That's asking too much."

Out on The Intercept

Then he shifts his sight to Ralph on his milk carton, "And you... before you open your mouth, I can't afford to give you any time off. You were going to ask, right, kid?"

"Of course, boss. It's the stuff reputations are made of."

After lunch, they all do some fishing. It's fun and there are some good catches.

Chapter 8

Tailing Dr. Wilson

Fifty-five East Seventh Street is in the heart of New York City's East Village. In 1978, it's not necessarily a pretty part of town, but, certainly, one steeped in the arts. Each night, just one block north, street vendors are bountiful on St. Mark's Place. They hawk locally produced crafted jewelry, paintings, funky clothes, etc. Up-and-coming artist types, including students from nearby New York University, along with curious out-of-towners, most of them young and from the surrounding suburbs, roam the street. Music can be heard overhead from open-windowed apartments, especially at this time of year, as fledging musicians flaunt their stuff. It's a part of town where Dr. Wilson feels comfortable—a home away from home. It vicariously gives him the feeling of being part of the creative scene, a contrast to his other life, yet sharing with it, perhaps, the quality of an underlying seediness. For it's an older section of town, its buildings slowly decaying, only camouflaged by the energetic crowds of unique individuals and newly conceived artistic wares.

The Catch!

It's morning as Steve takes his post across from Dr. Wilson's apartment. It was agreed that he would follow the doctor on his own this day and report to Johnny on developments.

The streets are bare and smack of decrepitude. He has a coffee and a newspaper and is situated on a set of stairs in front of another residential building. There he waits to see where the doctor will go.

Then, as usual, late in the morning, he steps out from the vestibule of his apartment house and walks briskly in a westerly direction. Steve waits until he is half a block away, then gets up and discreetly follows. 'I'm glad he didn't hail a cab,' he thinks to himself.

Johnny is on the phone at home. He's taken another day off from work. Dressed neatly and comfortably, he wears a burgundy short-sleeve, knit shirt, and blue jeans. He's made sure his hair is combed and he savors the prolonged, fresh scent of the fragrant shaving cream he used earlier that morning.

"So, I'll give you a call, if we're on the move... Terrific, Michael... Talk to you later."

Not long after putting the phone back in its cradle, Johnny's doorbell rings. It's whom he's expecting, Robin. When he opens the door, she's there, a picture of refinement in a canary yellow summer dress and he welcomes her in.

"I see you really want to go through with your idea," Johnny says, eyeing the dress.

"I do! I think this color should work well, don't you?" she asks stepping inside.

"Perfect. I won't lose sight of you in that. But, you know, I still can't believe you volunteered and came up with this plan. I would never have asked you to do this."

"You don't get anywhere without a little daring in this world, and just following your doctor hasn't been working, right?"

"True."

"What a cute place," she declares while being led down the hall past the living room.

"Thanks... not everybody appreciates it." He stops at the archway to the den. "Have a seat in here."

The den is a room that's always slightly disjointed. It's stuffed with all types of interesting, but incongruous things. Rather than being distracting, though, there seems to be a relaxing quality about it that brings order to the variety. It's meant to be comfortable, not formal in a way that would make a guest feel on edge. It's an ideal spot to put both Robin and Johnny at ease.

As she enters, she notices some of the prominent features: a dart board in one corner of the wood-paneled room with the usual damage done by errant tosses; bracketed wall shelves, displaying trophies of days past; a small standing bar, complete with shelves below the counter; a big twenty-one inch TV atop an old, Blaupunkt console radio; a wooden cable spool used as a coffee table with scattered sports magazines on it; and a big comfortable reddish-brown leather couch with a matching, stuffed leather chair. The floor is covered almost entirely by an oval, rustic-colored rug. There is a lot more around, but she already has the flavor of the setting.

"Make yourself at home," he says."

The Catch!

Robin nods an appreciative thank you and sits down on the stuffed leather chair. After she unpretentiously crosses her legs, Johnny can't help but gawk and be in awe. *What a silken quality she has, beyond the obvious physical beauty.*

"Excuse me," Johnny apologizes. "I'm not used to having someone so... fine... here. You're just gorgeous, really gorgeous."

"Thank you," Robin says, looking away to graciously savor the moment and deflect attention. Then focusing in on the surroundings, she says, "This is the homiest room I've ever been in."

Johnny goes with the change in subject. "Thanks. It's filled with many favorite things going way back."

He notices that the old Blaupunkt radio has caught her attention. "That was a wedding present my folks received way back when. As a preschooler, I remember my mom listening to it all morning doing chores around the house. Still works. Sound is great."

She smiles as her sight lingers on it a moment longer. Then her eyes wander back to his. "Well, what now? I can't wait to start.

"We should be hearing from Steve soon. He was set to hang out near Wilson's apartment the last time he checked in. Wherever he follows him to today, say to a restaurant or whatever, he'll call and we'll hightail it over there. That's when you can work your magic, while I stay close. In the meanwhile, how about some lunch?"

"Here?"

"Sure. Here. I can whip something up. After a few years of living on my own and TV dinners up the kazoo, I decided to try a little razzmatazz in the kitchen. The

Tailing Dr. Wilson

razzmatazz was cheaper than eating out, but it took a while before I could make something without a return address."

Johnny puts a hand to his stomach and feigns nausea to make his point.

"Hmm, sounds chancy, but okay. I'll try one of your first-class concoctions. What do you have?"

"A choice of sandwiches – peanut butter and jelly...."

Robin laughs, amused. "You call that razzmatazz?"

"... or one with a delectable spread I make myself."

"Hmm, this delectable spread... it doesn't come with a return address, does it?

"Nope."

"All right, I'll have that. It must be good. Peanut butter and jelly sandwiches are tough to beat... What is it, by the way?"

"I'll let you know after you try it," Johnny says on the way to the kitchen.

Caught up in the silliness, Robin makes a quick sign of the cross in anticipation of the worst.

When he comes back a little later, he leads her to a seat at the kitchen table. At each of the two settings is a plate with a sandwich neatly arranged with potato chips. "How about coffee for later?"

"That would be great," she says, eyeing the sandwich as she sits down.

Johnny goes to the counter to brew the coffee. Out of the corner of his eye, he sees her still looking at the sandwich.

"Go ahead. Start."

"Do I detect fish?"

"Could be. Take a bite."

After taking a tentative one, chewing and swallowing, she admits, "It is fish. It's good!"

Johnny grins, turns the coffeemaker on, and sits down. "I chopped up one of the ones from the catch yesterday. The other gook in there is a Sloper secret, but don't be surprised if you begin to feel a little mellow."

"Don't tell me. Peanut butter wine," she deadpans.

"Close. A shot of whiskey. Just enough to bring out the flavor. That reminds me. Would you like a beer?"

Robin prepares to take another bite, holding the sandwich in both hands. "No thanks. I'll just take this straight, no chaser," she says with a rueful smile.

At that moment, Sir Steve feels like the character Popeye Doyle in the movie, *The French Connection*. He's on a subway heading uptown, barely able to keep up with Dr. Wilson and, at the same time, keeping out of sight while switching trains. He has no idea where he's going and is glad it's the train doing the moving now, giving his overweight frame a chance for a breather. At stop after stop, he's kept the man in the distinctive gray tweed suit at the other end of the semi-packed car within his peripheral view. Finally, at 161st Street in the Bronx, the station for Yankee Stadium, the doctor gets off with almost everyone else. Steve takes his time, then saunters out onto the platform and inconspicuously keeps up his pursuit.

Back in Johnny's kitchen, Johnny asks Robin, "So, Michael's been a friend of yours for several years?"

"Yes, a loyal one—very supportive when I've been in need of some."

"Oh, like for what?"

"For instance, the fashion industry can be quite cutthroat. Once, when I wrote a critical piece, I got some

Tailing Dr. Wilson

poisonous backlash which shook me up. Michael helped calm me down just by his presence."

Johnny nods, waiting to hear more.

"You know, just being there for me, re-enforcing what I already know—that what I write comes from a genuine heart, nothing to feel bad about."

"Sure, I can understand that. With me, he's said things that are startling at times, have made me uncomfortable, yet make me think."

"He certainly can have that effect on people."

Johnny's phone rings on the kitchen wall, interrupting the conversation. He gets up to answer it.

It's Steve in a phone booth outside Yankee Stadium. "This guy never works, Johnny.... Oh, yeah. I guess I have kinda funny working hours myself.... At Yankee Stadium....Yep, there's a day game at two.... Bought a general admission ticket for the upper deck.... All right.... All right, I'll meet you here when you get here." Steve visually scans the area around the booth. "I'll be just inside Gate 6."

Johnny puts down the phone and looks over at Robin still seated, their eyes meeting. "What do you know about baseball?"

Before he and Robin depart for Yankee Stadium, Johnny fills Michael in, calling him at the office where he's working.

It isn't a long ride to the Bronx—up the Jersey Turnpike, across the Hudson River on the George Washington Bridge, then over to the Major Deegan Expressway and they are there. Within 40 minutes they are parked, and in line to buy tickets at an outside booth.

As arranged, Steve waits just inside Gate 6, beyond the turnstiles. When Johnny and Robin pass through, he

The Catch!

informs them that Dr. Wilson is sitting in the left-field section of the upper grandstands.

He then leads them up the many ramps that traverse back and forth to the level providing access to where the doctor is. From there, beneath the grandstands, they pass the food concessions and eventually enter a tunnel. It leads out to broad daylight, where row upon row of sloped seats overlook the stadium field with its clay infield and beautifully manicured, green grass.

At the end of the tunnel, Steve points out where Dr. Wilson is seated. Dressed in the grey tweed suit, he sits a few rows down and diagonally to their left, empty seats all around him.

"Okay, great," Johnny says to Steve. "We'll take over from here. Will you stay for the game?"

"The game? On a day like this? Nope. A spin in one of your speedboats sounds more like it."

As soon as Steve departs, Johnny turns to Robin. "You can still back out if you want."

"What? And waste the time we've already spent?"

Johnny nods. "All right then. I'll go down first. Don't forget, I'll stay close, but if we ever get separated, call me at home as soon as you can."

A few moments later, he sits in the row behind Dr. Wilson, a few seats to one side. The doctor doesn't notice as he intently fills out a scorecard for the upcoming game. Minutes later, Robin comes down Wilson's aisle juggling a hot dog, a coke, and her own scorecard.

The doctor isn't aware of her until she sits down two seats away and announces aloud, "It's certainly beautiful up here!"

Looking slightly annoyed, Wilson glances over, but his expression immediately changes to one of delight upon seeing her and her infectious smile.

"Yes. I wouldn't sit anywhere else," he says, keeping that delight contained. "You have a clear view of the whole field, even of a bird or two.... A Yankee fan?"

"Well, sort of," she says fumbling with the things she's holding.

"Wait, I'll help you out."

He folds down the seat between them. Then he takes her scorecard and places it on it, freeing up one of her hands to put the coke into a cup holder. "Commendable, isn't it, that the stadium renovation included these?"

"Yes, quite handy. They should put them in cars, too," she says.

Wilson wags his head, impressed. "Not a bad idea.... So, what do you mean by sort of a Yankee fan? They're starting to look good. They may catch the Red Sox."

"Oh, that.... I'm a New Yorker, so I guess that makes me one, plus it's the Yankees, not the Mets. They're usually the better team I always hear. But that's not the real reason I'm here."

"Oh, spying on me?"

Johnny cringes in his seat.

"No," she says with a giddy laugh, "I've been stressed lately and a girlfriend told me coming here for a day game is a nice way to relax. She also said to keep an eye on a player named Lou something."

"Piniella?"

"That's him. She says he's a good ballplayer and a heartthrob, too. I'm Robin, by the way."

"James. Nice to meet you."

The Catch!

"My pleasure, James."

"Your friend is correct. Weekday games draw fewer fans, making it more comfortable, especially being way up here in the nosebleed section. And I suppose the ladies do like Pinella.... Do you know how to use your scorecard? I was just filling mine out."

"No. Could you show me?"

"I'd be happy to. When you finish your hot dog, we can rearrange our seating."

Can't believe how well she's handling this!

A few minutes later, Dr. Wilson is side by side with Robin, acting every bit a gentleman while going over the intricacies of keeping score.

It's silly, but I'm beginning to feel jealous of this guy.

When the lesson is over, Robin and Dr. Wilson settle back in their seats. Batting practice is over and the ground crew is doing its final fussing of the field before the start of the game.

Knowing there's still a chance to chat before game action begins, Wilson subtly looks her over and comments, "You're of mixed race, aren't you?"

Robin, not knowing how to take that, responds matter-of-factly, "Yes, you're observant."

"Hmm, thought so. I've always found mulatto girls to be a finer shade of chocolate." Said similar to how a gentleman would in expressing appreciation for a fine piece of art, it takes a second before it sinks in.

Despite being shocked to numbness when it does, Robin puts the damper on any simmering anger and smiles, "I'm proud of both my parents, so I'll take that as a compliment."

Tailing Dr. Wilson

After a period of silence between them, the doctor asks what she does for a living. When she tells him about her freelance writing, he inquires, "Do you travel a lot?"

"A fair amount, but there's quite a bit to cover here in New York. And I've gotten to the point where I can be more selective about where and when. How about you? You look like a businessman. I'm sure you're on the go quite a bit."

"A little. Right now, I'm in New York, but I'm from Vermont, a doctor on a research assignment. I've gotten to enjoy and know the city pretty well during my free time."

"Who gets a day off now and then?" she says, questioning the irony of him being at the ballpark in the middle of the day.

"Now and then," he says hesitantly as if he's startled by her observation, then explains it away. "In medical research, there are periods when you just have to let things develop on their own before going back to examine results and analyze data."

"Sounds important. What are you working on?"

"That's a closed door," he says with definiteness. "Top secret. Government project. Sorry."

"I understand, but is it exciting? I mean is the outcome going to be big news?"

"Big news?" he says introspectively. He doesn't look at her now. His eyes stare out into space. "To me it is."

"Will I be reading about it one day?"

Dr. Wilson seems more distant, his words becoming ponderous, and carefully chosen. "I assume not. It's more a big deal on a professional level, something the majority of the public wouldn't care about."

"Why top-secret, then?"

The Catch!

A long pause. "You're pretty inquisitive," he finally says, the weight of his words sounding somewhat menacing.

This time Robin is visibly shaken, but quickly recovers, "Sorry, I'm always doing that, forgetting sometimes that I'm not on a writing assignment, digging for info."

Wilson, believing her apology, turns, looks into her sorrowful eyes, and smiles, dropping the threatening disposition.

"That's all right," he starts again in a much easier vain. "It's just that the public questions so much. They love to jump on any opportunity to interfere whenever they don't completely understand something."

"Sure, that can make things uncomfortable," Robin adds innocently to keep the conversation going.

"Uncomfortable? Unbearable at times!" he says, tension creeping back in. "Then government officials get into the act to check things out and before you know it nothing goes smoothly. Pressure mounts and those fuckers begin to haunt you, feeling justification is on—" He stops, suddenly realizing he's getting carried away.

"Now, it's my turn to apologize, my dear," he says, shaken by his lapse in poise. "There certainly are more pleasant things to talk about."

And they do, right up until game time. But both Robin and Johnny, who's been listening in, now know something is troubling about this man.

During the game, the banter between Wilson and Robin continues, but only about what's going on down on the field. The former relishes his role as a baseball authority, leading to numerous moments of mutual kidding, regarding his overzealous wisdom-sharing, due to her knowing practically nothing about the sport.

Is she still on my side? If so, she's playing her role extraordinarily well. If she'd only give me some sign occasionally that she's on my team, not the highfalutin Wilson's.

At the game's end, Robin and the doctor come across as any happy couple would who've had a great time at the ballpark.

"That was fun," she says as they get up from their seats.

"It was," he replies, smiling, as organ music plays to accompany the stadium's departing crowd. It had swelled by the time the game had begun. "Do you have to rush off?"

Robin takes a few seconds to consider this. "No, I guess not. I took the whole day for myself."

Good move! But why do I still feel envious? Get over it! Be ready to follow them!

"You know, I've felt out-of-place working in the city. Hardly know anyone. It would honor me if I could take you to dinner."

"I'd like that very much," is her well-played, gushing response.

"Great," Wilson says, encouraged. "Is there a particular place you prefer?"

"No, but..."

"What?"

"No, I'm being silly."

"Go ahead. Say it."

"Well, just that I've always been fond of Brooklyn."

"Brooklyn, huh?"

"No special restaurant. It's just that I had a girlfriend who lived in Brooklyn Heights. I loved the view of the bridge and the Manhattan skyline from there."

"Well, I happen to know that area fairly well. We'll go there then."

The Catch!

Nice work, Robin!

Moments later, Robin and the doctor leave their row and are in the aisle headed to the tunnel leading them back under the grandstands. Johnny follows and catches Robin giving him the okay sign behind her back. *Thanks for that! How silly of me to think she'd be falling for Wilson's cavalier charm?*

The Yankees had won the game with an exciting finish, atypical of the slow start they've had this year. The fans now make their way gleefully out of the stadium. Boisterous and full of frolic, they can't just file orderly toward the exits. They run, dance, sing, shout and shove their way along. By the time Johnny reaches the tunnel, Robin and Wilson are almost to the other end.

Once through the tunnel, his eye catches Robin's canary yellow dress, but he's lost more ground. They are way across the floor about to access the zigzagging downward ramps. With more room to move, he dodges through the throng at a quickened pace, making up some of the distance. At the mouth of the first ramp, the crowd thickens again. Looking down its length, he can see they're about halfway to the next bend.

Unfortunately, after each pair of ramps that goes down, there's another juncture, allowing bodies to pour onto the ramps from a lower level of the stadium. When they reach that next level, the crush is substantial, the distance between Robin and Johnny widening. He can no longer make up ground. The crowd is packed too tight.

Meanwhile, Robin is unfazed by this, yet wishes to keep Johnny in sight. The last time she had a chance to glance back, she couldn't spot him. Now she has to wait for the next turn to try again.

Tailing Dr. Wilson

As Johnny rounds the corner of the next ramp, he catches a smidgen of yellow at the far end. Then a head turns and it's Robin's face momentarily in view, still maintaining its coolness. At the last instant, their eyes meet just as she rounds the bend below him.

Outside the stadium, fans pour into the plaza from the open gates. After a while, Robin and Wilson appear among them, the latter taking a good look around the area.

"Sorry to say," he says. "I think we better take a train. A taxi will get stuck in traffic."

"Sure. That's undoubtedly best," Robin says, wondering if the short pause will allow Johnny to catch up. Glancing back, she realizes he hasn't exited onto the plaza yet.

This is crazy. My heart's beating a mile a minute. I may lose her stuck in this mob! Why did I let her do this? She says she can take care of herself, even if we got separated. But I can't give up! She could be in danger. Who knows what Wilson is capable of? That comment about mulatto women—chilling! What? From a genteel-looking medical researcher? Uncle Gene's suspicions are probably right!

Momentarily, Johnny squelches his negative thoughts about the situation as he reaches the exit gate. From there he hurries from the pack to a clearing where he hopes to get a better view and sees the yellow dress. It's all he can make out. It's across the plaza, moving toward the subway entrance.

Run is all he can do. And run he does, dodging and often brushing against people, leaving not a few startled in his wake. Three-quarters of the way to the entrance, where he last saw the yellow dress disappear, an older woman steps in his path. He sees her in time to let up steam, but can't avoid bumping into her.

"Sorry," he says hurriedly while grabbing her by the shoulders to keep her from toppling over.

She responds with a machine-gun burst of expletives, but so consumed by the urgency of the moment, Johnny says nothing further and continues on.

When he reaches the subway entrance stairs, he has no idea if he still has time. Anxiety, due to the possible futility of his hustle and the feeling of losing sight of someone newly special in his life, suddenly results in a recurrence of the knotted sensation in his gut. His hand goes there as he doubles over and comes to a stop. *Why now, damn it?*

Precious moments of his pursuit slip by, but the pain, never reaching its previous intensity, soon subsides and he descends the stairs.

Besides graffiti scrawled everywhere, it's dark and dingy as most subway stations are, but Johnny quickly adjusts to it and rotates in place to scan the jammed space. It isn't long before he sees her. She's squeezed in among the crowd on the platform near the track. Dr. Wilson is pressed up against her from behind, his arms at her sides.

The echo of a train is rumbling somewhere in the subterranean distance, getting louder and louder by the second. *No time to spare. I need a token! Can't risk getting caught jumping the turnstile.*

Instead, Johnny gets in line at the token booth, a line moving reasonably fast. Keeping one eye on the platform, he sees the crowd tighten as the echo of the incoming train becomes a roar. When there is only one person ahead of him online, he turns his attention to the booth. He can now hear the squeal of metal wheels against the metal track, the sounds now free of the reverberation of the tunnel as the train pulls into the station.

Tailing Dr. Wilson

The woman in front of Johnny speaks only Spanish and the token seller has trouble understanding her. Impatiently, he looks back toward the track. The train, in all its colorful graffiti-painted glory, is stopped. He watches as the doors open.

I've waited long enough!

Abruptly, Johnny leaves the line and sprints for an unoccupied turnstile and leaps clean over it. Immediately, a transit cop comes out of nowhere and grabs him by the arm.

"Over here, buddy! You're getting a fine." the cop says as he jerks Johnny away from those waiting outside the train. "We've had enough of you Yankee fans abusing the transit system. Let me see some ID."

Meanwhile, a trickle of people departs the train, followed by a wave of humanity moving toward the doors. Dr. Wilson raises his hands to the back of Robin's arms and, exerting pressure, guides her through the throng.

Johnny tries to resist the hold on his arm but quickly realizes he could also be charged with resisting an officer. Instead, he gives in and looks past the cop to witness the train doors closing, Robin visible through one of its windows, packed tightly inside.

God, I hope she really can take care of herself!

As Johnny continues watching, the train slowly moves out of the station.

Chapter 9

Waiting for Robin's Call

------※------

I feel terrible! Who cares about getting a ticket and being fined? I'm pissed that I let the pain in my gut slow me down… and miss that train, damn it! And how irrational to think that Robin might have fallen for that sick guy? Can't be true. I know that! But I'm so goddamned taken by her, I can't help but feel somewhat defeated.

Johnny's gut, spurred on by these thoughts, has begun to act up again as he arrives home and gets out of his *Falcon*. The fact that he knows Michael should be waiting at the house doesn't help. He's already filled him in on what's happened from a pay phone in the Bronx. And, sure enough, he's there, sitting on the front stoop with his arms folded, propped up on his knees, observing Johnny on his walk across the lawn towards him.

Johnny silently mutters an obscenity to himself, then says in a depressed tone of voice, "Hope you haven't been waiting long, Michael."

Michael ignores his concern. "Are you all right?"

"Sort of."

The Catch!

"Don't take it so bad. Robin can handle herself. She has lots of experience dealing with all kinds of people."

Johnny reaches the stoop. "You two certainly are in agreement about that!"

"I can't say I'm not concerned about her, but I know she follows her heart. That's the most important thing. So, whatever happens, is probably what's supposed to happen."

"That's an unusual way of putting it."

I'm distressed with the possibility that Robin may be in jeopardy, and here's Michael, a man I hardly know, whom I can sense from the little I do know, is someone who values life and the purposeful living of it more than anyone I've ever met, and he's suggesting that I shouldn't worry about Robin, nor kick myself for what's just happened?

Michael pats him on the shoulder and says, "Let's go inside, check your answering machine, and if nothing's on it, we'll wait for her call."

His inner calm is so grounding. A relief, too! I was afraid he'd be angry about this. He continues to leave me in awe!

They go inside and find nothing on the answering machine, then settle down in Johnny's den, the only light illuminating the room coming from a fluorescent lamp over the bar.

After a while, Johnny offers him some coffee and the two of them sip from mugs in silence. Michael is sprawled out on the floor, his back propped up against the sofa. Johnny sits on the edge of his leather chair.

In Brooklyn, Robin and Dr. Wilson are on a sidewalk in front of a rowhouse with the number 11-33 marked near its porch door, which Robin seems to take note of while the doctor hails a cab.

When the taxi stops, they get in and Dr. Wilson tells the driver, "Take us back into Manhattan, please."

In the meantime, while Johnny continues to sip on his coffee in silence, ingrained images of Michael, and especially Robin, pass lightning-fast through his mind. *As much as Michael continues to intrigue me, the thoughts of Robin are beginning to possess me.*

"You really love Robin, don't you? Johnny asks.

Subtle evidence of adjustment to the break in silence appears on Michael's face, then quickly subsides. "Of course. There's a Love Nature intrinsic in all of us. When it's stirred by another human being, you feel it."

Johnny nods in agreement. "Sure, I've come to understand that." *But with Robin, the added physical attraction is just out of this world!*

Johnny puts down his coffee and leans back in his chair and closes his eyes. Eventually, Michael, still on the floor, propped up against the couch, closes his eyes, too. They stay that way for over an hour.

Inside a Manhattan restaurant, blues music can be heard as Dr. Wilson pounds on a door marked *Ladies*.

"You've been in there a long time, Robin. Time to come out," he demands.

Johnny, who's been napping, suddenly opens his eyes and sees Michael's are also open. *Now might be the time to bring up what I've been thinking about. The stillness seems ripe for bearing fruit. Listen to yourself—bearing fruit! What? Me?... Philosophizing?*

The amused look on Johnny, due to his thoughts, soon turns serious.

The Catch!

"There's something I haven't talked to anyone about," Johnny begins. "For some reason, it seems okay to run it by you."

He looks to Michael for reassurance.

Michael straightens his back against the sofa front as if to indicate that he's all ears. "Go ahead. Shoot."

"I started writing down my thoughts the day I was home recuperating from that night of partying a week ago. One of the things becoming clearer, yet perplexing to me, was that I no longer felt good about the life I've been living. Most would say it's a great life – the marina, the ladies, the booze, the image of bravado I manufacture, as you pointed out once – and the repetition of all that. It's never felt completely satisfying. I think getting to know you has been helpful in making me aware of that. It was kind of freeing to put it down on paper, but I can't figure out what would make me feel satisfied."

"Maybe knowing what's not leaving you satisfied, and dropping those things, is a good start."

"Okay, but then this thing came up with the heirloom, and you two involved. Unexpected things seem to be happening. I haven't been able to pursue it."

Michael smiles empathetically. He then looks out into space and speaks softly, reassuringly. "From my own experience, I find that answers come from the sheer wanting of them. It's not the sort of thing to get too analytical about. You could end up with something you don't want. Be open to the unexpected. If you're honest with yourself in intent, you'll know what's well and good when you see it. It'll resonate with you and feel absolutely right."

A pause follows. *That's unusual! I feel a reverberation in my body from him saying that. Is that what he means by 'resonate?' However, I have more questions to ask, like where does all this philosophical advice come from?*

But instead, the phone rings breaking the stillness. After a startled instant to identify the intrusive sound, Johnny springs out of his chair. As he reaches the table where the phone is, he stops in place. "It's gotta be Robin. It's only right that you answer it since you're best of friends."

Michael gets up and Johnny hands him the phone's receiver. "Hello," he says, his voice betraying some concern.

"Michael, thank God! It's so good to hear your voice," comes the response.

"Robin, where are you?"

Johnny, thinking fast, grabs a pencil and pad he's had ready. As Robin relays the information, Michael repeats it back. "Manhattan... the Lower East Side... *Life in the Hood Tavern*... All right. We can look it up."

Robin is excited, "Please hurry. He's been harassing me most of the night. I have to get out of here. He's still waiting in a booth near the front door. I'm calling from a hallway where the restrooms are. I'll be in the Ladies' Room. Knock three times, pause and knock three times again."

"Got it," Michael says, eyeing Johnny as he finishes taking down the information.

After getting the location of *Life in the Hood Tavern* by calling 411 for information, Johnny and Michael are on their way.

Chapter 10

Robin's Ordeal

I feel supercharged. This is getting exciting and that ache in my gut is again a thing of the past. So glad Michael is with me this time.

Michael by contrast is somewhat contained, yet very present. Johnny is focused on only one thing—getting there fast, and, at one point, Michael suggests he slow down and the warning is heeded. Otherwise, they don't talk.

They take the nearby Holland Tunnel into lower Manhattan and within twenty-five minutes they're on the Lower East Side. Michael now helps Johnny navigate the confusing, meandering streets in this part of town, giving directions, using a New York City map open on his lap.

"This part of the city is extra dirty," Johnny says observing the filth all over. It looks like nothing's been cleaned in a while, including graffiti all over the place."

Michael nods in agreement. "Hopefully it'll all change soon. Carter's Federal loan guarantee could turn things around after Ford told the city, according to one headline,

The Catch!

to *DROP DEAD*. Otherwise, a bankrupt New York would probably have repercussions throughout the country."

"Hmm, I guess I should pay attention to stuff like that."

"It helps when it's time to vote."

Meanwhile, two men in their fifties are staked out inside an older model, blue *Chevrolet* across the street from *Life in the Hood Tavern*. The somewhat bored man in the passenger's seat fiddles with the car stereo. Behind the wheel and staying alert is a man with a distinct ugly scar etched on his left cheek.

"Relax! He's with a broad. He'll be a while," says the bored man, after tuning in music to his liking.

"I'm not so sure. She didn't look like the type of gal who'd take to a place like this."

"You'd be surprised who comes to places like this."

"Really? What do I know? Hey, what are you listening to, anyway?"

"What? You don't know the blues? Goes with this part of town."

"The blues, huh? Better than disco," the driver comments sarcastically, still observant of the goings-on across the street.

"The way he was gazing at her before... it gave me the feeling he'd be keeping her a long time."

"If he isn't in a rush to take her to bed. Besides, it might be the blues for us, if we miss something. We have to be prepared, Jack. The doctor is important to us. We don't want to blow it the first-night keeping watch."

"Why don't we go in there, then? Act the part. Have a drink or two," Jack says cockily.

The scarred man winces at the suggestion, which stretches the crease on his marred countenance. "I'd rather give the doctor his privacy. Our job is not to be so visible, remember?"

Just then Johnny's *Falcon* comes down the block. When they spot the tavern, they pull over across the street from the *Chevrolet*.

The scarred man takes extra notice when Johnny and Michael urgently get out of the car and enter the premises.

Once inside, the atmosphere does bring to mind the blues, not to mention the soothing voice of Billie Holiday playing over the sound system. It's shadowy and smoke-filled, an older establishment that seems as heavy as the brick that lines much of the interior walls, their joints sloppily filled with mortar and painted charcoal gray. Yet the patrons are fairly well-dressed sophisticates. They murmur among themselves at small round tables, enhancing the somberness of the mood and suggesting that any edginess of day has been tucked in and put to bed.

Outside across the street, the scarred man turns to Jack, "Keep your eyes open. I'm gonna check something out."

As he departs the car, Jack raises his head off the seat's headrest, straightens up, and shakes off the laidback mood that the blues station brought on. "I guess I've got to work sometime," he mutters mostly to himself.

Inside the tavern, Johnny and Michael cross through the vestibule into the main room. Dr. Wilson is visible in profile. He sits alone at a table, looking intoxicated and seemingly morose as if he's sifting through alcohol-obscured thoughts. The preoccupied, bustling wait staff and the contained conversations at each table, allow the two to move inconspicuously toward an adjoining room.

The Catch!

The scarred man's taut, middle-aged frame is already swiftly and stealthily moving across the street. He gets there just in time to sneak a peek through a window to see Johnny and Michael, already past Dr. Wilson, continuing out of sight into the other part of the tavern.

The adjoining room is separated from the main one by a half wall, also of brick, topped by a steel trellis. A four-foot opening in it provides access. Once Johnny and Michael pass through, they notice an archway in the rear leading to the hallway which Robin described.

Outside, the scarred man pauses, wondering what to do next, then takes a microcassette recorder out of a pocket and records his description of Johnny and Michael, plus the license number of their car.

About then, Johnny and Michael enter the hallway at the rear of the establishment. The patterned, tin ceiling, which hovers over the entire place, stands out in the smaller space as they approach two old, solid-wood restroom doors, marked *Gents* and *Ladies*. They stop at the latter. Johnny then does the honors and gives the designated knock.

Within moments Robin opens the door with trepidation and steps out. She quickly slides into Michael's arms for a hug. "Oh, God, you couldn't have gotten here too soon."

Michael responds with a tender squeeze. Then she embraces Johnny, too. "It's good to see both of you," she says in his ear, the whisper of her breath igniting his insides. *Whoa! Feels like being shot into orbit!*

Robin steps back anxiously. "Let's get out of here. He's still here, isn't he?

"Uh huh," Johnny confirms, slowly coming back to earth, her stirring effect on him taking its time to wear off. "Uh... he looks quite soused."

"I don't doubt it. I think he's been nursing his failure to hit on me," Robin says with a sigh.

A moment of uncertainty passes before Michael takes charge. Looking at Johnny, he says, "Why don't you walk out with an arm around Robin? I'll follow."

There's no need to say another word. It's the perfect thing in this circumstance. Johnny feels drawn to Robin and she needs to feel physically protected. Johnny stretches an arm around her, then gently pulls her firmly to his side, once again experiencing her sublimeness against his body. Now feeling secure, she looks sideways at him with a contented smile. The three then begin their walk out of the tavern.

I feel so empowered being part of this threesome! Kinda like a manning up I've never known before. Total fearlessness! Still gotta be cautious, though.

Robert Johnson, the great blues musician from the 1930s, now plays over the sound system as they approach the front door of the tavern. Between them and it, is Dr. Wilson, still seated as before. This time he's faced in their direction, head bowed gazing at the dark substance in the glass in front of him. Then the doctor looks up in his stuporous state. His view is blurry, but soon it's clear enough to make out Robin and the man latched on to her. With that recognition taking hold, he slurs the words, "Good night, dear," and nothing else.

Johnny, Robin, and Michael continue on and out the door.

The Catch!

Once outside, they hurry to the *Falcon*. As they scramble inside, Robin declares emphatically, "I hope I never see that man again!"

The scarred man, back behind the wheel of the old *Chevrolet* is observing with his window down. His pulse quickens upon hearing and seeing the woman who had been with Dr. Wilson, leaving with the two men he had deemed suspicious. Moments later, the *Falcon* pulls away from the curb.

It's a nice building on the Upper West Side, complete with a glass-enclosed lobby featuring lots of potted trees and plants, not to mention a twenty-four-hour, manned security desk. It's what Robin calls home.

Not long after, Johnny and Michael sit at the round kitchen table in her comfortable apartment. Johnny's already noticed some nice original paintings on the walls. "The only time I splurge is when I see art like these reasonably priced," she explains, before going over to the stove to prepare tea. It's her first words since they left the *Tavern* and drove uptown.

When the tea is ready, she silently fills three cups, pouring from a porcelain pot over each of their shoulders, then fills her own. Finally, she sits down between the two. A creamer and sugar bowl are on the table, but nobody moves. The two men's eyes are focused on her, eager to hear her tale. Instead, she motions to the condiments. Reluctantly, Johnny goes ahead and takes some of each for his tea. Michael takes just cream. When they're done, Robin raises her unadulterated cup to her lips and takes a sip. The others do the same, their eyes still glued on her.

Putting the cup down, Robin presses her lips together in momentary thought. "Okay, here's what happened. I think he took me to the house you're looking for."

Johnny lights up. "No way!"

Michael beams proudly. "I knew it. Just leave it to Robin!"

"I know you were headed to Brooklyn," Johnny says, "a brilliant bit of improvisation at the Stadium on your part, but how—?"

"I guess I was acting a bit like a doll to draw him in," she teases, deviating momentarily from the serious tone.

Johnny smiles at her playful remark, then says, shaking his head, "I'm sorry I couldn't keep up with you two as you headed to the subway."

"It actually was better that way. I didn't have to wonder whether you were nearby, or not. I also have plenty of confidence in dealing with things on my own… up to a point."

Johnny nods, swallowing his chauvinistic pride and obviously happy that she ended up unharmed.

"Anyway, once in Brooklyn Heights, we looked around and found a nice Italian restaurant."

"And?" Johnny says, trying to stay patient.

"Dinner was okay. He was being very debonair at first, not revealing much about himself, obviously trying to impress me."

"Of course! Anybody would," Johnny says.

Robin glances his way. *Did I just see a pleased reaction? Could be, but hard to tell.*

"We had talked about taking a walk while we ate. Then, out of the blue, he says, 'Why don't we stop at a nearby house of a friend of mine?' I said I didn't mind, but before long, once we left the restaurant, I got the message…"

It's then that the defiance begins to sound in Robin's voice.

"...he was eager for a roll in the hay there. He kept hinting as we walked. I'll spare you the awful ways he put it... I kept myself busy looking at street signs to remember where we were, not discouraging him because I was hoping this place was going to be on State Street where your uncle said he was going that night."

"And?" Johnny asks.

"Sure enough—State Street! It was then that I could especially sense him getting geared up for a good time, the way he got so quiet before reaching the house and started breathing deeper as if to contain his excitement."

Robin takes another sip of her tea and sets herself before revealing the rest.

I'm suddenly realizing how sensitive, yet strong and bold, she is. I'm being drawn to this woman like none before!

At that moment, he notices Michael, who's sitting very stoically, catching Robin's eye with a wink and a slight grin. *What a bond they have!... But just how far did Wilson get trying to hit on her? I can feel the gut acting up again.*

"It was house number 11-33 on State Street, near Sycamore Lane, or Sycamore Street. Sycamore something, anyway," Robin continues.

"It was grey, I think. It was difficult to tell in the evening light. It was also one in a string of attached houses," she says. "Rowhouses," she adds, being more specific with the terminology as if warming up for the harder details.

"So, when we get there, this gruff, low-life, looking guy answers the door. Nothing like James, Dr. Wilson, at all. He looked surprised to see us and it was obvious James held some kind of rank over him. That's when James asked me to wait while he stepped inside for a minute. When he came out a little later, he said it was okay to go in. Well, at that point, I knew I'd accomplished what we wanted, so I told him I didn't like the looks of the man who came to the door and would feel very uncomfortable going in there."

Atta girl!

"That's when I noticed his attitude changing. He tried some gentle coaxing at first, but I could tell that a kind of fury was building up in him. He came across as somebody who always gets his way. And when he doesn't, it gnaws at his giant ego."

Robin takes a big breath, then slowly exhales. "Anyway, I stood my ground, even though I was getting more alarmed by the second. Fortunately, he knew there wasn't much he could do about it, standing outside and all, a pretty awkward situation for both of us. So, when he finally said 'Let's take a cab to the city for a nightcap,' I went along with it. The fury in his eyes settled down some then. And I was hoping it'd give me time to figure out a way to get away from him."

Whew! She really can take care of herself.

Michael, unflappable so far, sighs to indicate his own relief.

"The cab ride confirmed that the subtle hints he was giving me, *were* pointing to what I thought. I guess he figured I'd be more comfortable away from that house and could get cozy with me during the ride, putting his arm around me as if he possessed me."

She looks down for an instant in disgust, then over at Johnny again, whose own arm had held her tenderly.

"Then he started telling me, as an option, we could always go to his apartment and have our drink there, squeezing me a little extra for emphasis." Robin literally

The Catch!

squirms in her seat as she remembers. "I felt it wouldn't be a good idea to refuse him outright. That might have set him off, and things may have gotten worse fast. I couldn't even consider bolting out of the cab because he was holding me so tight. Instead, I tried to keep him in a good mood. I said, 'Let's go to the tavern first, then your place later.'"

"Good thinking," Michael says, "So nothing happened then, I hope?"

"That's right. You two saved me! At the tavern I allowed myself to be calm and think things over. We each had a drink and I thought he might soften up and agree to take me home. Not a chance. He just got more insistent about going to his place, letting his charm slip and treating me more like a disobedient pet. Eventually, I said I needed to use the restroom. He said he did, too, and accompanied me there. When he was done, he hung outside the *Ladies'* room door, waiting for me, then calling for me, relentlessly. Meanwhile, a few women went in and out." She laughs at the thought. "He apologized to each of them as they left, saying it was time for his wife to go home with him.

"Finally, after about fifteen minutes of not hearing anything, I took a peek out the door. He was gone, but he hadn't left the tavern. I stuck my head around the corner of that hallway and could see that he was back at our table in the front room. That's when I called you. The timing was good because he came back while you were on your way here and harangued me some more."

Michael reaches across the table and takes one of Robin's hands. She then reaches out with her other hand and takes one of Johnny's.

Robin's Ordeal

"I would have walked right out of there, but I feared he might go after me, and it being late and hardly anybody on the street, I knew I'd be powerless against him if he caught up to me. Besides, I'm sure he was ready for something like that."

"There wasn't a back door?" Johnny asks.

"There was an emergency fire door. It was one of those with an alarm. He would have heard it go off."

"I noticed that," Michael confirms.

"Fortunately, there was that phone by the restrooms!"

"That was fortunate!" Johnny agrees, and Michael nods in accordance.

With that, Robin closes her eyes and tilts back her head, letting out a sigh, reinforcing the fact that her ordeal is over. When she opens them, Michael gently squeezes her hand in his and says, "I'm glad you're okay."

She gazes at him and smiles a smile for a good friend. Then she shoots Johnny a look with an unmistakable twinkle in her eyes. He meets it for a moment or two, then looks down. After a pause, respectful of the unified feeling between the three of them, he declares, "We now have something to work with. All we need is a plan."

Chapter 11

Michael's Prescient Advice

It's late the next day. Johnny is at his desk on the office phone when he dials his uncle. Ralph has already left for the day, but Michael is nearby.

"We know where the house in Brooklyn is, sir. And we've devised a plan to snoop around and see what we find."

Uncle Gene listens intently as his nephew describes in detail the plan Johnny and Michael have put together.

"That's good, John—imaginative. Kudos to you!"

"Thanks, Cap," Johnny says, trying his luck at being less formal. Unfortunately, it brings only silence. Johnny instantly regrets the slip and knows his uncle must be fuming at his end of the line. Peripherally, he can see Michael is also uneasy with this casual approach.

Now with remorse sounding in his voice, he says, "What I should say, sir, is that this has all been very exciting and it's meaningful to me being involved. So, thank you!"

"That, I appreciate hearing, John," Uncle Gene says, his anger subsiding as the words come. "The plan sounds good, but don't do anything that could endanger yourself."

"Yes, sir. I'll be aware of that."

"All right, then. Thank you for filling me in. Let me know tomorrow how it goes."

After the call, Johnny looks out the office window at the bay. Evening is settling in at the marina. The water is a reddish glow as the sun descends in the west out of sight from his view. It's quiet, yet the feeling from the phone call still lingers on, unsettled in his brain.

God, I treat him awful a lot of the time, don't I? When I look at it honestly, Uncle Gene doesn't deserve that, despite his irritating quirks! I've got to change that attitude—now!

Johnny swivels in his office chair to face Michael, who's also admiring the view outside. "Guess I gotta put that thing on!" he says, gesturing to a navy-blue suit hanging from the bathroom doorknob.

Michael still has the one on he wears for work. He gives Johnny a look that says, 'when you gotta, you gotta.'

After donning the suit, Johnny pats the left side of his chest, hitting something solid inside the jacket. "Have you got yours in place?" he asks.

Michael taps the same area, "It's there."

"Good," Johnny says, moving to the door. "We're ready to go."

Michael, on the contrary, stays in place studying him. He seems on the verge of something, a restlessness enveloping him. "Maybe we should have a word first," he finally says.

I should have known. He's been a little odd since he arrived, not saying much. I don't get it. Everything seems to be in order, the plan straightforward. Does he want to back out?

"About the plan?" Johnny asks, instead.

Michael's Prescient Advice

"No," Michael says, drawing out the sound of the word. "I suppose we can go over that on our way. I hope you don't mind, there's something else I feel impelled to talk about. Can we sit a minute?"

"Sure."

The urgency in Michael's voice prompts Johnny to do just that. After re-seating himself, he waits in baffled anticipation.

Michael settles on a stool he brings over from the pantry area.

"Is this about the possible danger?" Johnny asks.

"In part, of course."

"Okay, shoot."

"I don't want to sound like a preacher. Nobody likes to be preached to, but as I said once before I get intuitive promptings, and they're seldom wrong."

"So, you've got one now?"

"I do and it feels like a strong one."

Johnny looks closely at him, involuntarily not blinking. Michael is looking at him, too, or is he? He's as still as ever, and his focus, although seemingly on Johnny, has an unearthly look about it, as if he's doing something inwardly. *It's as if he's tuning into something like an automatic tuner on a radio receiver, zeroing in on a difficult frequency.*

Johnny finally blinks hard, as if to determine if this is real. When he reopens his eyes, nothing has changed.

"I get the feeling that you've reached a crossroads," Michael begins.

A crossroads? He's going to say something that's challenging again. My heart's pounding.

Michael continues, "You've been making attempts toward a major shift in the way you engage the world."

"Uh-huh. Sure," Johnny responds, going along with this.

"It's evident in the conversations we've been having. Yet, I don't think you know what you're really encountering. Your motivation has been sincere and well-meaning and I think that everything that's been happening to you has been leading you in the right direction for finding your answer to true satisfaction. One's authentic nature works that way. You can go with it, or against it. In that regard, you've begun to follow your authentic nature's desire to reveal itself. It's a path many have taken, yet few take it to fruition."

"Hmm, very mysterious. I don't understand."

"You don't have to understand completely because life *is* a mystery. But there's a pivotal point when there's a thought-altering realization, which I came to myself. It's then that it's best to act according to the demand of the new perspective you've attained. Instead, most retreat to the comfort of an unchallenging, yet dissatisfying existence, despite what they have come to know. As for you, I feel that you are on the verge of discovery. If you decide to continue, I feel you'll surely be graced with the answer to your quest. However, you will no longer be able to rely on your old ways of getting by. The danger, a danger of a different kind, is that the challenges will be greater than ever before. You've got to be strong and unwavering to meet them, never falling back on conventional means dictated by the weaknesses of human nature."

This is unbelievable! Where does he come up with this stuff? Is it really Michael talking? All I can do is look at him with a big question mark on my face.

"You have a great spirit, Johnny. It was evident even on the softball field, despite the grandstanding. And, recently, you've been questioning yourself, which is good for enabling change. For some reason, and I don't know why—I'm feeling that what we are about to do tonight is crucial. There may be no turning back. It may not be obvious at first, but I think the repercussions could soon be evident and you'd be forced to make critical decisions that would have you confronting your years of acquired weaknesses. But, if you stay the course by following your good intentions actively, I feel you'll be guided in a way beyond what we, as humans, can comprehend."

"Is that where the *mystery* comes in?"

"Yes, surrendering to the Unknown always is. But there's no boost from that mysterious Source when there isn't purposeful living. The outcomes are always same old, same old."

Johnny hangs his head respectful of what's being said. *This is weird but strangely feels right and humbling. Is it the next step in my transformation?* "Hmm, all I can say is I'll just take your word for it. Everything you've said to me in the past has rung true, as this seems to."

"Good, because I feel it's important that you know this before we continue. I have no qualms about going with you. I just warn you that you had better be 100 percent certain that you want to go on before we do so."

His words are like a hazy cloud, which I'm sure will soon dissipate and everything will be normal again. But something else tells me it isn't going to be that simple—my own premonition!

"Are you trying to say that snooping around this house, besides possibly being physically dangerous, could mess me up even more in another way?"

"For one, on the surface, what we are about to do is undoubtedly illegal, although we know it's for a good cause. There is some justification for going ahead with it, but there may be some repercussions as a result. I feel, though, that if there are repercussions, they can be overcome as long as you are solidly committed to going forward with the inner, heartfelt changes you want to make. Otherwise, there may be karmic consequences to deal with. And, yes, don't ever downplay the physical danger. You always have to be on guard against bodily harm when you go out on a limb."

"What does karmic mean? I've heard that word before, but have no idea what it means."

"Simply put, it's the universe's way of *sticking it to you* for not doing what's right in your heart."

"Oh… think I get it, but how do you know this stuff?" Johnny inquires, looking at Michael in awe.

Then the unearthliness of Michael's demeanor breaks and he smiles at Johnny, looking like he's really seeing him. "Let's just say for now that my sensitive nature gives me a different insight into life than most. Sorry to scare you. I was feeling that was necessary to be said."

"Well, thanks," Johnny says as a grin breaks out on his face.

"So, shall we carry on?"

"Are you kidding? Of course."

Chapter 12

The House on State Street

The vintage *Falcon* parallel parks into a lone space on State Street, approximately a block and a half from the rowhouse numbered 11-33. It's dark out now, but street lamps provide just enough light to read the house numbers located on every front door.

So, here we go. It's a crazy plan, but lately, especially after hearing what Michael had to say, I feel buoyed by something inside me that I've never felt before.

"Wilson should be well into his usual night on the town," Johnny says, as he douses the lights and pulls the key from the ignition.

"Are you sure he won't be coming by here?" Michael asks.

"No Steve to warn us, but I doubt it."

Michael bows his head in self-contained thought. "That's not totally comforting, but it was good to hear Steve got a job."

"Working regularly for me must have given him incentive. Unfortunately, he's too bushed, like most normal folks, to do this sort of thing at night now.

"As for Wilson, he's only been here once since we've been following him—last night, which had everything to do with Robin doing her thing. Every other night he's amused himself in Manhattan, or caught a game at Yankee Stadium."

"Good. It sounds like the odds of him stopping by can't be that great."

Then, without further ado, the two of them get out of the car and take two bubble-wrapped paintings on loan from Robin out of the trunk.

The night air is refreshing and the street pleasant, by no means desolate. A moderate amount of traffic passes by regularly. It gives the impression of a safe neighborhood.

Michael, keeping in mind their vulnerability, says, "Let's be prepared for anything."

Johnny nods, his face mirroring the necessary caution.

It isn't long before they're standing at the front door where Robin had been the night before. Johnny pushes the doorbell and they hear a loud buzzing sound from inside. Within moments, a window shade, not far from the door, is pulled back a smidgen. A face appears, then is gone. Footsteps are heard approaching the door and a man in his late 40s, with dark eyes and thinning black hair, opens it the width of the attached chain. He looks just like the guy Robin described—a gruff, low-life.

Looking at them suspiciously, the man behind the door demands in a voice confirming his coarseness, "Yeah?"

Johnny jumps right in. "We're here to see Dr. Wilson. He's expecting us."

"Wilson ain't here!" the man growls in response.

Without missing a beat in their well-rehearsed plan, Johnny counters, "He said to wait for him in case he was late."

"I didn't hear nuttin' about this. Who are you guys?"

"I'm Ed Harper," Johnny announces. Pointing to Michael, he continues, "and he's Dave Hanson." The gruff man's eyes go up and down on Michael suspiciously.

"We met James last week at the theater. He told us about the heirloom he had on exhibit recently and his interest in fine art. We brought a painting from each of our collections for him to view."

"Really?"

"He said this is the most convenient spot for us to meet. He said he works out of this house occasionally."

With an incredulous stare, the man finishes sizing them up. "Where are yous guys from, anyway?"

"New Jersey," Johnny says without giving it any thought.

"Wait here a minute."

With that he closes the door, shaking his head. "Lou!" he shouts as he hastens from the vestibule to an archway to the kitchen, which is quite large and modern. "Lou, did you hear that, two guys from Jersey?"

Lou does not look like a low-life. A man, also in his 40s and nicely dressed, he looks like he has some smarts. He sits at the kitchen table sipping coffee and reading a copy of the *New York Times*. A small, portable black-and-white TV sits on a counter. It's on with the sound low, a baseball game playing on its screen. "Yeah, I heard it."

"What do ya think? One of 'em is Black."

"Doesn't matter. We both know Wilson is an art enthusiast. We'll have to let them in and wait. If only he'd call in more often, we wouldn't be in the dark about everything."

"I don't like it," the gruff man complains, puffing himself up. "Last night he stops by unexpectedly wanting to get laid with some broad. Now, this! This stuff makes me nervous. He used to be more careful."

"I don't like it either, Pete," Lou says, thinking the situation over as he turns to another page in the *Times*, "but he's the boss and our meal ticket. Besides, the house was set up to pretend to be other than what it is, especially for unexpected visitors. And, don't forget, we'll be out of New York sometime soon. Just let them in while I try the doctor at his place in the city."

"You know he's hardly ever in. Why don't you just beep him?"

"Emergencies only. Remember? I got hell the last time."

"All right, all right. I'll let them in."

"They can bide their time in the living room."

A short time later Johnny and Michael are seated on a loveseat, among other couches and chairs, in a large living room, apparently set up for optimal viewing of a large screen TV in one part of the room. On its walls are some exceptional-looking, traditional paintings, but, mostly, there are photos and framed newspaper clippings, all sports related. Both of them scan the room, taking it all in.

"I bet one of the paintings here was on exhibit at that heirloom show," Johnny says to Michael.

The rest of the room is formal with a stone fireplace and expensive-looking furniture, including a marble-topped, coffee table in front of their loveseat with assorted sports magazines scattered on it. The overall feel of the room is like that of a private club, only smaller.

"I wonder what's with these guys living here?" Johnny comments as he peruses magazines in front of them.

The House on State Street

"Maybe they're caretakers for a sports club."

"Could be. We know Wilson's a Yankee fan."

"The one who let us in looks more like an enforcer of some sort."

"Who knows—maybe to take care of trouble; the other one to oversee everything."

In the kitchen, Pete has returned from escorting Johnny and Michael inside. He watches as Lou takes a small handful of peanuts from a bowl and puts it in his mouth.

"Was he in?" Pete asks, mouthing the words.

Lou shakes his head as he motions for his companion to come closer. By the time he's done chewing, Pete is within earshot of his whisper. "I got his answering machine… We'll let them hang for an hour. If the boss isn't here by then, show them the door."

"Uh, huh," Pete responds, his attention drawn to the open newspaper still on the table. "I guess I can live with that…. Say, what's this? Lefty Phillips wants a new contract? He didn't even break even last year."

'Yep. Ever since Catfish Hunter signed that big one with the Yankees, everyone wants a bigger chunk of the pie."

As the discussion turns to a disgruntled athlete's pay, Pete is loud enough to be heard in the living room, compared to Lou's more lowkey retorts. While they're preoccupied, Johnny quickly surveys the scene.

Across, and to the left of where they are on the loveseat, is a staircase going straight up to another floor. To the left of the staircase, he notes, there's a hallway that goes to an area out of view. Just to its right is an archway to a good-sized dining room. And, to the right of the archway, is a shorter hallway with a swinging door to the kitchen. It's

The Catch!

in view from where they're seated and is currently held open with a door stop.

Inside the kitchen, the conversation has escalated into a full-blown session of that common, American male practice of shooting the breeze, a practice spurred on by the current popularity of sports talk radio.

Johnny is now ready to do something. He nudges Michael and slowly gets to his feet, then pulls back the left side of his suit jacket and takes a walkie-talkie out of an inside breast pocket.

Michael nods and does the same.

"Make sure the volume is turned very low," Johnny cautions, whispering the words.

After they turn both walkie-talkies on, they return them inside their jackets and give each other a thumps-ups. Johnny then continues on, walking over to the shorter hallway and the open kitchen door.

"Jackie Robinson was the spark to the '55 team, I tell you," Pete insists. Lou doesn't bother to answer. He's looking at Johnny who's standing at the kitchen archway.

"What's up, Mr...?

"Harper, but Ed is okay."

"Well, what can I do for you?" Lou asks, matter-of-factly. Pete turns to glare at Johnny.

"Sorry to bother you, guys. Is there a bathroom I can use?"

"Down the hall on the left, Ed-dee," Pete says with a mocking tone, and immediately turns back to Lou. "You name a better ballplayer than Robinson that year."

But Lou seems more concerned about Johnny. "Pete, why don't you be a good host and escort our friend to the bathroom? Then check your baseball statistics book before coming back. It'll show Robinson wasn't the NL MVP in '55."

"How much do you wanna bet? It had to have been Robinson!"

"Sure, you're on—fifty bucks!"

"You're on for ten."

"Hmm, doesn't sound like you're so sure now."

Pete shrugs his shoulders, annoyed, and doesn't respond. He turns to Johnny instead. "Okay, Ed-dee! Let me show you to the can." Then he shoots Lou a poisonous stare. "It may take a while to find that sucker. It hasn't been unpacked since we've been holed up here."

On their way, Johnny asks Pete, "What is this, some sort of sports club?"

"Nice guess, Ed-dee! The shitter's right here," he says, pointing to the bathroom door.

After Johnny enters, Michael, still sitting on the loveseat, listens as Pete's footsteps continue further down the hall. He hears the creak of a door, then the creak of another. Michael gets up to take a look. Seeing light pouring out of a room through an open door at the end of the hall, he realizes the second creak must have been from another door inside that same room. He figures it must be to a closet to find that statistics book.

Now, with an eye on the kitchen doorway, Michael reaches into his jacket and pushes a button on the walkie-talkie. Bending his head toward it, he whispers, "The guy who escorted you is now in a room at end of the hall, door open, but out of sight. Otherwise, coast clear."

Within seconds, Johnny silently exits the bathroom and closes the door behind him. He tiptoes down the hall back to the living room and gestures upward to Michael.

The Catch!

He then proceeds to noiselessly ascend the staircase, occasionally steadying himself on the darkly stained, wooden banister until he reaches the second floor.

Upstairs is barren compared to below. A narrow hallway has four doorways, its walls bare, except for old-fashioned wallpaper. It's musty, too, and Johnny doesn't look surprised when the first room he enters is totally empty.

Downstairs, Michael waits patiently, again seated on the loveseat. He hears Pete rummaging in that same room down the hall. Then there's the sound of something heavy plopping down on the springs of a tired, old mattress. Knowing Pete is hunting for a packed-away book, Michael figures that it's a box of stored-away items that's been plunked down on the bed. He continues listening as softer plop sounds emanate from the room, conjuring the image of Pete dropping books, one by one, onto the bed in his search.

When the softer plop sounds end, he hears an, "Ah-huh!" recognizable as Pete's guttural, growl of a voice. Soon after, there's the riffle of pages turning, first briskly, then slowly, then stopping, silence. A long pause, followed by noise suspected to be the box being repacked, slower now—the desire to hurry no longer evident. A kerplunk sound is next, as if the same, supposed box is being put down, perhaps in a closet, because what follows is the familiar faint creaking sound of a door, this time undoubtedly closing. Then there are the somber-like, less confident, sounds of meandering steps coming back down the hall toward the living room. There's a pause part way. Then they begin again and soon enough Pete emerges into view.

The House on State Street

"Can't believe your friend is still on the pot," Pete says with an inquiring look at Michael.

"A lot of junk food, I guess. He's a salesman. Eats on the road all the time."

"Well, I hope he knows to open a window when he's through."

Just then a faint throat-clearing sound comes from Michael's breast pocket. He clears his own throat to mimic what the walkie-talkie produced. "I hope he will," he says. "I may have to go, myself if we're here much longer."

Pete grunts in response and continues his trudge through the living room. Michael keeps an eye on him as he walks back to the kitchen dejectedly.

Without looking up from his newspaper, Lou says, "I was right, wasn't I?"

Pete hesitates.

"Don't want to cough up 10 bucks, do you?" Lou taunts him.

"Let's make another bet, so I can win it back," Pete counters while irritably kicking the kitchen doorstop out of position, allowing the spring-loaded hinges to swing the door closed.

With the sounds of a deadened, full-scale debate on sports now resuming, Michael hits a button on his walkie-talkie inside his jacket and whispers, "A close call, but the coast is clear."

Moments later, Johnny's legs are visible as he works his way quietly down the stairs. When his upper torso and head descend below the ceiling line, he points in the direction of where he's just been, and mouths the word 'Nothing'.

Before he's all the way down, he, too, hears the muffled sounds of the continuing absurdity happening in the kitchen and makes a face cognizant of that. When he reaches the bottom of the stairs, he gestures to the hall on his right and heads that way.

Besides the bedroom Pete rummaged in, there's another one on the left just past the bathroom. Johnny enters. It's apparently for guests, the light in the hall allowing him to make out what's in it, a neatly made-up bed, an empty chest of draws, a chair, and a closet—bearing mostly unencumbered hangers, one with a bathrobe. There's also a desk with nothing on it, except an ashtray, holding a couple of cigar butts. *Hmm, probably where Wilson has his flings. I can imagine him smoking a cigar in that bathrobe after sex.*

Johnny quickly dismisses the unwelcome thought and moves on to the other, bigger room. The door is open as Pete left it. He enters and flips a light switch to get better illumination, then closes the door. A fast scan reveals this one is definitely being used. It has two bunk-size beds, a single bureau, a desk, two chairs, and a louvered door, probably to a closet.

The beds exhibit two different personalities. One is semi-neat, with a blanket covering the entire mattress and a pillow centered at one end. He shifts his attention to the other. It has filthy sheets, a worn-out bedspread, and a pillow, no case, all jumbled together on a mostly uncovered mattress. *This one's gotta be Pete's. Matches his fine disposition.*

Keeping his disgust in check, he begins to systematically search the room. Dropping to his hands and knees, he checks under each bed. He moves all kinds of junk and garbage around under the unkempt one until he's satisfied that there's no evidence of the missing heirloom. Next

The House on State Street

is the bureau. He goes through it draw by draw. Besides clothes, he finds various other items —porno magazines, Vaseline, cheap cigars, even a tube of hair coloring, but, so far, not a shred of anything indicating stolen property.

Meanwhile, Michael endures the escalating racket in the kitchen. With the door closed, he can't make out more than the combativeness in Pete's voice. Then, all of a sudden, the kitchen door swings open and Pete comes hurrying out, followed by Lou walking at a normal pace.

"You'll see. It was the Braves who won that year. The book'll prove it," Pete shouts, huffily.

"I've got to see the dumbfounded look on your face when you find out you're wrong again," Lou coolly responds.

Michael is briefly taken aback as they pass in front of him. Regaining his composure, he reaches into his jacket, finds the walkie-talkie's button, and fakes a sneeze, "A-choo!"

Hearing the pre-discussed danger signal over his walkie-talkie, Johnny closes the last of the bureau draws. *Damn! Gotta find cover!*

Sure enough, the sounds of two sets of footsteps coming down the hall catch his attention. *Gotta find cover—fast! The louvered door!*

In two steps he's there and opens it. In the next instant, he steps in, immediately recognizing it as a walk-in closet. Clothes hang from poles on his right and left. A few scattered boxes clutter the floor between him and another door at the opposite end, which he can see has an old skeleton key in its keyhole. A moment later, he closes the door behind him and all is dark. *Stay calm! And keep moving, damn it!*

And Johnny does, the danger of tripping on a box very present in his mind.

"Did you leave the light on in here before?" he hears Lou question Pete, leaving no doubt that they're now inside the bedroom.

"I dunno, maybe," Pete says, uncertainly.

"Where's the book?"

"It's in the closet. I repacked it."

"That was dumb! We'll leave it out this time."

Johnny staggers forward in the blackness, tiptoeing around boxes that he only has a mental image of. Unbelievably, he makes it to the opposite end without mishap, his hands quickly locating the doorknob and skeleton key nestled in the lock.

How I do get out before they...

"How many times have I told you to keep all of your junk under your bed?" Lou scolds. "And why don't you toss stuff like that Burger King bag?"

"Sorry," Johnny hears Pete say without contriteness, "the bed must've moved when I looked for the book before."

Pete then kicks items back under his bed. Inside the closet, Johnny turns the key to unlock the door in front of him with trembling hands.

"I'll throw some of that other stuff out later," Pete promises.

"It's always later with you!"

The discussion gives Johnny the extra time he needs and distracts them from hearing the click sound as he turns the key in the door's lock.

Wondering what's happening and still sitting on the loveseat, Michael suddenly sees something vague in front of him. He gets to his feet to get a better look. Inside the

The House on State Street

dining room, only partially illuminated by lamps from the living room, he sees a door swing open. Quickly, a human form slips through. Then, just as swiftly, the door is shut without making a sound. It takes only a moment before he realizes it's Johnny.

Where am I? Wait, there's Michael! Adjusting to the surprise, Johnny shrugs his shoulders at his friend, as if to ask, 'So here we are. What next?' Then he answers his implied question by taking a closer look at his surroundings.

Like the living room, the dining room is well-appointed. Expensive, modern wallpaper covers its walls, adorned by several brass light sconces. A nice mahogany oval table, surrounded by eight matching chairs, is centered under what looks like a genuine crystal chandelier. Nearby is a serving stand, also mahogany, and conveniently on wheels. The walls have original paintings, many of sports legends, done with conservative, somber colors, much like the ones in the living room. There's an open liquor cabinet in one corner, fully stocked with an assortment of bottles. And then there is the mahogany China cabinet on the opposite wall with glass doors. Seen inside are fine crystal goblets and dinnerware. But something is odd about the cabinet on closer view. Johnny wouldn't have noticed it, except for the fact that he's looking for something unusual. The cabinet appears to be sitting on a three-inch platform, painted a similar mahogany-like color. That's only the first thing that seems unusual. Stepping sideways to see it from an angle, Johnny notices vertical molding on the wall behind it, a few inches in from the cabinet's edge. He goes to the opposite side to take a look and sees the same thing. Then he goes down on his hands and knees and gets a closer look at the platform.

The Catch!

At ground level, he sees what appears to be the bottom of wheels. Taking a look over at Michael and scratching his head, he gets back up on his feet and tries to move the cabinet. It does so easily and he continues to roll it away from the wall.

Michael, in the meantime, has gotten a better view, standing at the archway between the two rooms. Within moments, he sees what's revealed as Johnny moves the cabinet totally away from the wall. It's a door. Instead of having a knob, there's a shiny, built-in security lock with a keypad.

Michael, ever alert, notices that the sound of voices has moved from the space where Johnny has exited, back to inside the bedroom. He steps back away from the archway and, no sooner has he uttered the words, "I think they may be coming out soon," than voices start to reverberate down the hall.

"I told you I knew my baseball, you numskull! The Yankees were unbeatable in '58," Lou says with satisfaction.

He and Pete are moving steadily toward the living room at a reasonable pace. However, to Michael, it seems like racewalking. Johnny won't have enough time to move the cabinet back.

"Like I said before. You don't get the complete story from the book. Milwaukee had the more color—"

Suddenly, Michael steps up to examine an exceptional painting, hanging just to the left of the staircase. He's right in the path of the two men who are just a few steps away. "Excuse me," he says with a touch of naivety, "is this part of Dr. Wilson's collection?"

Both Pete and Lou stop short.

"Not ours to say. Why?" Pete growls.

"I wouldn't bother getting into that," Lou mutters to Pete. "Let him ask the doctor if he shows up."

"Oh," Michael says, feigning surprise.

"C'mon," Lou says and brusquely goes around Michael, followed by Pete.

Once by him, though, they stop again upon seeing Johnny out of the corner of their eyes. He appears to be pacing in the dining room with his hands clasped behind his back. The China cabinet is back in place, Michael's timing was perfect.

Knowing, they must be staring at him, Johnny turns their way. There's a pause as they look him over, Pete with particular curiosity. "A bit restless after your little episode?" he says as gruff as ever.

Johnny tries to hide his surprise at the assessment, "Huh?"

"Your constipation, bud! I'd get myself some bran flakes." He glances at Lou. "A prune or two should do the trick, too, right, Lou?"

Lou doesn't respond as he gazes around the room.

"Oh, sure… good advice," Johnny says, his words accompanied by an easy laugh to hide the flood of relief that he feels.

But Johnny and Michael aren't completely out of the woods. Lou's gaze has detected something out of the ordinary—the China cabinet isn't quite hiding the door behind it as it did before.

"Did you guys beep me?" It's Dr. Wilson a little later. He's on a pay phone in a hallway at a concert hall. The sounds of an orchestra play in the background.

After Lou explains the situation, Dr. Wilson gives him a directive, "You said they're from New Jersey, so have

The Catch!

Pete check around outside and get the license plate numbers of any car from there, pronto! Before they leave!"
Approximately an hour after they arrived, Johnny and Michael are escorted to the door of 11-33 State Street. Fear had gripped them both only twenty minutes before when they heard a phone ring in the house. They wondered about the possibility of it being Dr. Wilson. Now they still don't know.

"I'm sorry the doc didn't show, fellas. Dems the breaks," Pete says with a peculiar grin.

"You didn't hear from him at all?" Johnny ventures as the front door is opened for them.

"Of course not. I would have told yous. Oh, the phone call... yeah, that was about something else. Nothing to do with yous."

"Well, what do you think?" Johnny asks with a troubled look after he and Michael are settled and on their way in the car.

"I think that may have been Dr. Wilson who called. Pete's explanation sounded phony."

"Right—evasive."

The vintage *Falcon* goes one block to the next intersection and turns onto Atlantic Avenue in the direction of the Brooklyn Bridge.

Johnny continues, "It's just odd, if that *was* Wilson on the phone, why didn't they do anything about it."

"You never know," Michael cautions. "If that was him calling, you'd think... I wonder if we're being followed? They were plenty suspicious of us in there."

Johnny checks his rearview mirror. "Hard to tell."

Michael twists in his seat to double-check. After about thirty seconds, he says, "Nobody's following. Nothing

The House on State Street

unusual back there." He turns back to Johnny, "By the way, what did you make of that hidden door?"

"A lot! Did you see the recessed, combination lock on it?"

"I did. And no doorknob."

"Makes for a tight fit of the cabinet against the wall. Obviously, they're hiding something."

"Considering where it's situated, I'd say that's a door to a basement."

The car travels across the Brooklyn Bridge, cuts through lower Manhattan to the Holland Tunnel, taking them into New Jersey, then through Jersey City down to Bayonne.

Back home, Johnny invites Michael in for a nightcap. Inside they discover a message from Uncle Gene on the answering machine. He's eager to hear what's happened that night and wants a call back no matter how late.

"How did it go, John?" Uncle Gene answers, barely after one ring.

Johnny gives him a thorough description of the night's events as his uncle listens in silence. Finally, when he's finished, the older man says in his booming voice, "Good job, John. You've really come through. Your timing is excellent, too. I just got the name of a New York police detective from a law enforcement friend of mine. I think you've gone as far as you should go. Give him a call. My friend thinks there's enough suspicion that he just might take on the case and do so without involving the media.

Johnny jots down the name and number of the detective and promises to call first thing in the morning at the office.

Michael stays for the offered nightcap, then leaves. When he's gone, Johnny lingers alone in his den. *What a day! It's probably best that this detective does take over. Things have escalated even more after what we've learned today—those guys at the house, the weird atmosphere there, the mystery of the hidden door, etc.*

Then there's Michael's unusual advice before we left to go out! He humbly shakes his head in amazement, thinking about him. *He's so wise for his age. And, the one-time cocky me hanging on to every word! How different my life's been of late!*

Chapter 13

Surprise!

We learned a lot last night, although I have a sneaking feeling there's a whole lot more to find out. For now, I'll contact that detective and see what he says.

These are Johnny's thoughts as he steps from his car into the cool, heavy air at the marina parking lot, barely noticing the man. It's not odd for strollers and joggers to be out early for a little exercise during the summer. This is before the onset of the scorching heat that comes on suddenly about mid-morning this time of year. Some of those pause by the marina to take in the sea and the accompanying boats, peaceably bobbing in their slips, while they absorb the sounds of the seagulls and slapping water amidst the mild rush of a salty breeze. This man seems to be no exception. It's only his extraordinary bulk that stands out.

However, unbeknownst to Johnny, as he makes his way to the marina office door, it is he, not the panorama, that the man is focused on. He remains positioned there a little longer, observing with a menacing expression on his face, then turns on his heels and leaves.

The Catch!

After Johnny enters the office, he continues right out to the back deck and sees a familiar figure lying on one of the piers down below.

"G'morning, Ralph!" he shouts.

Ralph raises an arm and manages a wave, then feebly shouts back, "Morning, boss."

Johnny takes the walkway down to dock level and over to Ralph who's comfortably sprawled out on his back. Being unmerciful, he says, "A few cool rays before busting butt, huh? Nice! Likely to be ninety, ninty-five today with deadly humidity. Weather to grunt to."

Ralph arches up his back and neck in his remaining moments of relaxation. "Thanks for the sympathy, boss. I already heard the weather report. Just wish it could feel like 7:30 in the morning all day."

"Don't worry, fall is just around the corner. You'll be back at school, far away from the nasty, sticky air and, unfortunately, Martha Highland in her skimpy bikini."

"Come on, boss, don't torture me… But since you're on the topic, I actually prefer Michael's friend, Robin, in a one-piece."

Johnny makes a face and comments, "An older woman over Martha? You're growing up, Ralph."

"Yes. Maturity. How sweet it can be."

"Ah huh," Johnny mutters, gamely. He then grabs Ralph by his wrists and swiftly pulls him to his feet. "And mature grown-ups get up when it's time to work, instead of letting their imaginations run wild about beautiful, older women!"

"And yours hasn't been running wild, boss?" Ralph teases back, while not giving in to the show of force, turning it into a spirited bit of tug-of-war.

Surprise!

"Ah-ha, speculating about your elders is bad enough, but have you forgotten who the boss is?"

Ralph reduces his struggle to a few half-hearted attempts of resistance, then gives in. "All right, all right, we can't let the empire deteriorate and crumble to the bottom of the bay, can we?"

"Now you're talking," Johnny says as he lets go.

The two laugh and take a few moments to catch their breaths.

"Let's get some coffee in the office," Johnny says as he leads Ralph back up the walkway. "You could use some and I had a late night. I also have an important call to make."

A look of remembrance crosses Ralph's face, "Oh yeah, phone call! There's a message on the answering machine from last night. It's from the curator at that museum in New York."

"What?"

"Probably about your missing heirloom. I wrote down the name and number inside."

Johnny steps up his pace to the office. Then, after a quick glance at his watch, he slows down. It's only 7:40—too early to be calling anybody.

It's after 9:30 a.m. when he finally gets through. Ralph is nearby eavesdropping, pleased at his timing in the midst of his tasks.

"You've got to be kidding!... I don't believe it!... Nobody knew 'til now?... Wow, I see…. That must be what my uncle took…. I'll let him know right away…. No problem. I'll get there ASAP to pick it up…. Thank you!"

Johnny puts down the receiver.

"They have the heirloom?" Ralph asks, not without excitement.

The Catch!

"They do," Johnny says, in a way that implies the joke's been on him. "How do you like that? They labeled the bubble-wrapped heirlooms incorrectly. An archeologist from Wyoming just got back to New York to retrieve his. He had an old fossil on display at a different exhibit at the same museum. When he removed his bubble wrap, he found our figurine inside. His fossil must be the rock Uncle Gene ended up with. Hope he didn't throw it away!"

"At least we've got ours," Ralph says, and adds with sophomoric wisdom, "What would the empire be without its leader's rightful inheritance out of wraps and on display?"

"Ours?"

"A slip of the tongue, but it was beginning to feel that way."

The next evening Michael and Robin are at Johnny's home together for the first time. They've been told the invite is for a special occasion. After serving them an excellent champagne in the kitchen, he leads them down the hall, stopping just before the doorway to the den.

"And now the reason I asked you to come."

He opens the door and gestures for them to enter. On display, in a makeshift way, is the heirloom. It sits on Johnny's coffee table, which he's moved to the center of the room with lamps around it, their shades tilted to direct light in its direction. Its 14-inch, gold-plated figure glitters in the wattage, along with the jewels which ornament it.

More breathtaking than can be described with words, both Michael and Robin gasp. The sculpture's small size bears no relation to its beauty, in its depiction of something being profoundly sounded.

Surprise!

Johnny lets their awe linger in the air for a while, then breaks the silence. "After all the fuss, it turns out it was never stolen, or missing, for that matter. It was mislabeled in the museum's storeroom the whole time. Anyway, with all the good-intentioned help you gave me I thought you'd want to see..." *They're not listening. They're transfixed on the heirloom, totally in awe of it! Kinda what I expected!*

"It's incredible!" Robin breathlessly raves.

"I agree—wasn't prepared for anything like this!" Michael concurs.

"The inscription! I've got to know what it says!" Robin says enthusiastically. "Michael, can you read it out loud?"

Michael nods in acceptance and squats down in front of the figurine without blocking the others' view. Then he reads what's on its base in a voice that resonates.

"Catch the Glory!
Catch the Sound!
Stand tall and catch the Pitch,
Know the Love Unbound.
Then be the Pitch
And sound the Pitch.
Be the answer to the Call.
To be Love Unconditional
The Catch is All!"

When he's finished, Michael quietly gets up and steps back to where he was.

Whoa! Feeling flush all over! Once again, it's like an electrical charge is running through me as I stand with these two.... The figurine's come alive! Something in that face—so passionate, so inspired.

"He must be sounding the Pitch," Johnny says.

"En how!" Michael confirms.

Michael's reading gives it significant new meaning for me. I feel elated like never before.

"I think it's found a new home," Michael says, his tone in keeping with the reverent feeling in the room. "Perhaps your uncle will let you keep it here."

"That would be ideal," Robin adds, in support.

After Michael and Robin depart, Johnny returns to the den and lingers before the sculpture in lieu of restoring the room to the way it was and takes in a deep breath. *An exhilarating few days and exceptional times with Michael and Robin. And, oh, is Robin ever fine! But better than having the hots for her, is the energy boost generated whenever I'm around these two!*

And the heirloom—the new feeling I have about it, changes things. I'll talk to Uncle Gene about where it will end up. Once decided, I know that can't be the end of it. I've gained a lot from this, topped off by incredible, physical sensations, especially from this evening. I don't know what the future holds, but I know it will be different and mysterious, and hopefully pleasingly so.

After contemplating in silence, Johnny reluctantly returns the den to its original order.

The next day at the marina Johnny is on the phone with his uncle, pacing the floor with the long extension cord going every which way. He's hardly slept overnight, but that won't deter him from what he's about to ask. In the meantime, though, he has to submit to his uncle's inquiring mind.

"Did you put the sculpture someplace out of sight as I told you, John?" By contrast, Uncle Gene is seated at his desk at the naval base in South Carolina, looking as firm and established as ever. The naval yard looms through a

Surprise!

picture window behind him, the drab colors of its military vessels in sharp contrast with the sporty-looking ones docked outside Johnny's marina.

"I did. First thing this morning I went to my bank and had it stored away in a safety deposit box."

"Great—the best place for it for now."

"I guess I'm learning from you. I have to admit your constant haranguing has done me some good over the years. I'm starting to appreciate the value you've been in my life."

An embarrassed Uncle Gene doesn't know what to say. It isn't too often that he's praised this way.

"Thank you, John. That means a lot to me. I've always seen your potential."

The vulnerable tone in his voice clearly comes through. However, it's imperative to his own sense of self-demeanor to change the subject. Dwelling on compliments, especially ones tinged with sentiment, isn't part of his make-up.

"You know, it's amazing the way things turned out," he continues, dropping all trace of emotion. "Wilson not having anything to do with it and all."

Johnny continues to pace. "You're right. That whole episode was pretty bizarre. He's definitely a strange character. And those guys at the house were nothing short of creepy."

"Well, you don't have to bother with them anymore. It's a good thing we never got the police involved."

"Right. What a mess that would have been." *Okay, now get to the point!*

"By the way, sir... about the heirloom... you know, it's quite... I guess I'm surprised that I suddenly feel very proud that it's ours. And I'm sure you can't wait to get it back... but just in case there's any chance, I thought I would ask—do you think I can keep it here?"

Uncle Gene is momentarily taken aback. Despite the seeming security of the established setting, something in Captain Sloper's foundation is shaken. 'How dare he make such a request?' is his first reaction. But just as quickly, his own inability to do the sculpture justice rises up bare before him from its oft repressed state.

"Well, John," he says eventually with a tremulous voice. "I'm sure that's a fair consideration, especially since it seems to have some importance for you."

The intensity of having dared to ask has resulted in a bit of absentmindedness on Johnny's part. In moving about with the phone's extension cord, he ends up having it wrapped around a leg and snagged on his chair.

Uncle Gene continues in a somewhat concessionary air. "You know, it does mean a great deal to me, too, John. But, as I said once before, it's true, I just don't have the home for it."

Johnny grabs the opening. "I've got the home, which really is thanks to you getting me on my feet. I can have a showcase built for it here in my den."

His uncle relaxes a little. "It sounds like you've given this some thought."

"Yes, sir!"

"I'll tell you what. You can have it in your possession for the time being, but you must promise to keep it locked in that safety deposit box until the showcase is built, one that encloses it in impenetrable glass and is wired for security."

Surprise!

"It's a deal. It will probably be costly, but I agree—that's just what it deserves," Johnny says getting further twisted in the phone cord.

"One other thing, John," Uncle Gene is back to using his authoritarian voice. "I would consider settling down. Stop all the gallivanting you do and, maybe, think about getting married."

At this point, Johnny, still moving about and focused only on the phone call, is tangled up in the phone cord. Suddenly aware of this, he lets himself plop down, somewhat gracefully – kerplunk – into his chair without losing balance.

"I agree. The gallivanting has to stop, sir. But marriage? I'll have to give that some thought."

Chapter 14

Romantic Interlude

Good God, I hope this goes well! She did agree to go out with me, after all. I've got that going for me.

It's Johnny's first date with Robin. It begins with a scenic drive along the Jersey shoreline and a stop for an informal dinner of mussels and beer.

She is tepid about the beer, hardly taking a sip. And, in general, things aren't easily comfortable between them. To him, she seems so refined. Although dressed casually in a blouse and skirt, Robin is nonetheless impeccable in appearance. Nothing is out of place – her hair, her makeup, her lipstick – right down to her perfectly laundered, wrinkle-free apparel. Besides that, she smells of roses, fresh roses. The pungency of wafting beer just doesn't compare.

However, by twilight, the effect of the falling sun and the relenting heat on the coastline mellows the uneasiness between them. The sound of waves petering out, as low tide sets in, adds to the ensuing tranquilness.

Johnny suggests a barefoot stroll on the beach and she complies, taking off her shoes before stepping on the sand

and easing his mood some more. *That's better—a shoeless Robin, so contrary to her prevailing air of perfection.*

It's apparent that nature's day-ending unfolding is pleasing to both of them, and Johnny, who usually operates with an anything-goes-forwardness, finally takes her hand as they walk in the wet sand along the water's edge.

"You know, I don't really know how to be with you," he gently confesses, surprised at his own admission.

"Why would that bother you? You seem to be able to handle most everything else quite well."

"Thanks, but I almost feel like a country hick who got lucky and got to go out with a princess."

"Well, you can stop that sort of thinking. I don't feel like her royal highness around you. You make me feel very much at home."

"Appreciate hearing that," Johnny says. *But isn't that compliment another example of her perfectness?*

They continue to walk in silence. *This is unbearable. Where does it go from here? I can't just leave her as an object of desire.*

Out of the blue, he decides to let go of her hand.

"Hold it right there," he says and continues ahead for a few yards, then squats down with his back to her.

"Come on. Hop on," he beckons, his arms stretched out to his sides, ready to catch her legs.

Robin doesn't move. "Johnny, I have a skirt on," she protests with a laugh.

"You are 'her royal highness!'"

"Oh, that's it—a test!"

"Ah huh. The moment of truth." Then he booms out as if querying all of creation, "Is she real beneath the surface of that flawlessly-appointed, exquisite bod of hers?"

Romantic Interlude

"Bod?" she asks on the verge of giddiness.

"All right, I apologize for the informal terminology."

"I only meant that word. The rest was fine, actually very fine. But bod..."

"I agree. That one isn't deserving. 'Divine visage' is more like it, yet seemingly untouchable and unpiggybackable," he continues in a teasing vain while maintaining his crouched position.

"Thank you for being so polite," she responds, the gaiety unmistakable, "and making that revision!"

"You're welcome.... You know, I can't believe you would consider a skirt getting dirty or wrinkled at a time like this," he says deliberately, ignoring her cracking facade. "What—with a piggyback ride in the offing?"

"It could be embarrassing. Skirts do ride up, you know."

"And reveal virgin thighs?"

"Something like that."

"Don't worry. Nobody's going to see anything. It's only you and me. And I've got my back to you."

"Well..." she teeters in the weighing.

"All right," he says, obviously faking resignation. Then he begins to tentatively rise from his squatting position. "I guess Jersey guys have some peculiarities that just take time getting used to."

Robin knows that he has manipulated her perfectly. She can't disappoint him, but it will be on her terms. "Get back down in that crouch!" she orders.

Pleasantly blown away by her sudden compliance, Johnny does as he's told. But before he's totally back in position, she lurches forward and using all the force she can muster, leaps onto his off-balance back, tipping them both over into the wet sand.

Immediately, the smell of roses consumes his senses and the warmth of her pressing body arouses his desire. *Seize the moment! Twist around, embrace her, kiss her, and…!*

Instead, in her state of silliness, she demands, "What kind of ride is this? We're not going anywhere. Giddyap, piggy!"

All right. My turn to comply. Later for the passion stuff.

"Hold on tight," Johnny says, getting to his feet with Robin holding fast. She's snugly attached—arms around his shoulders and legs wrapped firmly around his waist. Then, as one, they splash along the surf as he jogs as best as he can under her weight.

The rest of the evening they are inseparable—her head eventually resting against his chest, his arm holding her against his side. That's the way they stay for most of the walk back to her place, talking breezily all the while, right up until they get there.

Not long after, the setting is New York City—a sun-soaked outdoor restaurant. Across the street is Lincoln Center, the city's prime hotspot for artistic endeavor. The fountain at its heart is like an oasis in the early evening heat. Johnny sips on an iced coffee through a straw, then focuses in on Robin across the small, round table from him.

"The Big Apple, a sidewalk café, and an alluring woman," he muses. "Is it a dream? I never cared much for the city before now."

Robin, with a touch of aloofness, looks down at the table, then around at the surrounding scene. A peaceful smile adorns her lips as she returns to Johnny's steadfast gaze.

"Only if you're looking through the eyes of a dreamer. I wouldn't try to make it anything more than it is."

"Ah shucks, princess. Dream or no dream, I'm having fun with you."

"And I with you," she says, but not before averting her eyes again. Then she looks back up at him and continues, "but I want you to know, regarding this 'princess' business, that, yes, I was born with the proverbial silver spoon, etc., and I do like a certain amount of sophistication, but I don't like the phoniness exhibited by many of those who were born under the same circumstances. Then there's you—I love it that you're so real and down to earth!"

Wow, that was unexpected!

Johnny takes a moment to relish it, but then says, "I appreciate hearing that, but I know I still have some rough edges to me."

Robin says nothing, but she continues looking into his eyes while reaching across the table, supportively putting one of her hands on top of one of his.

Later, he walks her home. They are hand-in-hand when they reach her apartment building. *I still hardly know her, yet I know she's no ordinary woman and I want to be no ordinary man. I've got to be respectful, though, despite desiring more.*

Reaching the building's door, they turn toward each other. There's a pause between them. *I know she's reading my mind.*

Then Robin quickly kisses him on the lips and steps back. She will be the one to make the decision.

"I'd invite you up, but the place is a mess and it's late. I had a great time, though. How about you?"

Getting the drift, Johnny smiles, steps up, gently cradles her head in his hands, and gives her a quick peck on the lips, then says, "So, I'll see you, Sunday?"

"Yes. Looking forward to it."

Sunday wakes up fresh. It's early September now. The nights are succumbing to the changing season. They bring chilled breezes that carry over into morning, then ease as the day wears on without the normal summer wallop of hot, soggy air. Better yet is that Johnny doesn't have to rely on his old a/c compressor in his cherished car. He drives into the city with the *Falcon's* convertible top down, filling his lungs with invigorating clean air.

Robin waits in front of her apartment building, ready to go. The allure of the refreshing sun-kissed day has drawn her outside to relish its beauty.

There, she reflects on the new man in her life. Despite her usual discipline of detachment when it comes to men, he's been making an impression. And, now her body can't help but tremble with anticipation, making her wonder if she can keep herself in check for what lies ahead. Good judgment mustn't be left behind in the dust, she tells herself.

Because it's a Sunday when most parking restrictions are lifted, Johnny is easily able to find a spot for the *Falcon* near her building. After putting the top back up, he and Robin head by foot over to Central Park. In one hand he holds a multicolored, bird-shaped kite.

"I've been looking forward to flying this thing ever since Michael gave it to me for my birthday," Johnny says as he and Robin come out from under a London plane tree into a large open field in the park. The field is so large that, even with several ongoing touch football games, not

Romantic Interlude

to mention frisbees being tossed and people frolicking with dogs, there's still plenty of space to launch his kite.

"Hold onto this for a moment," he says, handing it to her, leaving him with the ball of string that's attached to it. "My father showed me an odd, but good way of doing this as a kid."

He then unwinds a few feet of string, after which he tosses the remaining ball as far as he can out into an unoccupied area. "This'll give me a string burn. Should have brought a glove, but I won first prize years ago at a Cub Scout event doing it this way.

"Now, when I start sprinting, let go," he adds as he hustles over and picks up the string about twenty feet in front of Robin.

"Here we go," he shouts and starts running, holding the string tightly. Feeling the tug on the kite in her hands, Robin lets go. It immediately shoots up into the air like a bird taking flight. Then, as Johnny runs, he loosens his grip, allowing the string to slide between his palm and thumb, the kite rising even more dramatically. When it reaches the desired height, he slows to a stop and alternately tightens and loosens his grip, controlling the kite as it interacts with the breezy air.

Robin watches from the spot where she let go. Besides being amazed at the kite's quick ascension, seeing the fun and contentment in Johnny's eyes as he maneuvers under it, enhances the bond she's been feeling with him. She then jogs in his direction.

"That's amazing!" she exclaims, skipping like a schoolgirl the last few yards.

He sees her out of the corner of his eye, as he keeps the bird-shaped kite in flight. Then she's upon him, wrapping

The Catch!

an arm around his torso and laying her head on his chest. Once again, she smells of roses and the show of affection melts his insides.

"I love it. What a spectacular sight—you and your kite!"

"Great fun, huh?" he responds, putting his attention wholly on her.

"Ah huh," she says, looking up into his eyes.

Then, beyond the face that smiles back down at her, Robin sees the kite out of control. Johnny, seeing her startled expression, looks skyward, but it's too late. The kite plummets to the ground, like a bird hit by buckshot. He shakes it off with a sheepish grin.

"Oh, well."

At the end of a day of kite flying, row boating, and seeing the sites offered at the park, followed by dinner at a sidewalk cafe, Johnny and Robin arrive outside her apartment building.

This time, when they face each other, Robin asks, "Want to come up before you go home?"

Johnny's pulse quickens, "Sure."

Minutes later, the apartment smells of lemon herbal tea brewing in a stainless, steel pot. Two sets of cups and saucers are already arranged neatly on the kitchen table.

Robin is over by the cupboards reaching for a box of vanilla wafers on a shelf. Suddenly, she feels the gentle caress of Johnny's arms encircling her waist from behind. After the initial surprise and leap of pulse, she relaxes back into his arms as he kisses her neck.

Within moments, he turns her around, and after an initial dazed pause, their lips meet. Quickly they're lost in passion—he the pursuer, she succumbing.

Romantic Interlude

Next, as one, they move slowly by the table, down a hallway, and through an archway into her bedroom. She's practically being moved totally by him, his embrace nearly lifting her off the floor. All the while, they continue to kiss—slowly, deeply.

Then in a gentle tumble, they fall onto the bed. Tenderly, he caresses her, touching her intimately. She's being totally receptive now, letting him lead. He pauses, then moving his head and upper torso back as if to get a better look at the object of his affection, he reaches forward to unbutton her blouse. For the first time, he knows what he feels isn't all about sex. He wants her for something intangibly deeper, which he's never experienced with a woman before.

Then Robin's body stiffens just a little bit as he releases her top button. *Did something just happen? Is everything all right?*

He goes ahead and unbuttons a second one. She doesn't resist or move for that matter. *I know. She's just bracing for what's coming, the consummation of the special bond we've both been feeling.*

But, then, as his sweating hands reach for another, she grabs his wrists and wails softly, "No!"

Johnny is stunned. He looks at her and her unexpectedly pained eyes.

"No?" he repeats, startled by his own shaky voice.

"It isn't right."

"Why? I love you. You must know that."

"I know, but you have to stop," she reiterates, easing her grip.

"You're only kidding, right?" he whispers with a cooing softness.

The Catch!

Johnny's body aches to fulfill the act and his hands again move toward her blouse. She resists by tightening her hold.

"No!" she wails, this time louder and more insistent.

Johnny now has no doubt about how serious she is and feels agitation building within him.

"You're the only woman who's ever been real to me. It has to be right."

Her voice is panicky. "I don't know how to explain this."

"What is it, Love?"

Robin's eyes turn inward as she lets go of his wrists.

"It's a feeling I've had all along. Before, with the kite, reinforced it. When you were flying it, you were soaring, too, without me... until I got in the way. Maybe we're meant to do this someday, but not now."

"I thought you–"

"I thought we'd just have some tea and talk. I didn't expect... but I should have known."

"I don't get it," Johnny says too sharply, then dips his head and closes his eyes. *Maybe I do get it! She might just be right.*

Robin takes one of his hands in hers to placate him. He opens his eyes, hopefully. "All signs seem to point to you being on a path, perhaps unbeknownst to you, destined for something special. Something I have no right to interfere with! That's all I can say." *I hear her, but I don't want to accept it, not now anyway!*

Rage builds on Johnny's face. *Here's this gorgeous, penetrating woman who makes me feel like no other woman has ever made me feel and there's to be no union, no act to show my appreciation, to communicate my never-completely expressed love?*

Romantic Interlude

He rises to his feet, numb, and steps away from the bed in silence. Then an eruption—his body shaking in frustration, he lets out a loud unintelligible sound.

Robin sits up on the bed. "I'm sorry."

Johnny's eyes are pained now, too. He looks at her for an instant. *I just can't bear this!* He turns to leave the room. Robin doesn't move. Soon she hears the apartment door slam shut and, from the kitchen, the rattling of the empty tea cups on their saucers in his wake.

Outside Robin's apartment building, it's an angry man who emerges onto the street. Ambling slowly, with no certain destination, he walks right by his car and down the block until the street intersects with Broadway.

The evening is as comfortable as the day has been. At least there's that. Being Sunday, it's the last chance for relaxation before the start of a new work week and Broadway still has a fair number of people swarming around. When Johnny reaches the intersection, he turns the corner and heads south.

The activity, the bright lights—almost feel like insulation for my self-pity. Waves of pain course through my body as if my insides are being purged. I'm hurting, yet, at the same time, I'm beginning to accept it. It might be necessary.

Johnny sees peripherally what's happenings around him on the sidewalk—the different varieties of people present. *I know they're there, but it's as if they aren't there!* He picks up his pace and strides sprightly through it all in his encased state.

And on he walks, ten blocks, twenty blocks, the impact of Robin still percolating powerfully within him—the mix of the sexually alluring image of her with her blouse still partially open, together with her innate, loving nature so evident beyond the visual,

She cares about me. I know that. She's been courageous to be so honest with me, and herself. But, oh, how I could get lost in making love to her! How satisfying and sweet that would be! But she said it would be interfering with me. I can only accept the feeling that she might be right. Yes, I've got to accept that!

He slows his pace and begins to listen to the sounds he's hearing and absorb what he's seeing as he approaches Times Square. The lights are brighter and flashing in the dimming evening light. Now he really notices how varied the people are—well-dressed out-of-town couples, clinging to each other, absorbing the pulsating artificialness; diners seen through windows, savoring their wine; less-elegantly dressed minorities having fun, or looking for action of another kind; the homeless; the obviously drugged and those of the oldest profession mingling nonchalantly.

Then, like a mirage, out of the corner of his eye appears a beautiful, bright-eyed, Black prostitute wearing her garish attire as if it's royal garb. She notices his appreciative gaze and makes eye contact, accompanied by an easy, soulful smile.

Right then, he stops in his tracks.

She stops, too, across a subway grating separating them on the wide sidewalk. Then she raises a spiked high heel, drawing attention to it, as well her well-shaped legs in fishnet stockings. "You know I can't walk on the grating in these," she says.

Romantic Interlude

Totally taken by her earthy beauty, he dares to take a couple of steps toward her, close enough to be within touching distance.

"Well, are you going to ask me on a date?" It's said almost as if she wants him as much as he lusts for her.

His eyes continue to admire her for a moment, yet caution rises up within. Then, he says with a voice he can feel is true to something deep inside, "You're gorgeous!... But brief flings aren't my way anymore."

The enchantress before him pauses in place, then, in an apparent gesture of genuine understanding, she widens her smile and pats him on the shoulder. Then, spike heels, fishnet stockinged legs and all, she continues down the sidewalk.

He watches her for a second, or two, or three, as those hips and legs ease with silken fluidity through the crowd and disappear.

Strange! It feels like I just experienced something awesome.

Suddenly there's a shuddering that passes through Johnny's body. *Wow, there it is again! The sound, the high-pitched singing from the time of the catch—more of a sensation now, like a vibration playing throughout me.*

Chapter 15

The Sound at Carnegie Hall

Autumn is now in full evidence this night on Manhattan's West Side. There, in its midst, Johnny comfortably makes his way on foot down Seventh Avenue, the cool, fall air rescuing him from the fate of drowning in his own sweat. *Ah, this is better, much better!*

Only an hour before he was donning a tuxedo for the first time in his life. Wearing one was something Michael had suggested. It would make him appreciate the upcoming experience more, so he said. But, the heat of his revved-up body had gotten trapped beneath the garment, causing discomfort. Now, the tension of the day and the tuxedo's sweltering oppressiveness have subsided.

As he goes, he takes notice of the multi-colored leaves that blow about the sidewalk and the striking hues the bright city lights form on lampposts, shop windows, cars, etc. *Such extraordinarily impressive colors! Or have I just never paid much attention to this sort of thing?*

At one point, he takes time to glimpse at his reflection in a store window. *Lookin' pretty smart…. But, watch it! Don't let it go to your head.*

The Catch!

Finally, he turns a corner onto Fifty-seventh Street, and there it is—across the way, Carnegie Hall. The old concert building, in all its grandeur, is buzzing with activity.

The main event this evening is displayed on a large, full-color poster behind glass. It's at the end of a series of others spread out uniformly around the building to highlight upcoming performances. Tonight's will feature a choir from Canada called the Aurora Singers. Michael and Robin told him about them months before.

I wonder what this'll be like? They told me they have a unique sound, singing only a cappella with voices so highly trained that they often seem to be accompanied by instruments.

Johnny is here because of their strong encouragement to join them. The poster shows the group, numbering only twelve, posed on an elegant staircase with their conductor in the foreground. They are all formally dressed – gowns and tuxedos – as they stand bright-eyed and erect, giving the impression of discipline, quite contrary to the look of the modern bands Johnny is more familiar with.

The whole atmosphere around the Hall is energized and Johnny feels it, involuntarily raising the level of his anticipation. Michael and Robin are already there and he spots them waiting on the front steps. He hasn't seen the latter for a few weeks, ever since he walked out of her apartment, but there is no animosity on her face, and he finds it easy to give both a hug after Michael initiates.

Once inside, Johnny surveys the crowd around him in the hall's lobby. Most of the men are dressed formally, if not in tuxedos. Robin wears a classy, evening gown, looking more like a princess than ever.

The Sound at Carnegie Hall

Moments later, they're inside the main auditorium and he's wowed by the chandeliers and the ornamented multi-level tiers of seats overlooking the stage. Though it's not a sellout, about two-thirds full, the audience seems super excited about the performance. Once settled, he continues to take in the visual extravagances, right up until the singers walk on stage with their conductor already vocalizing their first number.

Not being used to their sound, Johnny is having difficulty enjoying it. It's unique all right—with lots of highs and lows, sung quite spiritedly. And the conductor is quite animated, the singers' eyes glued to every direction he gives.

They're obviously highly trained, but this is really different—kind of unsettling. Those high notes from the women are really, really high! They're like lightning bolts of penetrating sound, making direct hits on me. So much for the soothing music, I was expecting!

After that first song ends, Michael, Robin, and a good portion of the audience applaud enthusiastically. Yet Johnny can see there are a few who are equally as uncomfortable as he is. *At least I'm not the only one having trouble with this.*

Michael then leans over and whispers, "A little different than you're used to, huh?"

Johnny nods with a the-jury-is-out expression.

"Just hang in there, guy. It'll grow on you if you're open enough to give it a chance. Don't try comparing it to anything else."

So, in an attempt not to disappoint his respected new friends, Johnny tries hard to find some enjoyment in the performance. *Well, they're dressed pretty sharp, but wouldn't they feel freer dressed down a little? That conductor really gives it his all, but why should he be in such control of the singers? And, wow, they really do have incredible voices, but why can't they sing something more with-it?*

The harder he tries to like the concert, the more he questions it and the more he sweats and churns inside. And, then, that pain in his gut, which he thought was history, makes a return appearance.

At intermission, he looks for some water, finds a fountain, and discovers that it doesn't extinguish the inner turmoil. He then makes his way over to the men's room and splashes water on his face from a running faucet. While he dries himself off, he looks at his reflection in the mirror and suddenly perks up. *I'm going to go back and not even try to like it!*

And he does just that. After intermission, he goes back and listens to the next song without judgment.

You know, now that I'm used to their style, it's beginning to sound acceptable. No longer yearning to hear something which emulates his favorite tunes, he's allowing the newness of it to be absorbed within him.

Then he focuses on the conductor. *It's interesting watching him as he points and lunges toward each singer to draw out the varied sounds I'm hearing.*

Then the dreaded happens. The conductor turns to the audience before another song and says, "Now it's your turn." He teaches them the song's chorus, having the singers sing it, then them. He's very playful in his approach, but this exercise makes Johnny extra uncomfortable. *Now he's is trying to tell me what to do! I'm not a singer!*

So, Johnny doesn't participate. Michael notices and whispers to him. "Why don't you drop whatever you're thinking and enjoy yourself."

"I don't sing!" Johnny whispers back, stubbornly.

As Robin looks on, Michael whispers again, "Don't take it so seriously. You can sing, even badly, and still be a man."

Johnny reluctantly nods. *All right, I'll try to make them happy.*

And, so he sings, not particularly loud and not particularly well. Yet, something seems to change as he goes on—an air of confidence coming forth as he concentrates on his singing, having cleared his opinionated thoughts. *You know, this isn't too bad. I'm actually liking this.*

By the time the conductor is through eliciting audience cooperation, Johnny is belting out the song's chorus as loud as anyone.

Right after that, the finale, the major work of the ensemble, begins. It's quite rich and varied from the start. It's slow, then fast, bold and vibrant, then soft and gentle. Yet, throughout, the tension is so tightly intact that one can't help but admire the singers' steadfastness.

I'm really feeling it now! Getting goosebumps, of all things! Me singing definitely helped! And, it's as if there's some purpose to their songs, some meaningful intent. What specifically, I don't know.

Then, most of the way through this last work, it happens. At the end of a particularly intense passage, the sound shifts into high gear. It comes fast and furious, and the pitch skyrockets to new highs. It's then that Johnny's attention is drawn back to the softball diamond

The Catch!

when he first heard the siren-like sounds at the time of Michael's catch!

What's this? Sudden light-headedness, the light in the hall intensifying, and the sounds of the singing... they're penetrating right through me. Just like that day!

As a result, Johnny's entire body trembles slightly! His self-awareness stays intact, though, saving him from the embarrassment of losing his balance.

Then another shift—one of relief from the high-pitched siren-like sounds, yet the song continues a little longer, ending with a strong, lower-pitched, more grounded ending.

The audience sits silently for almost a minute. No one moves a muscle, yet they, as a whole, have been energized to a barely containable state. When the conductor, who has remained facing the singers, turns to the crowd, one man stands up a fraction of a second before the others. His eyes meet those of the inspired maestro in a moment of admiration and shared euphoria. They're Johnny's. And as he breaks into applause, so does everyone else, rocking and shaking Carnegie Hall for minutes on end with an extraordinarily long ovation.

Chapter 16

The Heirloom on Display

It's mid-afternoon of a weekday, a rare time for Johnny to be home. In the driveway is a beat-up van with commercial plates parked next to his gleaming, recently polished, *Falcon*. On its side, written in bold, is:

David Haraway & Company
Security-Plus

Inside the house, Johnny is in the den ready for a demonstration.

"Here we go," says the man next to him in workman's clothes as he rotates a newly mounted, dimmer switch. Across the room, against one wall, a light goes on and brightens within a glass-enclosed cabinet. "Pretty impressive, isn't it?"

"Awesome, Dave. Perfect."

"Thanks. If anybody tries to tamper with that glass, Mr. Sloper, an alarm will go off at the office and we'll have law enforcement down here, pronto."

"Security-plus," Johnny adds with a grin.

The Catch!

Dave chuckles, "Yep, Security-plus!"

After Johnny sees Dave out, he heads back to the den to gaze at the heirloom one more time before leaving for work. Now he can give it his full attention which, in the glow of the new lighting during the demonstration, had made such an impression on him.

Whoa! Am I not used to being home at this quiet time of day? Or is it that – along with the figure, poised and erect while seeming to sound something powerfully important – that the siren-like singing from the time of the catch, and the Carnegie concert, comes back to me, giving me that pleasant tingling sensation, again?

He steps closer, looking quizzically at the figurine, totally consumed in the moment. Then he reads anew the inscription, concentrating on the words.

"Catch the Glory!
Catch the Sound!
Stand tall and catch the Pitch,
Know the Love Unbound.
Then Be the Pitch
And sound the Pitch.
Be the Answer to the Call.
To be Love Unconditional
The Catch is All."

He stands there for a few minutes after he's read it. Finally, he breaks out of this state and looks at his watch, bringing him back to earth. He then gets himself together and leaves to go back to work.

In his East Village, New York apartment, Dr. Wilson is on his kitchen phone. "Lou, better send Oaf out again, this time to put a scare into that Sloper character. We

The Heirloom on Display

have to be sure all our bases are covered for the upcoming transition."

"Sure. I'll send him. How about the other, Black guy with Sloper?"

"Scaring the shit out of the one ought to be enough. You know, the ole two-birds-with-one-stone..."

Chapter 17

Standing by with the Light

The sun is setting earlier these days, and as Johnny pulls the *Falcon* into the marina parking lot, he's aware of the reddish glow being cast across the horizon.

He also notices that both Ralph's and Michael's cars are in the lot. Michael is there because he was recently hired to do the marina's books on an intermittent basis.

But, instead of going inside, Johnny decides to walk down the sandy slope that runs alongside the building, and around back, to check on the moorings for the boats in their slips. As he does this, he lets his senses take in the freshness of the bay air while being peripherally observant of the beautiful, changing night sky.

He finds one sailboat isn't tied up as snug as it can be, so he pauses, unwinds the rope, and redoes it with a flourish. When he finishes, his view of the horizon is obstructed by a figure towering over him. He looks up to see the man, the same humongous one who once stood just outside the marina observing him. Now the look on his face says trouble.

The Catch!

Johnny is startled and it takes an instant for him to regain his composure. No sooner has he done this, than the intruder speaks with as much animosity as his expression implies. "What kind of place is this?" he demands.

Johnny gets to his feet quickly, containing his rising anger as he makes up some of the vertical distance between them. He points and says, "Well, there's a sign over there that says it's a marina and I'd say from the look of it, that's probably what this is. Can I help you?"

The man's face tightens with enhanced meanness at the response and ignores the question. Instead, he comes up with another of his own, "Mr. Sloper, aren't you?"

"That's right!" Johnny says. "I must be the guy who runs the place, according to that other sign on the office door."

The man is now totally infuriated at Johnny's seeming indifference, his cheeks crimson red, seemingly ready to spurt blood through their pores. But he manages to gain a reasonable amount of control to reply. "Very funny. I was sent to check this place out. I hope you're the accommodating kind. You'll have to be unless you'd like to see this place destroyed."

"What?"

This time the man just glares at him, spits onto the wooden decking, and glares some more. After an appreciable amount of time, he turns and lumbers away. Johnny watches as he takes the same route he did coming down, the power in the big man's limbs and upper torso evident as he goes.

Then Johnny sighs. *What the...?* Johnny takes a few deep breaths, giving his senses a chance to come back to earth.

Who was that guy? Is he nuts? Or could it be the mob trying to move in on me and my thriving, little business?

Meanwhile, in the office, Michael works at Johnny's desk. Ralph is close at hand, returning boat keys to the key rack on a side wall.

"We'll be locking up soon," Ralph says, taking charge in Johnny's absence.

"That's quite all right. I'm just about through," Michael replies, staring at a pile of paperwork scattered on the desk. "I've finally made some sense of this."

Just then, the outside door on the deck side of the office opens and Johnny appears.

"Hey, the boss is back," Ralph exclaims.

But Johnny says nothing. Michael peers up from the desk and registers immediate concern. "You look like you've seen a ghost."

Johnny stops next to the desk. "It's nothing. Just a character I ran into outside... How do the books look?"

It's obvious to Michael that Johnny's withholding something very troubling. "What kind of character?"

Johnny hesitates, then says, "I'll tell you later. Just give me some time."

"All right," Michael says, going along with that. "As for the books, they're not bad once I caught on to your unique way of bookkeeping," he kids.

This relaxes Johnny some. He grins and color comes back into his cheeks. "I knew you'd figure it out. I just hoped the doodling wouldn't throw you off."

"Only when they obscured numbers on the page. But I must admit... drawing fireworks to highlight the month's gross is a nice touch."

"Like that, huh?" Johnny says with a laugh.

The Catch!

"Keeps it interesting for the CPA."

"The empire's finest artist," Ralph interjects as he heads for the door to go home.

"Hold on a sec, Ralph," Johnny says. "Don't go just yet."

"Come on Leonardo! It's another romantic, Indian Summer night."

Michael laughs, amused.

Johnny holds up a finger to Ralph to wait, then directs his attention to Michael. "You know Ralph's right. It's a beauty of a night to be out on the bay. How 'bout we shoot the breeze on the *Intercept*?"

It occurs to Michael that it might be more than just shooting the breeze. The incident with the unknown character outside, perhaps, is ready to be discussed. "Sounds terrific!" he says, allowing enthusiasm to hide his anticipation of what's to come.

"Great, let's do it," Johnny affirms, then turns back to Ralph. "How about some overtime, Casanova, baby?"

Twenty minutes later, the *Intercept* is well out into the bay. Ralph pilots and, at Johnny's order, keeps the vessel cruising slowly and quietly. The sun has long set by now, but the lights from New York City highlight the horizon and get closer.

Johnny hands Michael a glass of cognac out on the deck. "It's nice to try out the stock once in a while."

"Thanks. I appreciate being out here on a night like this," Michael says, beaming.

Johnny looks at Michael closely. *He truly takes nothing for granted.*

"Tell me, was it tough growing up Black and gay."

"Probably even more so now that I'm no longer the little innocent I was growing up with – God bless them – protective parents."

"I can only imagine. In what ways?"

"For instance, when I wanted to live in Manhattan a couple of years ago, I couldn't get a decent apartment even though I was making good money, so instead I decided to settle in Jersey."

"You like the city?"

"Love the city—the cultural things it offers, the multi-ethnicity of it, and so on. Only, if you have the means and want an apartment in a good part of town, being black makes it very difficult."

Johnny grimaces, knowingly.

"For example. Have you heard of the Thumper real estate family?"

"The name sounds familiar. I'm sure I've heard it on the radio."

"You've probably heard the name, Ronald Thumper. He's coming to the fore in the real estate business. He's been attempting to clear the family name of racial discrimination. So, after they settle a court case – without admitting any wrongdoing, by the way – I go and apply for one of their advertised rentals, and am told it's already taken. Fine, but when I ask if anything else is available, I'm told they're all taken. Yet the ads for them continue to this day in the newspapers."

Johnny shakes his head. "Terrible."

Michael smiles without regret. "I look at it this way. You just have to roll with things that you don't have the means to change by making the best of the situation you're in."

The Catch!

Just then, a restless Ralph shouts down from the helm, "Where are the girls? How about if we dock near some action, boss? That's the Big Apple coming up—with all the lights!"

"Just take it slow and easy, kiddo," Johnny shouts back. "We're gonna put off your reputation earning one more night."

Then to Michael, he adds, "I better give him a shot of cognac to keep him on our side. He's a good kid—invaluable, really."

"I've noticed."

"I was surprised when he passed up going back to college to hang around here. He seems to love the marina."

"It could have something to do with the company he keeps. You treat him very well, you know. In fact, I'd say you're probably his role model."

"I wouldn't go that far."

"Why not? What other man does he spend most of his day around? And who allows him to mature by giving him so much responsibility?"

"That responsibility was given to him out of necessity," Johnny says, shaking his head. *Starting with when I was completely out of it after the pool party.* "but I see what you mean."

"For that matter, I wouldn't be surprised if his desire for some *action* with the ladies isn't something else that's rubbed off on him."

Johnny wags his head, regretfully. "Hmm... well, at least I'm not that way now. But thanks, I know what you're saying. Hold on a minute while I get him that drink."

Johnny goes into the cabin and pours another cognac for Ralph, then proceeds to deliver it. Meanwhile, Michael stays on deck and watches him from the railing. The look of appreciation in Ralph's eyes when Johnny gives him the cognac is another indication of the special bond between the two. The corners of Michael's mouth curl up, pleased to see this touch of warm-heartedness.

When Johnny returns, he and Michael gaze out over the railing at nothing in particular. The tranquility of the moment is temporarily enough. Then Johnny says, "I'm glad we could do this. It just felt like a good time to chat."

"Sure, I'm all ears. Did you want to begin with the character you had a confrontation with before?"

"God, that almost skipped my mind. Yeah, I couldn't believe it. This huge guy surprises me while I'm checking the moorings down on the dock. Must have tiptoed right up to me."

"And?"

"He was a mean S.O.B. Threatened to destroy the marina if I didn't cooperate."

"Cooperate?"

"That's all he said. I don't know what he meant by that. He just said it and walked off."

"Maybe you should report it to the police?"

"I don't know if that'd do any good.

"Why?"

"I don't have anything substantial to tell them, besides a description. I was pretty cocky with the guy and didn't bother to follow him. I could have gotten a license number if he came by car. A little shortsighted, I guess."

Michael scratches his chin, "I see."

"Also, it could be a mob warning. Maybe a shakedown coming. I've heard plenty about racketeering in the area. Fortunately, up 'til now, I've never been pinched. But if

The Catch!

that's what it's about, I'll be better off waiting and seeing. The mob can strike fast and ugly if they even think you're a threat to them."

"Right. That could be damn serious," Michael concurs, then pauses and stares out into the night air as if the empty stillness holds an answer. "Somehow, I don't think it's the mob. Do you think it could have anything to do with Wilson?"

"I'd like to think that's behind us, but could be a possibility."

"Just be careful," Michael says, shaking his head. "Something's fishy. Please keep me informed, if you don't mind."

"No, I don't mind." *In fact, it's great having Michael for support. I value his insights and I have no doubt he knows when to keep things confidential.*

"Let's get more comfortable before we talk about what I originally wanted to discuss," Johhny adds, pulling up a small, round table, which was recessed into the deck. Before long, they're seated with refills of cognac.

"Remember the day we met?" Johnny begins, as a gentle breeze generated only by the movement of the boat helps define the mood.

Michael nods. "Of course."

"I had an unusual experience when you made that catch," he says in a confessional tone of voice. Johnny then goes on to describe how he tumbled to the ground after failing to make the catch, then watched from that vantage point, looking into the blinding sun as Michael made it in such a surreal way, including it appearing to be in slow motion.

"That is unusual," Michael says.

"The eeriest part of all this – and I don't know if it was because I was dizzy after I fell to the ground, or something else – is that I heard what sounded like high-pitched singing, this sound repeated over and over, siren-like. I'm sure it was my imagination or something, but it sounded real at the time and the whole thing had quite an effect. It was like 'you are hearing this and seeing this and from now on things are going to be different.'"

Michael raises his eyebrows in response. For the time being, he's speechless, just letting it sink in.

Then Johnny continues, "Now the odd thing is, I'm sure I heard the repeated sound again, several times, at the most unusual moments. It just would come to me in my head... and, at times, it even seems to pulsate within me! But what blows me away is that I'm sure I heard the same thing when we went to that Carnegie Hall concert. All of a sudden, there it was in the last song, loud and clear. I could feel its vibration go right through me. It was only then that I was able to fully appreciate the concert.

"Anyway, I can't explain it. The feeling that comes, whether I'm hearing it in my imagination, or live, like at that concert, is quite enjoyable – thrilling, actually – but I also feel on edge as a result, kinda on the verge of something, never quite comfortable.

"And there's been this change I've felt, especially after I made a fool of myself at that pool party. I already told you that that incident made me consider what characteristics I need to change about myself. Anyway, as a result of all this, including being involved with you and Robin, I've begun to be more aware of things – skylines, sunsets, smells from the bakery – that sort of thing…. I don't know what to make of all that?"

Michael's been taking this in with great interest, sipping on the cognac periodically. Now, he puts it down and interjects with that voice that doesn't conform to general conversation.

"I think it's a good sign, a sign that you may be coming to Pitch. I believe you're beginning to get in touch with the real you."

Johnny has the look of 'what?' in his eyes. *Hang on! Listen to everything he says.*

Michael continues, "At least it appears that way. It's interesting how this all coincides with the inscription on your family heirloom."

"I've been wondering about that. The time I had you and Robin over and you read it. That was quite an experience, too. How does it all relate? I'm not sure I get it. Have any idea?"

"The inscription on the figurine said, 'Catch the Pitch.' That's what I believe you've been doing, the Pitch, referring to the frequency associated with Love in its truest manifestation within a man, or a woman. In other words, I feel you're discovering your inherent Love Nature. Trust me, most people never do. They think they have, but they haven't. Being more sensitive, more aware of things – both of beauty and, also, what isn't of beauty – is part of it."

I feel like I'm waking up from a dream, finally facing reality. He's hitting home because I've always thought of sensitivity as a weakness. I've tried to keep a strong male persona, but sensitivity doesn't seem like a weakness in him.

"How do you know all this stuff?" Johnny asks. "That time at the office—just before we went to Brooklyn, the warning you gave me then. Where did that come from?"

"I told you before. It's intuitive. And I feel there's more I can tell you. I think you're ready. The fact that you were just able to reveal, at last, what you experienced during that game, points to that."

Michael pauses to take another sip of the cognac. Johnny feels bare. His friend has even read his past reluctance to completely express what he'd been consciously holding back.

Then, after re-engaging Johnny's eyes, Michael says, "I spent many years influenced by a teacher of philosophy, or what you might call a spiritual guide. Robin, too. He was a great man, no longer living, but if there's anything said by me that is right-on about what you're experiencing, and has been of any value or help to you, it's owed to what opened up to me during those years I was able to be in his presence. It helped me develop a more fine-tuned awareness beyond ordinary, daily life—much like what's beginning to happen to you."

"It sounds like you two gained a lot."

"We both owe a lot to him—what he taught us and the example he was. As for the Aurora Singers, Robin and I have found the man who conducts them comes from the same stream of understanding. The singers have been his expression of that in public."

Johnny shifts in his chair as he struggles to understand.

"What do you mean by the same stream?"

"Ah, now we get to the heart of all this. The stream of people who know at their essence is something special, a universal Divine Nature—no separateness from God, now or ever."

Johnny seems to be taking his time mulling this over and Michael gives him time to let his words sink in. Then

The Catch!

he says, "And, most importantly, those people are in agreement that it is ideal to align their mentality, their thoughts, to that Divinity and let It live them."

"So that conductor is in touch with that special Essence?"

"More exactly put would be to say he's become that Essence, or Divinity in manifestation. And we all are capable of that."

"In manifestation?"

"In other words, if you think of a mind and body as an instrument, he has allowed his to be played by the higher, intuitive Force of his Love Nature, instead of ignoring that the Force exists and trying to get by with the limits of logical reasoning only. It's a form of surrendering to a Higher Power, letting yourself be guided intuitively. People may not realize it, but the saying, 'May the Force be with you" in the movie Star Wars, which was a big hit last year, is exactly in line with what I'm talking about."

"Really? Star Wars? Haven't seen it."

"You might want to. It seems like a wacky sci-fi movie, but it actually can be understood as more than that."

"Okay. I will. Now, are you saying that this guy, the conductor, is perfect?"

"First of all, I wouldn't use 'guy' in relation to someone so accomplished. Yet, being human, he may not be perfect all the time, but the evidence of his creativity with music certainly bears that Mark of manifested Divine Essence. Everyone is capable of living their lives bearing It, too."

"How about your teacher?"

"He was the most perfect human being I've ever met.... Are you understanding what I'm saying?"

Johnny nods. "I think so," he says slowly. *My mind is beginning to numb up with all this.*

"How does that explain the sound I've been hearing?"

"There's a Frequency, a Pitch, that corresponds with that Divine Essence—which is innately inseparable from what appears as you in human form. And, thus, that Frequency is capable of being perceived. Yet, it is universally ignored due to the noise of the mind, created by so many worldly influences. For example, the so-called music that stimulates the senses, but never reaches your heart, or your own thoughts when they are personally oriented. You, though, may be starting to experience that true Pitch.

"As for the Aurora Singers, the conductor, a man undoubtedly living true to his Essence, has been able to reveal that true inner Pitch through them, kind of like osmosis, as a result of their dedication in working with him."

Johnny suddenly wells up with spontaneous recognition. "Your way of putting things is different than what I'm used to, but I feel what you're saying is correct. It explains a lot."

There isn't much else to say. Johnny has told Michael everything he planned to. And he's satisfied—just short of being overwhelmed. They stay quiet for a while, enjoying the night and the easy breeze. Ralph occasionally looks down at them from the helm, not knowing what was said, yet feeling, along with them, the peacefulness in the air.

I'm feeling that reverberation again. It feels good!

However, over a short period of time the mood changes.

Sure, I'm feeling good, I think, but what he's told me is so new! It's all pretty jumbled in my brain. Does he really know what he's talking about? It's nothing like I've heard before!

Most would think Michael is far out compared to everyone else. What the—? My gut—the ache is coming back!

Then Johnny hears something irregular.

What is that? The reverberation is going haywire? Wait…, no, it's the Intercept's engine.

It is the *Intercept's* engine. It's sputtering, shaking out of rhythm. The boat then lurches as its power diminishes dramatically. Then, all is still, except water slapping against its hull.

"Damn," Johnny swears as he looks up to the helm to see Ralph already staring back at him perplexed. "I'll be right back."

Michael watches as he hurries over to the helm's ladder, shouting, "Emergency lights!"

Ralph quickly hits a switch that darkens the boat, except for areas where a few dimly-lit lamps remain. Then he makes a few futile attempts to restart the engine.

When Johnny gets to the flybridge, Ralph squeezes over to make room for him. Immediately, he puts his attention on the control panel, fiddling with a couple of knobs.

"Crank it again," he says.

Ralph complies, but it still doesn't start. Repeated efforts are to no avail. Dejected, Johnny tells Ralph to stay while he returns down the ladder.

Back on deck, he says irritably to Michael, "I'll have to check the engine."

"Anything I can do?"

"I don't even know what the problem is yet!" he says irritably.

Michael follows him as he enters the cabin. In the light of the few emergency lamps lit, Johnny moves a few things around in the semi-darkness. Then he opens a pair of doors on the floor, exposing the engine.

Getting down on his stomach, he tries to get a close look at the inner workings. Unfortunately, the shadowy light makes viewing the compartment impossible.

Johnny gets up on his knees and whirls around to a nearby wall cabinet. After opening its door, he reaches in and pulls out nothing.

Where's the damn flashlight?

Annoyed, he rummages around until he finally discovers it on a lower shelf among some canned food.

Temporarily relieved, he tests it. No light. Annoyed again, he shakes it hard in a show of anger. Still no light. "Damn! The batteries are either dead or corroded."

He then opens the flashlight up and takes out the two batteries inside. He rubs the ends of each against the other, hoping to scrape away any possible corrosion. After returning them into the flashlight, it now works.

Then, holding it out to Michael, he says, "Here, just point it wherever my hands are."

The engine block is hot to the touch and Johnny's first contact produces an unhesitating, "Damn it!"

Eventually, by manipulating the right parts – and avoiding the engine block itself – he's able to make a determination. "Gas isn't getting to the carburetor."

"Is it something you can fix, or do you need to radio for help?"

"We'll see. I don't want to radio if I can help it," is the tense response just before Johnny touches another hot spot on the engine. He shakes his wounded hand in the air. "Damn it to hell!"

The Catch!

He proceeds now in a fury, not helped by a mind that's still unsettled from all the new things Michael said to him. *Now we're stuck at sea, at night in the middle of the bay, and I don't know if I can remedy this, damn it!*

With a jerk, he pulls off the outgoing hose on the engine's fuel filter. Then he yanks off the in-going one. With the freed filter in hand, he gives it a shake to break up any possible clog inside, then he reassembles it the way it was.

Once again, he manually manipulates the linkage on the carburetor. After a brief period, some gas squirts into the carburetor's barrel. Feeling relieved, he looks up at Michael and says, "Yell up to Ralph and tell him to try it again."

Michael sticks his head out the cabin door and delivers the order. Ralph cranks it once—no go. Then a second time. The engine comes alive with a roar. However, it sputters and stops running a few seconds later.

"Try it again," Johnny screams at the top of his lungs from his prone position, not bothering this time to use Michael as a go-between.

It's a needless command for Ralph is already re-cranking it, but now it's giving no indication of starting at all. Finally, silence as he gives up.

The silence lingers until Johnny blows his fuse! With an assortment of expletives, he lets it be known to the world at large how disgusted he is with their predicament, and that the problem had better not boil down to a bad fuel pump.

There's a pause as the tension of the flare-up dissipates. Then Michael asks unperturbed, "Is there anything else you can check before concluding that the pump is faulty?"

Johnny, who is up on all fours now, looks over his shoulder at Michael holding the flashlight as if he's forgotten he was there. "I suppose," he replies sheepishly.

"Well, I can stand here with the light as long as you want."

Johnny blinks once and a change appears to come over him. *Suddenly, it's like a guardian angel is hovering over me. Like magic, Michael's calm seems to have cleared the air of my foul mood, and the baseless doubts that just sprung up! So, what if I can't reconstruct what he just explained? My gut already told me it all rang true. That's what counts, not whether it fits in with what I've known to be this crazy world.*

After this one-hundred-eighty-degree shift in his outlook, and with a voice now warm, without strain, Johnny says, "That's great. Thank you. I'll take a better look at the filter."

Johnny disconnects it again. This time he has Michael point the light so he can see into the in-going end, a quarter inch in diameter, cylindrical protrusion.

"Hold on. I think I see something."

Johnny takes a small folding knife out from a pants pocket. After removing its thin blade from its casing, he slides it into the narrow opening and proceeds to drag out a curled-up piece of leaf that had fit snugly inside.

"There's the culprit. Somehow that leaf ended up in the gas tank, then the filter. Problem solved."

Chapter 18

Dr. Wilson Again

Over the next couple of days, Johnny looks like a new man carried on a wave of energy.

The things Michael has told me have come back little by little. The more I repeat them to myself and begin to understand how they apply to me, the less let down I feel about life. It's changed my whole attitude.

Everything he does happens without obstruction or strain. He's light on his feet, too, having the spryness of a younger man. And when he views himself each morning in the mirror, he sees how different his face appears—relaxed with no dull eyes or pensive creases.

I've realized how so self-centered I've been all along. Could this humbler way of looking at things help in how I relate to others? I'd think so! There's anticipation, too, since I don't know where it will lead.

Then an unusual thing happens while driving home from work.

I'm feeling uneasy—puzzling because I can't figure out why.

The Catch!

Johnny's thoughts are then interrupted as the *Falcon* approaches his house. Lounging on the front stoop are two men. As he gets closer, he can tell they've spotted him and are anticipating his arrival. When the car stops in his driveway, one of them is standing with his arms folded and muscles twitching. It's the giant of a man who threatened him at the marina. The other one sits on the steps, looking composed, smoking a cigarette.

Johnny gets out of the car and self-consciously closes the door behind him, his uneasiness escalating. Nevertheless, he approaches the visitors, keeping a wary eye on the familiar bigger one, while determining that the other, of average build, looks more brainy than brawny. When he's within ten feet of the stoop, he stops and asks, "Can I help you two?"

The composed one takes a long drag on his cigarette as if he's a character out of a 1940s film noir movie.

"We work security for Dr. Wilson's research project," he declares, exhaling smoke. "I'm sure you know what I'm talking about. We've been keeping an eye on you since he found out you and your friend were snooping around the house in Brooklyn."

Johnny, caught by surprise, plays innocent. "What?"

The bigger man reacts with disgust. "Don't fool with us you damn, piece of–"

"The one on State Street, Brooklyn," the composed man says, cutting him off. "Ring any bells, Sloper?"

Okay, stay calm. Just go with it. "Oh, that," Johnny says.

"Oh, that? Suddenly you remember?"

"It was a mistake."

"Mistake or not, the doctor now wants to know what you were up to."

Dr. Wilson Again

"We're here to persuade you," the big guy snarls as his neck muscles bulge with the definite impression of wanting to get physical.

"Encourage you is more like it," the other man corrects before doing some hacking due to his smoking. He then clears his throat. "My buddy sometimes gets a little cross unnecessarily."

No need to be intimidated. Just tell the truth. "It's a long story," Johnny volunteers.

"Save it! The doctor wants to hear it from you directly. He's at home in the city tonight, expecting your call. Do you have his number?"

"It so happens I do."

"Call him then—now!"

"Sure," Johnny says apologetically. "It was all a misunderstanding."

"Don't tell us. He's waiting on you. If he doesn't hear from you, though," the composed man continues, nodding with a creepy smile toward his unruly companion, "you'll be seeing us again."

With that, he takes a last drag on his cigarette, drops it on the ground, and hacks some more, before crushing it with a heel. He then gets up off the stoop, carefully brushes off the seat of his pants, and walks away. His companion follows, displaying his powerful strut, giving Johnny one last killer stare as he's on his way.

Johnny doesn't bother to see where they're going. He goes directly inside the house. *I should have settled this weeks ago.*

A minute later, his telephone is pressed to his ear in the kitchen. After two rings, it's answered at the other end, "Hello."

The Catch!

"Hello. John Sloper calling. Dr. Wilson?"

"Yes, Mr. Sloper. I hoped you'd call." The voice has an edge to it. Dr. Wilson is seated at his dining table. In front of him are an open two-hundred dollar bottle of wine and a meal specially delivered from one of New York's most prestigious restaurants.

He puts a palm over the transmitter part of his phone and gestures with his head to a finely-sculpted, mature woman at the other end of the table. She immediately understands what he wants, and gets up in her pricey, little black dress. Her expression betrays how humored she is by the clandestine nature of the call. When she's out of earshot, Wilson then gets back to the business at hand.

"Are you still there, Sloper?"

"Yes."

"I'm sorry I had to send some of our security personnel to insist you make this call."

"I'm the one who's sorry... about the delay. I owe you an explanation."

Surprised by Johnny's contriteness, Dr. Wilson, nevertheless, says firmly, "You ought to be! What was that snooping about—false names and all, a few months back in Brooklyn?"

"It's related to my Uncle Gene, Captain Eugene Pierce, who you know."

"Gene Pierce? He's your uncle? What's he got to do with this?"

Johnny goes on to explain the story about the missing heirloom and his attempt to find it. He's as brief as possible, just giving Dr. Wilson the facts about what made them wrongly suspect that he had stolen it. He then tells him that he'd been tailing him and finally discovered the

Dr. Wilson Again

house in Brooklyn the night Wilson went there with some woman. He doesn't mention that he knows the woman, Robin, nor that it was a setup. When he gets to the part about his and Michael's ruse at the house, Johnny asks just how it was that Wilson came to know where he lived. They were sure no car tailed them that night.

"Let's just say my security detail is very protective of me and does its job very well. We actually watched you long enough that we discovered that the woman you saw me with that night on the Lower East Side was Robin, a friend of yours."

Johnny has trouble hiding his surprise. "Yes. She is a friend. I was hoping to keep her name out of this," a sudden nervousness causing his voice to crack.

"And, undoubtedly, you were the one escorting her out of the tavern that night with your other friend, named, Michael."

"Your guys did a lot of digging, didn't they?"

"One can't be too careful when it comes to top-secret government projects. Your uncle told you I'm involved with important medical research, right?"

"Yes, he did," Johnny says. "You've got to admit, though, considering all the facts, it was reasonable for us to think you might have had something to do with the missing heirloom."

"Hmm, you're right, my behavior may have come across a little strange the night of the museum dinner. But who knew your figurine would go missing?"

"A coincidence all right, but what was that all about, by the way, suddenly jumping out of his car and taking off to Brooklyn?"

The Catch!

"What was that about?" Dr. Wilson repeats, seeming unsure himself. He pauses as if he's trying to recall that evening. "Right, I remember. Another researcher had unexpectedly flown into town to compare notes on our project. A message came during dinner at the museum that he was going to be at the house in Brooklyn. Our lab is there in the basement, and also where our data is kept. The plan was to go home first to freshen up, but, while en route with your uncle, I realized there wasn't enough time for that. So, I changed plans and grabbed the taxi to Brooklyn. I didn't explain it to Gene because, being such a good gentleman, he would have offered to take me there, which would have been way out of his way."

"I get it," Johnny says, nodding, "but I'm left wondering about a few other things."

"Like what?"

"Why is that house made to look like a sports club?"

"Just a decoy for unexpected visitors, like you, to disguise the important research going on there. My security guys are also a decoy, made to look like caretakers for the phony club."

"Okay, got it… but the biggest question is why did you wait several months before confronting me?"

Dr. Wilson pauses again, then says, "We checked you out for a while, but you, nor your friends, Michael and Robin, ever approached the house or did anything suspicious since. So, we decided to let it go for the time being and just fully concentrate on our work. It's been a busy time, you know."

Busy? He was all about town like a man on vacation. But why stir up trouble?

Dr. Wilson Again

Instead, Johnny continues with the same line of questioning. "But why look into what we were up to, now?"

"Because the project is wrapping up, and I, and the project coordinators, are making sure there's no threat to upset the applecart. I doubted there was, but we had to be sure."

"I see," Johnny says, letting himself be easily convinced, hoping to draw the conversation to an amicable end. "I apologize again for not coming forward to straighten this out myself."

Johnny's sincerity, and the believability of his story, are testament enough for Dr. Wilson. He no longer has any doubts about what his intentions were. Chuckling to himself, he says, "You know, your actions did leave us pretty uncomfortable for a while, never knowing if there was some kind of crazy conspiracy at work. We were ready to contact the F.B.I."

"Yes, I get it," Johnny says, humbly.

"So, you also get that our project in Brooklyn shouldn't be talked about, right?"

"Of course."

"And nothing about that house, either. It was picked for our work because it doesn't stand out."

"I totally get it."

Then Dr. Wilson says something totally unexpected, "It so happens I'm something of a boating enthusiast. Perhaps you're sorry enough to let me take a complimentary boat out a time or two since you run a marina. A reasonable request, I'd say."

"Are you licensed?"

"I have my certificate from Vermont, my home state."

The Catch!

"Don't see why not, then," Johnny hears himself say, "that would be good anywhere." He obviously wants the uncomfortableness of owning up to his part in this ordeal to end as soon as possible. "Just call ahead to reserve one."

"I'm pleased to hear that, Mr. Sloper."

"Please, call me Johnny."

"All right. Thank you, Johnny."

Johnny gives him the phone number at the marina and the call ends.

Oddly, being so accommodating doesn't feel quite right. Hope I'm proved wrong.

Meanwhile, in New York, a satisfied Dr. Wilson calls his lady friend back to the table.

Chapter 19

More Irritation

Sure, on the surface all the loose ends, due to the night of snooping seem to have been resolved. And a few free boat rides for Dr. Wilson to soothe things over seems reasonable. But, for some reason, I still feel troubled. Why? Something's strange about Wilson's overall behavior. Is he pulling the wool over my eyes? Is something else going on?

Johnny's increasingly pleasant, early morning drives to the marina, which had been sensorially alive to all the various accents of beauty around the Bayonne waterfront, are now eclipsed by these thoughts.

Fortunately, the day after his call, he's able to wend his *Falcon* through the streets by force of habit, rather than by conscious effort. If asked, he wouldn't be able to say what the traffic was like, whether there were any seagulls seen playing, or whether he remembers inhaling the wafting salt air as the *Falcon* got nearer to the bay.

Later, at the office, he's puttering around getting a pot of coffee going when Michael shows up for one of his agreed-upon unscheduled visits for going over the books. *Ah, Michael, my insightful friend! Gotta discuss the latest with him.*

Business takes precedence for the moment, though. There are the preparatory things needing to be done to open for the day, such as getting the cash draw ready, determining if all the boat keys are hanging on the board where they're supposed to be, and conferring with Ralph about the general state of the empire. In the meantime, as all this is being accomplished, Michael settles in at the space created for him at the end of Johnny's desk, adjacent to him.

Eventually, the basics are complete and Johnny instinctively goes over to the kitchenette for the now-brewed coffee. After being offered some, Michael agrees to join him over at the counter.

"I had some surprise visitors waiting for me at home last night," Johnny begins as he pours the coffee into two nautical-themed mugs.

Michael's interest is piqued right away. "Who were they?" he asks, concerned.

Johnny then lays out in detail all that occurred the previous evening, including how things were settled with Wilson, yet doesn't feel settled at all.

"That all sounds pretty ominous, despite the doctor's explanation," Michael says when he's finished. "Please, be careful…. Why not make the Star Wars slogan, 'Let the Force be with you,' be a reminder of your new perspective in life? And, you can always call me if you need someone to talk to."

"Thanks. I'll keep both in mind."

Michael's advice and promise of help, if needed, make me feel better. Yet, I know in my gut, that when it comes down to the nitty-gritty, it'll always be my responsibility, alone, to do the right thing.

By early afternoon Michael is finished with his work at the office and leaves for home.

A feeling of aloneness has begun to kick in, but thanks to Michael's presence, I feel confident that I'll be able to deal with things on my own.

Shortly after, things get busy at the office. It's the time of year when patrons want their boats out of the water and stored. Johnny's marina is a prime facility for that, storing on-premises, either in the boathouse or out in the open. People are in and out, sometimes three and four at a time, making arrangements to have their vessels taken care of. With that kind of traffic, Johnny can't be totally cognizant of everyone who's in the office at any given moment. At one juncture, as business finally slows, he spots Ralph quickly passing through and remembers something he wants him to do.

"Ralph, catch!"

Without slowing his pace, Ralph looks over to see a set of keys flying his way. In the midst of snatching them out of the air, he hears Johnny add, "Give the *Sea Lady* a good run. It hasn't been out for a while."

Ralph shakes the keys in his hand and replies, "I'll let it rip," then disappears out of the office.

"Thanks," Johnny utters, too late to be heard. Then he turns his attention to his last customer approaching his desk. Focusing on the man, he momentarily freezes.

"Dr. Wilson!" Johnny exclaims, leaving no doubt of his surprise.

Well-groomed as usual, the doctor wears nicely appointed casual attire, punctuated by the scent of after-shave. Overshadowing his general appearance, however, is the forceful presence of one who gets what he wants.

"Yes, it's me," Wilson says. "Naturally, I recognize you, too. The picture on your driver's license, which my security team dug up, doesn't do you justice. And, of course, my memory of that night at the tavern, when you rescued your friend, Robin, is a bit hazy."

"Again, I apologize for the big misunderstanding."

"By the way, is Robin your girlfriend?"

"I wish."

"Too bad. She's quite attractive," Wilson says, forcing a smile. "Bad evening for me, though. I really need to be the one to apologize. I was a fool that night, especially finding out later that it was a setup."

Wilson's forced smile turns into a forced, short chuckle as he seems to relive the events of that day in his head.

"Anyway," he says, returning to an even demeanor, "please excuse me for not calling ahead. I suddenly got this urge to take a boat out."

Wilson has already taken out his Vermont boating license and shows Johnny. "Boating is a little hobby of mine. I've been out on Lake Champlain many times over the years."

"A nice hobby," Johnny says, taking a pen out of the breast pocket of his shirt. "We have several speedboats available."

"Oh, no, not a speedboat. It's too chilly this time of year. Don't you have something like a small yacht with a heated cabin?"

Johnny hesitates. *He's awfully presumptuous, assuming our agreement would include a yacht. I'm not about to argue, though. The sooner I make good on my part of the deal, the better!*

"We only have one, the *Intercept*," he says, tapping his pen pensively on his desk. "How long do you want it for?"

"An hour, or so, at the most."

"Fine." Johnny says, looking relieved. Besides the *Intercept* being his prize possession, it's the most expensive to operate. "I'll show you the idiosyncrasies of this one, just in case you're not familiar with them."

Then Johnny picks up his walkie-talkie and asks Ralph to return to the office to watch things. "You can return to the *Sea Lady* later. I have to take care of something."

About ninety minutes later, Wilson is back, docking the boat with Johnny's help, having anxiously been waiting for its return.

"Excellent craft," Wilson tells Johnny, as they walk back up the wooden walkway toward the office.

"It's my pride and joy."

"Handles beautifully, lots of power, and the way that engine purrs...," Dr. Wilson says, concluding his praise with his best, within the confines of dignity, look of ecstasy.

"I guess you'll be wanting to go out in it again?"

"Sure. At least one more time," Wilson says, with that forced smile of his. "Maybe I'll bring a few friends."

"Fine, but I'll have to charge you after that."

"No problem. Another free one will be enough to even the score."

A few weeks go by. It's now November. Business is winding way down now—fewer rentals, more boats being stored, and some maintenance. It's when Johnny normally anticipates closing down for winter—maybe plan a vacation. But not this year.

The Catch!

Life for him has become routine again after several months of personal change and unexpected excitement. Things just aren't as rhythmical as they were for that short stretch after the evening boat excursion with Michael and Ralph. He seems to grow more and more irritable by the day. This is so, despite Dr. Wilson not having returned since his first and only visit to the marina.

He's alone this evening, sipping on his usual cognac as he begins considering his state. *Why do I feel so out of sync? Could it be I'm missing those things that used to bring me easy satisfaction? But do I really want to drift back into those old patterns of living? It's as if a pilot light was lit within me, a subtle flame waiting to be fueled so it can blaze hotter and brighter, torching what was old and lighting the way for the new. Unfortunately, that flame never seems to do anything but flicker.... Just don't ruin everything by letting it go out!*

As a result, he's been ending up in compromised situations. For instance, women. More than ever, he's attracted to them. *On one hand, I identify with what Robin brought to my attention: that a woman in my life might interfere with where I need to go. And that means a place where I feel deeply satisfied. And it sure doesn't have anything to do with sex because I certainly have had plenty of that. Nevertheless, I've still been dating impulsively, based solely on sex appeal, or, more selectively now, having seen something inwardly appealing; then quickly losing interest when the initial attraction doesn't develop into anything near to what I felt for Robin. She's become my gold standard for a woman, leaving me as dissatisfied as ever.*

More Irritation

Then there are sports and 'the guys.' There's been little time for either over the last few months. *Now that I'm less busy, maybe I should plan for something in my den.*

It's the heart of the pro football season and the upcoming Monday Night Football game is going to be between the local favorite New York Giants and the despised Philadelphia Eagles.

Let me do this. Invite the guys over to watch the game. Have a couple of cases of beer and snacks on hand. And I'll invite Michael. Haven't seen him in a while. The last few times he was at the office doing the books, our paths somehow didn't cross. Would he come?

Michael does agree to come and everyone, including Sir Steve and Rabbit, gathers in Johnny's den on Monday night with beer flowing and, generally, loud, raucous behavior the state of affairs. The game starts out very uneven—the Eagles scoring early and often. Disappointment is in the air.

Sir Steve, a diehard Giants fan, tries to change that and enthusiastically quips, "Like Yogi says, 'It ain't over 'til it's over.' Look at the Yankees. They came back this year!"

"He's right," someone else reaffirms. The Yankees had mounted an unbelievable comeback, defeating the Red Sox in a season-ending, tie-breaker game to win the American League pennant, and had recently won the World Series against the Dodgers.

"Sure, the Yankees had a great team," Rabbit says, making himself heard above the ruckus, "You always knew they had the potential."

Johnny grins to himself and shakes his head. *C'mon, Rabbit! You were the one who thought I was a loser rooting for them.*

Nevertheless, nothing goes better for the Giants, and attention strays from what's happening on the TV screen. Alcohol-fueled discussions of a trivial nature then break out and, fortunately, none of them turn ugly. Despite vulgar language, verbal put-downs, and ear-splitting noise, Johnny's buddies manage to keep from getting exceptionally rowdy. No bodies are hurtled across the room.

Eventually, the game ends, and one of Monday Night Football's announcers yawns and says, "Finally!" It's a signal for the guys to leave for home. The time for over-indulgence and rabble-rousing is over. For most, it's time to go hit the sack and get ready for another day of conformity. Within minutes, only Johnny and Michael remain.

I'm surprised at how shell-shocked I feel. I should have known that going back to something like this would seem unreal. Too bad Michael had to endure that. Tonight was a bad idea.

I'm left feeling somewhat mixed-up, between two worlds, desperately wanting to take a leap into the more deeply satisfying one.

So, in a dejected manner, Johnny begins to pick up beer cans around the den. Michael sits silently still holding what remains of his first and only one. Dazed by the evening's events, he's taking a moment to readjust.

Johnny looks over at him while picking up an overturned bottle that has produced a soggy area on his carpet. "How about a shot of cognac, instead?"

"Sounds good," Michael answers, rising to his feet, "but let me help you clean up first."

The two of them work in silence, putting empties back in the cases they came in. And, there's more than one puddle. They go around with paper towels to sop them up.

More Irritation

When done, Johnny sprays a room deodorizer to cover the pungent beer smell.

"Thanks for the help," he says with little energy and proceeds to the bar. Once there he sluggishly reaches below the counter for a decanter and two cordial glasses.

Michael, now seated, looks across the room in the opposite direction. With the others gone and the clutter picked up, his attention is drawn to the darkened display case which houses the heirloom. It has been inconspicuously present the whole time.

"Why didn't you have the heirloom lit up tonight?" he asks.

I knew it! The first thing he says is a direct hit. Nevertheless, Johnny offers excuses. "Glare on the TV. Besides, those guys wouldn't understand things like that."

"Oh? How do you know, if they're not exposed to it?"

"Maybe next time," Johnny sheepishly mumbles as he crosses the room to rectify the situation.

When he turns the light on in the case, the sculpture automatically becomes the center of focus, giving the room a different vibe.

As the light permeates the space around the display case, Michael senses a warming shift in energy, and for the first time that night, a chance for something worthwhile to happen.

After a few seconds of quiet, there's suddenly the distinctive sound of a piano. Michael's eyes go to where it's coming from and see Johnny bent over a small electric keyboard, which has always been there tucked away unceremoniously in one corner of the room. It's a simple melody he's playing by heart. When he's done, he turns to see the curious expression on his friend's face.

"I learned the basics when I was a kid. It's funny how that's stayed with me." Then he smiles what really isn't a smile, but a look of self-deprecation. "Piano lessons weren't for me, though. I didn't like being indoors. I was more inclined to go outside and play." The tone is bitter. "And play I did—all the way into manhood. I've become a playful, charming guy."

Michael doesn't move a muscle. The room, which a short time ago was a chaotic blend of bodies and noise, has shifted to one of silent anticipation. He waits as Johnny raises his hands off the keyboard. Then when the moment feels right, he says in a voice contrary to Johnny's, "That's true. You are. I wish I was so playful and charming."

Johnny makes a face to indicate a miscommunication. "You don't know what I–"

"No, I think I do. You feel like you've pretty much wasted your life so far, right?"

"Pretty obvious, huh?"

Moving awkwardly, Johnny moves back to the bar to finish pouring the cognac.

"Don't you realize it doesn't make sense to look back in a way that isn't beneficial to you in the present?" Michael says as Johnny picks up the decanter. "Being playful and charming aren't necessarily worthless traits if they're used purposefully."

"Purposefully?"

"Toward having a life not wasted," Michael says, making eye contact with him for emphasis. "If you're making a point about having wasted your life, you're obviously interested in the opposite. Isn't that what you're really after?"

Johnny grins reluctantly. "You're amazing!"

More Irritation

"Of course, being playful and charming isn't going to change your life by themselves. It's the intent that makes it worthwhile, or not. If you're only out to bed women, that's one thing..."

This naturally hits home to Johnny as he stands, waiting for more.

"... but, if your charm is genuine and is based on a soul response to something, or someone, then it can't help but reveal the spirit of Love inside you."

Johnny nonchalantly puts down the decanter of cognac without having poured a drop. He's irritated, yet he wants to stay focused on what Michael is saying. "I guess that's the formula for having a life not wasted?" he says flippantly, keeping eye contact.

"You know the answer to that already. It's not a formula. You can't live life as if you're following directions from a textbook. It's a Standpoint you accept through experience, which you seemed to have learned in your search for that," he says, pointing to the figurine, glowing magnificently in the display case.

"You know the Standpoint and that it has to be lived, so others can see where you're coming from and have the opportunity to feel a difference in their lives, too. It's obvious you've lost touch with what you really are. It's important you do what's necessary to get back on track."

Johnny lets that sink in for a few seconds, "Well, maybe you're right. I do remember feeling unusually okay for a while there, not too long ago."

"What happened?"

"A jumble of stuff—Wilson and that mess, not being able to get as close to Robin as I'd like, and so on. Then life just got back to where it used to be."

The Catch!

"You've just plain forgotten."

"Huh?"

"You've let things, events, control you and your thoughts. You've probably even forgotten the sound, that vibratory frequency you stumbled upon that put you in touch with your real Self, the God-Essence that lives us all.

"I know you know what I'm talking about. You felt It. You wanted to find satisfaction beyond the material, and your quest was answered. You have to acknowledge that. You haven't because you never ran with It. You never put It into practice. You never let It set. So, when the first unpleasantness came your way, you let your awareness slip until you're thinking It's gone when It isn't. It's only been misplaced by your mental discombobulation. Capeesh?"

"Oh, I don't know."

Michael then raises the intensity in his voice. "C'mon, Johnny. I don't mean to lecture you. I just want you to be happy within yourself!" he says firmly, without sounding angry. "You know better. I saw the change in you!"

"What kind of change? What do I know, really?"

Michael stands up, shaking his head. The heirloom blazes in its lit case before him, overshadowing the doubting figure of Johnny.

"You know the basics!" he says with increased volume, somehow maintaining warmth in his voice. He then gestures in the direction of the piano. "The basics to play out the melody of life. You've got to move with it, not block it. You've got to act from the perspective that we are not all just men and women living on this planet, but Man one with a Great Power ready to be manifested, day and night. When are you going to be that Man, the One you really are in Essence?"

More Irritation

Michael turns and points to the heirloom. "That's your heritage right there, as your uncle has said. It's there in the inscription. You've caught the Pitch. You know it. Now the call is to sound It by living It. It may seem difficult, but it's worth it!"

Johnny feels the purging heat from Michael's words, realizing his friend cares about him enough not to let him wallow in his own pity.

But Michael has already turned away, on his way out of the house.

"Hold on," Johnny says, his voice resonating with contriteness.

Michael stops upon recognizing that distinctive quality and turns around. With the new opportunity, Johnny once again picks up the decanter of cognac and hastily fills the glasses. Raising them both up, he approaches Michael.

"You're right."

He hands Michael a glass, who takes it and waits.

"Sorry about the bullheadedness. This is all new to me, but I know you're right—I have experienced what you said and appreciate your incredible support." He bows his head and looks up into his eyes. "I've never had a friend quite like you. Here's to friendship."

Johnny extends his glass toward Michael who reciprocates. The glasses touch and a crystalline tone fills the air.

Chapter 20

The Dirty Blue Car

Okay, last set. One... two...three... four... five... six... seven... eight... nine... ten.

Johnny finishes counting to himself, then lowers a barbell down onto the plywood. It's a Thursday evening, a week and a half later, and the little workout area Johnny assembled in the boathouse years ago is getting good use. It consists of a ten by twelve, wooden platform in one corner of the all-dirt floor. On it, cluttered about, are rust-marred weights and rumpled magazines. Also, often moved around for best reception, is a paint-stained, ancient radio ordered from a Sears catalog, circa sometime in the mid-sixties. It's plugged into the base of an adapted light bulb socket that hangs from a cable and is stapled to a nearby wooden post. The bare bulb screwed into it is all that lights the space. And what used to be three milk cartons, laid out in a line with a plank on top, has been replaced with a combination exercise bench and pulldown bar which Johnny picked up at Bradlees the year before. It was a floor model bargain for thirty-five dollars.

The Catch!

Now, with that last set of bicep curls, Johnny's workout is done and he sits down. He catches his breath while waiting for his pulse to return to near normal. He's pushed himself hard, doing at least ten reps and two sets of every exercise with little rest in between. His usual exercise – working around the marina and Sunday ball in the park – haven't amounted to much of late. The coming of winter has curtailed many of the marina activities and it's been a while since he's last participated in a sporting event. His pickup-game friends are well into the touch football season by now, but Johnny isn't ready to get back into that routine. As a result, it's necessary for him to step up his physical conditioning at the boathouse. And he's done just that, getting into possibly the best shape of his life.

After the short breather, Johnny readies himself to leave. Back on goes the old woolen sweater, long stretched out of shape and marred with permanent stains. It's a relic called for only when comfort, not appearance, is the criterion. Over the sweater he slips on a windbreaker, zipping it up and securing the outer snaps. Then he douses the light and makes his way outside. He heads to the parking lot, and when he steps onto its sandy surface, his feet feel how stiff it's gotten from the chilly air.

There's also a determined breeze to contend with. And as he turns his head to avoid the sting of it in his eyes, he notices a dirty blue sedan sitting across the street where a car rarely pulls over. Other than that being an oddity, he doesn't give it much thought as he gets into the *Falcon* and out of the breeze.

Realizing he needs gas on the way home, he pulls off the road into his usual service station. While the attendant pumps the gas (New Jersey doesn't allow self-service),

The Dirty Blue Car

Johnny leaves the car and enters the attached mini-mart to treat himself to his favorite while-the-tank-is-being-filled- pastime, getting a candy bar.

In the warm shelter of the store, he gazes out toward the pumps while savoring his snack. That's when he sees it again—the same dirty blue car. It's now parked on the side of the road near the station. Two men are visible inside, but they are too far away to make out clearly.

Why on earth are Wilson's men still watching me?

Johnny hastily stuffs the rest of the candy bar into a pocket, then goes out to the pumps and pays the attendant. The whole time he avoids looking in the direction of the car. Once in the *Falcon*, he drives back onto the main road. It only takes a glance in his rearview mirror to confirm the blue car is also moving, keeping pace behind him.

This goes on for a mile or so until he pulls into a parking space at a busy roadside diner. Getting out of the *Falcon*, he crosses the lot and up a set of stairs to the front entrance. Once inside, he passes a battered *Please Seat Yourself* sign before selecting a small window table. It conveniently faces the front parking area, which he discreetly checks out while making believe he's scanning a menu. Sure enough, the blue car is now parked in the diner's lot, the two men inside showing no sign of getting out.

In the meantime, a waitress appears and Johnny quickly places an order. After she departs, he glances out the window again and sees a man who seems to be patrolling the lot approaching the suspicious car.

The same scarred man who was outside *Life in the Hood Tavern* is behind the wheel. He rolls down his window.

"You can't park here unless you eat here," the man patrolling says with a Greek accent.

The Catch!

With a grimace, the scarred man turns to Jack whom he is paired up with again, and says, "I guess we eat here then. Let's go."

Once inside, the pair walk past Johnny's table and proceed to a booth further down the aisle where they'll be able to keep an eye on him.

"Well," says Jack as they're seated, "if he's never seen us before, he sure has now."

"What makes you say that?"

"Because who could miss that distinctive puss of yours? Everywhere we go, we get sideways glances."

"The price one has to pay," the scarred man muses. The expression on his face further contorts the deep scar that curves across his cheek from the corner of his right eye to his right earlobe. "By the way, just order coffee."

"How come?"

"Didn't you see what he was eating?"

"No."

"That's right. You were too busy watching people watching me. All he has is a slice of pie."

Within seconds, a high-spirited waitress appears at their table. They place their coffee order, but not before refusing her teasing advice to eat a proper meal. As she walks away, the scarred man watches her shapely legs as she sashays back down the aisle. His justification is so he can get a glimpse of Johnny who's temporarily blocked from view. Then abruptly, she makes way for someone coming the other way. Surprise! It's Johnny brushing by her and looking very intense.

"Uh, oh," the scarred man whispers to Jack. "Here he comes." Both men make like they're examining their placemats.

The Dirty Blue Car

Then two concurrent occurrences get their attention. One is the sound of heavy breathing directly overhead. The other is the presence of two fists firmly planted on the end of the table as Johnny hovers over them with much of his weight on his knuckles. His sweater sleeves are pulled back, revealing the veins and muscles in his forearms still pumped up from his workout.

"All right, you guys," he says in a hushed, fired-up voice. "What's this about? I thought I settled things with Dr. Wilson."

The scarred man, keeping his cool, says evenly, "Why don't you pull up a chair, so we can discuss this civilly?"

Johnny pauses a moment, then looks around for a chair.

In the meantime, the scarred man looks up in the air, then closes his eyes briefly, apparently wondering what he's going to say next.

When Johnny returns with a chair, he sits down at the table's end and crosses his arms on his chest.

"Well?" he asks, looking back and forth at the two of them.

The scarred man is ready, "Wilson just wanted us to keep an eye on you. It's important everything goes smoothly tomorrow night."

"Tomorrow night?" Johnny asks bewildered. "Is that when he's coming back to the marina with friends?"

The scarred man's sense of imperturbability seems to fade a bit. "Ah, yes. I figured you would have known by now."

"Well, I don't. Obviously, you know more than I do. What's up? What's so important that I need to be followed?"

The scarred man grins uneasily, avoiding Johnny's inquiring eyes. Jack stays out of it and looks on expressionless.

The Catch!

"The big operation," the former says.

"What big operation?"

"This is embarrassing. First, we get spotted following you, then we find out you don't know what's going over tomorrow. Tell me this. You did make a deal with Wilson, didn't you?"

"Yeah. I said he could use the boat. That's all. I don't know anything else. What's this big operation?"

The scarred man hangs his head, continuing to elude Johnny's eyes. "Look, we're in a bad position here. Wilson's our boss. If he didn't fill you in, we sure as hell can't. Besides, if he finds out you spotted us, our asses are grass. Why don't you just forget about this? Keep your end of the deal with Wilson and everything will be all right. Go ahead home. We'll just enjoy our coffee, maybe order dinner. It's obvious we don't have any real need to follow you."

"That's right," Jack finally contributes, barely changing his visage. Johnny looks at him, then back at the scarred man who now looks him in the eyes.

Relaxing his arms, he slowly drops them to his sides as he rises from his chair. Then he backs away a step or two, with a lingering stare, before turning around and treading down the aisle.

When Johnny gets home, he sits at the kitchen table. *What should I do? Should I talk to the detective Uncle Gene once recommended? I don't know of a specific crime, but I do know something awfully suspicious is supposed to happen.*

Above him on a bulletin board among an assortment of coupons, cartoons, and other bachelor-related items, still hangs the number for his uncle's contact, Detective Anderson.

The Dirty Blue Car

Should I, or shouldn't I? After a moment's hesitation, he picks up the phone and dials it.

"Is this Detective Anderson?... Oh, he's off duty, then.... Yes. Tell him John Sloper called from Bayonne.... Right, New Jersey.... I was referred to him by my uncle, Captain Eugene Sloper.... All right, I'll try him again tomorrow."

Chapter 21

Dr. Wilson Takes Over

Johnny is on his way to the marina the next day. His intention to call Detective Anderson first thing isn't looking good. He's running late and, unfortunately, a customer is waiting on his arrival. By the time he's helped load his speed boat onto a Florida-bound trailer, it's mid-morning.

The call is meant to be private, but Ralph is now in the office. He's finished taking care of all the outdoor, routine preparations for the day. So, Johnny excuses himself, leaving his dependable employee to service any incoming clientele.

He then takes a walk to a nearby deli with a phone booth just outside its dusty, front door. This time, when he gets through to Detective Anderson's precinct house, a more informed source tells him the detective is out-of-town on an investigation. A message can be left but with no guarantee that a call will be returned today. Johnny leaves one anyway. He requests that the detective call his home answering machine and provide a best-to-reach phone number because he probably won't be in later.

The Catch!

What should I do now? Call the local police? Let me think.... No, no—no go. They'll think it's a preposterous story.... I could use Michael's moral support about now.

He tries calling Michael at home, but there's no answer. *Shoot! He must be on the road working on one of his accounts.*

Should I even pursue this? The contractor's coming today, the only time it fits it into his schedule. Gotta be prepared for that.

After his return to the office, Johnny is kept busy the rest of the day. Mid-morning, the contractor spends two hours with him going over how to convert the office restroom into a bathroom with a shower and a few lockers. This will allow him to go directly to evening events from the office. Then he's occupied with end-of-the-week chores, including payroll. Interspersed, there are a few phone calls and a late-day customer asking about renting a couple of slips for the following season.

Soon enough, it's going on six o'clock, closing time. It's then that a long-time client returns in his own sedan cruiser. He's an older navy veteran, and his deal with Johnny has not only been for slip space, but for cleaning the inside of his vessel each time it's used. His trips are usually prolonged to get away from everything. And, according to Ralph, the messes he leaves behind are worthy of mention in the Guinness Book of Records.

When Ralph sees his boat approach, he groans. He was about to go home. Instead, he dutifully goes out to help the old sailor dock, expecting to spend the next forty-five minutes to an hour doing cleanup. But, when he returns to the office for the usual supplies, Johnny meets him at the door.

Dr. Wilson Takes Over

"Save it for tomorrow. Go ahead home."

"Tomorrow? Are they ice skating in hell?"

"He won't be going out for at least a couple more days."

Ralph is thrilled. "Terrific! So much for expediency, huh boss?"

"No. Expediency is still the rule. Tonight's an exception. You've got yourself a lucky break. Something's come up."

Ralph's demeanor then changes and he gives his boss a curious look. *Even the kid... no—the maturing kid, can see right through me! But whatever the inevitable is tonight, I can't let him be part of it. I've gotta face this alone!*

"I guess that's okay with me," Ralph says with rare reserve, somehow knowing not to ask questions. Then, allowing a concerned smile to appear on his lips, he adds, "Take care of yourself. See ya mañana, boss."

"Okay, Ralph, mañana," he says, as Ralph goes out the door.

Now alone, Johnny remains standing in place, thinking things over. *You know, nothing may happen at all.... Can't think that way, though. Can't be complacent. Gotta remain on guard.*

What if I leave the marina before anyone has a chance to come? Hmm, they could be lying in wait. Or, maybe they're just waiting for me to leave so they can do their thing without me? No, doesn't make sense. Wilson said he'd be back, a foolish thing to say if they were planning to break in? Besides, they'd go nuts trying to get to the locked-up keys without the combination.

At any rate, Johnny still has his end-of-day paperwork to do. *I might as well do it. If something is planned to happen, it undoubtedly will happen, no matter when I decide to leave.*

Johnny doesn't have to wait long. Within a minute after Ralph has left, he hears car doors shutting in the parking lot. Going to the office door, he sees shadows moving around in the early evening, autumn darkness. He's too keyed up to concentrate on how many. And, knowing he can be seen inside the lighted office, is an uncomfortable feeling.

He takes a step back when Wilson is suddenly clearly in view on his way to the unlocked door. In the next moment, the door opens and he's inside wearing a lightweight trench coat, open enough to reveal a glimpse of an extravagant silk tie.

Johnny is then taken aback when he sees a short, but powerfully built, expressionless, Asian man enter right behind the doctor. Wearing a bomber jacket over jeans, his fluid movements suggest training in martial arts. *Scary! Now, I wonder whether it was wise to face this alone.*

"Dr. Wilson, I've been expecting you," he says, trying to sound natural without considering his choice of words.

Wilson winces, taken aback. "You were?"

"Of course. You said you'd be back and here you are. Did you bring more friends?"

The doctor's features display not the slightest bit of cordiality as he continues inside. The Asian man stays by the door and catches Johnny's wary eye. "They're waiting outside while I take care of the preliminaries," Wilson answers, stopping at arm's length from Johnny.

"You should have called. It's too late to take a boat out now," Johnny braves.

Dr. Wilson's voice is ice. "Oh, that's too bad. Let's sit for a moment, please."

"I'm perfectly comfort–"

"Sit!" Wilson shouts forcefully.

Johnny fights to hold his cool as the doctor's demand resounds around the room. Under his shirt, sweat races down his sides. He looks at Wilson, and then at the now, intense expression on the Asian man's face.

In a show of defiance, Johnny takes his time rolling his office chair away from his desk, before sitting down to face the two men.

Wilson then steps up to him and, in an exacting tone, says, "Now, how did you know I was coming this evening?"

"I didn't. I only knew you'd probably come eventually. If I knew for sure it was tonight, I'd have told you to come sooner."

The doctor shakes his head gravely. "Forgive me if I'm not sure whether to believe you. In fact, I'm not sure about you, period—ever since you told me I had been followed for a whole week prior to that episode with your friend, Robin."

"Why's that?"

"Because, if I was being followed, you knew I wasn't working on a medical research project. And maybe you sniffed around long enough to know what tonight is about."

"Hey, I never gave any of that stuff a thought," Johnny says truthfully. "When our heirloom was found, you became a forgotten memory—until your guys came around."

"That's contrary to what we know," Wilson says.

"What *do* you know?"

Wilson moves around now, pacing, with the assurance of a prosecutor who has the goods on a woebegone criminal. "Want to know, huh?"

"Sure."

"I had your phones tapped since last week—your house and this office. We know all about your phone call trying to contact a detective."

Damn!

"How did you get in?"

"I deal with professionals who are good at that sort of thing. You can do a lot with money, my friend."

Johnny has trouble hiding the enhanced disdain he now feels for Wilson. "I should have known I was dealing with a total fraud the first time I saw your drunken ass at that tavern!"

Wilson barely winces, but the Asian man takes a step towards Johnny from where he's stationed. Wilson notices and says, "Stay where you are! I don't care what scum like him thinks of me." Addressing Johnny again, he continues, "Now, my next cause for concern. Why were you trying to reach a Detective Anderson last night?"

Johnny's voice can't disguise how alarmed he is that Wilson knows this, "All right, I did know you were coming today. I caught on to the guys you had following me last night and confronted them. They mentioned about something going down this evening."

Wilson stops his pacing. His look is incredulous for some reason—his assurance shaken, if only for a moment. "So much for secrecy among my men." He shakes his head. "I'll deal with that later."

Taking note of this reaction, Johnny feels his composure coming back under control. "They told me something was brewing, but they didn't tell me what it was about. That's when I thought this funny business was getting too close to home. I thought I should do something about it. That's why I tried to reach Detective Anderson,

Dr. Wilson Takes Over

who was a contact of my uncle's. And, since you were listening in, you know I didn't get through."

Wilson is silent for a moment as if his mind is just catching up to what's been said. "Yes... we knew that. But why were you trying to make calls on a pay phone today when you could have used the office line? Trying to reach that detective again, I bet!"

"I was still being watched, huh?"

A grimace takes up residence on Wilson's face. "Of course, it was especially important to do so today."

"I should have known not to believe the scar-faced guy about not needing to tail me anymore," Johnny says, shaking his head.

Wilson again pauses as Johnny's remark sinks in, then says, "Oh, him...." Then he reiterates with impatient, renewed intensity, "So, getting back to Detective Anderson—were you still trying to reach him today?"

The forcefulness of the question sends a shiver through Johnny. *You're fenced in, but just stay calm and stick to the truth.*

"Yes, but they said he was out of town investigating a case and would only return calls when he could. There was nothing more I could do."

"You're not bull-shitting me?"

"No."

"Who else did you call? You dialed twice."

Johnny shudders inwardly at another private detail about his afternoon that's been exposed. "A friend of mine. He wasn't in. If your spies watched closely, they would have seen that I didn't say anything. I got an answering machine that time. I hate machines. Didn't leave a message."

Wilson's facial muscles relax. Evidently satisfied, Wilson addresses the other pertinent issue bothering him. "Why did you go to a pay phone in the first place?"

"Privacy. The young man who works for me was doing stuff in the office at the time."

Wilson's face softens some more, and he says, as if to himself, "Okay, that's plausible. I think I believe you."

Johnny then dares to speak his mind, "It's obvious I don't know what's going on and I don't intend to know at this point. So, go on with whatever you're up to. Just don't expect me to volunteer my services."

Dr. Wilson, however, decides to tell him who's boss with cool-hearted deviousness, "I don't need your services," he says, emphatically, "because I'm taking over from here!"

A terrifying frequency seems to permeate every molecule in Johnny's body after this proclamation. Then Wilson moves about again, this time jauntily, flaunting his air of superiority.

The next words out of his mouth are enunciated to deliver the greatest effect. "Whether you know it, or not, Mr. Sloper, tonight is indeed a big night. Your boat will take my men out to sea to meet up with a vessel to make a rather large purchase. Cocaine—of superb quality!"

Johnny sees Wilson's eyes light up, similar to how a devil's would in his imagination. "Just what we've been looking for," the doctor continues, "to supplement our stock. Bought for a ridiculous amount, yet minuscule compared to what we'll get back on the street. It's thanks to your generosity in providing a boat that we're able to do this. It just so happens there's ample room on the *Intercept* to carry the new supply—along with the old. You see, it's

Dr. Wilson Takes Over

time to leave Brooklyn and the New York area behind. You can never stay anywhere too long, you know. So, after the rendezvous, the boat will meet us upriver. Then we'll seemingly disappear, but not our operation."

Johnny is stunned. "Why are you telling me this?"

Wilson stops his pacing and stands firmly planted in front of Johnny and looks down on him with all the willful intimidation he can muster. "I don't know. Maybe because I love to see the astonishment on people's faces when they have no control over the inevitable. Besides, you're not going anywhere. We're keeping you under our watch for a while."

Johnny goes pale, realizing his fate is probably in serious jeopardy, knowing what he now knows.

Wilson raves on, "So, for tonight, there'll be someone with you at all times. Then tomorrow you'll be going by train with us to Connecticut. There you'll have to wait a few days while we scoot. But don't worry, you'll get your boat back and nobody will get hurt. That is if you cooperate."

Wilson momentarily turns away from the apprehensive Johnny and glances back at the attentive Asian man, appearing poised to do what's necessary. Then, before even meeting the eyes of his captor again, he demands aggressively, "Now, Mr. Sloper, hand over the keys to the *Intercept*."

Johnny swallows hard and mumbles, "You've got it all figured out, don't you?" *How weak that must have sounded.*

"The keys!" Wilson shouts as loud as he can.

Every molecule inside of Johnny's body is permeated again, and not in a good way. He's never experienced such belittling, arrogant behavior. When the Asian man moves toward them, he senses it with a jerky eye movement, betraying his apprehension. Without delay, he gets up out of his chair. Fighting off the humiliation of defeat, he goes to the key rack, opens it with its combination, and removes the *Intercept's* keys. Dr. Wilson snatches them away in a flash.

The Asian man is now at Wilson's side. Holding the keys out to him, the doctor orders, "Take these to the men outside. Make sure they check the fuel level and damn sure that it's running okay."

Johnny watches as the Asian man gracefully moves his muscled frame out of the office. When the door closes, Wilson focuses his attention back on his captive.

"One more thing to consider," he says dryly. "Just in case you attempt to leave our company too soon, your friend, Michael, and the exquisite one, Robin, will be dealt with without regard to their health. Unbeknownst to them, they're being watched right now by two most unsavory members of my team.

"I don't want anyone to get hurt. I wouldn't go through all this trouble if I did. But when there is no other recourse...."

"Geezus!"

"Oh," Wilson responds with a change-of-pace chuckle, "you really have been innocent of what's been going on, after all!"

Johnny looks at him puzzled. "How did you finally come to that conclusion?"

"The way you said *Geezus* with such utter hopelessness," Wilson says, followed by maniacal laughter.

More than anything, this disturbs Johnny—the doctor's amusement at mocking his vulnerable state. Yet, the resultant sinking feeling takes him to another place and brings to mind Michael.

He said it's necessary to surrender to a Higher Power and allow the Star War's quote, 'Let the Force be with you,' be a reminder of that—remembering that Sound, that Feeling I first felt during the catch…. Of course, It's ingrained in me! I can hear It. I feel It.

Then the *Intercept's* engine starting up can be heard from outside in the quiet evening air. To Wilson, it justifies the villainous smile on his lips, yet Johnny is no longer under his spell.

"Hard to believe," he begins calmly. "A sculpture of significance to me is apparently missing. We look for it and run into a cocaine ring. Was it your stockpile of cocaine that was in the basement of the house in Brooklyn?"

Wilson relishes the question, "That's right, Sloper. But it wasn't enough to take us where we wanted to go. We'd been working on a bigger payoff. Then the opportunity came. It was initiated, believe it or not, the night your uncle was driving me home—when I met with a very important man. That was why I took a taxi to Brooklyn. We were meeting there, the headquarters for our operation. Crazy to think that your uncle Gene got so suspicious, thinking I'd swiped his heirloom."

The doctor lets out another sickly laugh. "What a coincidence that those series of events ended up with you involved. Then you trusting me with your boat!"

"You could have rented a boat anywhere."

"Think, stupid! Why would I show my face to just anyone and cause more suspicion when I can use your boat?"

The Catch!

Johnny takes this in but doesn't say anything. In the silence, the office door opens and the Asian man returns. "It's got a full tank and, as you can hear, it's ready to go," he informs Wilson.

"Good," says the doctor, a morbid, greedy grin on his face. "Tell the others to load the cocaine on, then come back and take Mr. Sloper home!"

Chapter 22

Under Watch at Home

———⋅⋄⋗⋚⋛⋖⋄⋅———

Despite feeling empowered in one way, I know I'm powerless in another. An attempt at being heroic could spell doom for my two friends. The thought of that could be paralyzing. Yet it isn't. Only if I let it be. Complying with Wilson's wishes is the best I can do for the moment.

These are Johnny's thoughts on the drive home while the powerfully-built Asian stranger sits beside him in the front passenger seat of the *Falcon*.

I can only let the scenario play itself out. In the meantime, gotta be prepared to take action should circumstances change.

Dockside, in the gentle waters bordering on the confines of Johnny's Bayonne Marina, the *Intercept* is all lit up in the dark, its engine purring. Wilson is there, and he and Lou, the nicely dressed man from the Brooklyn house, help push it away from its moorings.

As it smoothly heads out into the bay the two men turn and walk back down the dock.

"I kind of thought you'd be going on the boat," Lou says.

"No. Why risk having anything go wrong out there? I'm confident nothing will, but when you're in my position, you learn to steer clear of any possible implicating situations. If something goes wrong, others would go to jail while I'm free to start again. After all, nobody knows my real identity. Not even you."

"And you know, I'm perfectly okay with that."

Wilson senses Lou's weakness, "Of course. The money's been good, hasn't it?"

"No complaints, boss."

Wilson smiles at the respect, "Besides, I've got to talk to the whole gang when we get back to Brooklyn. They're going to have to keep on their toes tonight."

"Hmm. How about this Sloper character? Don't you think he could be trouble?"

"Certainly. You didn't think I'd just let him go, did you?" Wilson says, ridicule in his voice while patting something bulky under his coat. "I'll personally take care of him—away from the city, somewhere more secluded."

Johnny pulls his *Falcon* into his driveway, the Asian man at his side.

I wonder how different events would be if I was settled with a wife and kids at home, a home with cherished loved ones I was bonded with? I guess that's what experiencing real love is all about. I've probably missed the boat on that.

The gloomy pall which has come over Johnny's face suddenly breaks!

Stop it! Don't go there. Having a family might make a pretty picture, but I know dozens of marriages that just aren't that great—Fred's, for example. I'm actually better off alone right now. I'd rather face the consequences of this entanglement of my own making on my own. Besides, I know now that happiness, joy, or whatever you want to call it in the craziness of the '70s, is independent of whether one has a family or not.

Once inside the house, Johnny turns a light on under the watchful eye of his Asian companion.

That's where I'm at right now, and my dangerous-looking companion no longer strikes any fear in me.

As they continue inside, the Asian man, sensing Johnny's cooperative behavior, lets down his guard and looks around.

"Nice place," he says after they arrive in the kitchen.

"Thanks. I try to keep it that way for company," is Johnny's ironic, on-the-light-side reply, accentuated by the look he gives the uninvited guest before him. "How about a beer, or some wine?"

"Never touch the stuff. Got any juice?"

I should have known Mr. Martial Arts is a health nut. Nobody could look like him and not be one.

"How about a V8?"

"V8, huh?"

"I make a wicked bloody Mary with it."

The Asian man sizes Johnny up. "That hard stuff will kill you."

"I know. Moderation is my motto of late."

"Fine. I'll have a V8, but no alcohol."

Johnny grins pleasantly, gets a V8, and opens it with a can opener. For himself, he pours his usual cognac over ice. His guard makes himself comfy. He relaxes with his back against a wall and takes a gulp straight out of the can.

Johnny, too, leans back against the kitchen counter and puts a foot up on a chair. "I'm sure glad I got you over that other, big irritating dude," he says.

The Catch!

The Asian man laughs while Johnny takes a sip of his cognac.

"You must mean Oaf. Sorry, pal. He's relieving me around eleven."

"Oh, that hurts!" Johnny says, almost coughing up the cognac. "I'll just have to humor him, or better yet, sleep while he's here."

The Asian man's bulk heaves as he laughs some more. "You know, you're a lucky fellow. Nothing's gonna happen to you. Just keep playing it cool and nobody gets hurt."

"I guess that's the only choice I have," Johnny agrees. A few hours later, across the street from Johnny's house, a car sits under the shadow of a maple tree, its branches full of leaves showing their autumn colors. The tree filters out the illumination from two street lamps positioned equidistant from where the car is. A lone figure sits behind the wheel in the darkness. He curiously peers through his open driver's door window in the direction of the house.

Suddenly, seemingly from nowhere, a massive arm reaches in and wraps itself around the man's neck.

Within two minutes, the trunk of the car is open and the lifeless body of the man behind the wheel is dropped in. Meanwhile, Johnny is in his bedroom seated at his desk, a telephone to his ear. The powerfully built Asian man sits on the desk next to him.

"I'm going to have to go away for a few days, Ralph.... Yep, something's come up. I'll tell you about it another time.... At least it's a slow time of year.... You know all the procedures from other times I wasn't around.... Yes, he can help and I'll pay you more, like before.... Good! Glad you don't mind. Just promise me you'll carry on the way I would.... Great! By the way, the *Intercept* will be gone for a few days, too. I'll be bringing it back myself.... So, thanks a lot, young man. I know the empire is in good hands. See you soon.... Bye."

After Johnny hangs up the Asian man comments, "Good. No slip-ups."

Moments later, the doorbell rings. The Asian man gets up off the desk and looks at his watch. "Late as usual," he mumbles.

At the front door is a shaken-looking Oaf, the big guy who's harassed Johnny twice in the past. "It's about time," the Asian man complains.

Oaf glances down the hall and sees Johnny still sitting at his desk through the open bedroom doorway. Keeping Johnny in sight, he motions for his accomplice to come in close, then in a trembling whisper says, "Had to kill a man just now."

"What?! Who?" the Asian man asks incredulously.

"Somebody spyin' outside. Not one of us."

"Are you sure? How do you know he wasn't waiting for someone?"

"He was watchin' the house."

The Asian man mutters, "This could be trouble. Are you sure he's dead?"

"Definitely! Heard 'is neck snap."

"What did you do with the body?"

"Put it in 'is trunk," Oaf says, looking wild-eyed. "Never done anythin' like dat before."

"You're all shook up, man. Get control of yourself!"

Johnny observes, but can't hear what the upset is about.

What's going on? Drug business gone wrong? Unfortunately, this Oaf guy is about to spend the night. How's that going to work out?

He watches until the hushed voices regain some semblance of calm. The comparably, mellow Asian man then finally leaves, presumably to go home and rest up before the morning's activities.

As soon as he's gone, Oaf trudges down the hall to the bedroom, eyes on Johnny the whole way. He's one and a half times the size of his predecessor and more menacing, if only for the crazed look that's a permanent fixture on his face. And it's obvious, that besides his usual mean-spirited demeanor, something else is still bothering him.

Johnny can't resist commenting, "Brother, you look like you've seen some trouble."

"Watch your mouth," is the reply, accompanied by the trademark ferocious stare.

"Sorry."

Oaf ignores the apology and plops down on an easy chair next to the bed. The chair creaks under his weight, but to Johnny's relief, doesn't collapse. Across from him is a TV set on a nightstand. Aimlessly, he reaches over to the stand and picks up its remote with clumsy fingers. After some fumbling, he manages to turn the set on.

Johnny watches him and asks, "What time is that train coming in the morning?"

"Early," is his curt answer, eyes fixed on the TV.

Johnny feigns a yawn. "In that case, I'll get some sleep."

"Brilliant idea, buddy."

Johnny slips off his shoes and lays down on his back across the bed fully clothed.

Oaf, meanwhile, is twitchy. Flipping channels on the TV isn't enough to settle him down.

"Hey! Got something to drink?"

Johnny raises his head. "Most of a case of beer in the fridge."

"Take me."

Minutes later, they're both back from the kitchen, Oaf with an open bottle of beer in one hand and an unopened one in the other. They both settle back down in the bedroom—Johnny on the bed and Oaf back in the chair.

"I guess you're not a health nut like your buddy," Johnny says.

Holding up the unopened can, Oaf threatens, "How'd you like to wear this as a crown?"

"I'll take a pass on that," Johnny responds, closing his eyes.

In Brooklyn, unusual activity is happening. The house on State Street is all lit up. In the dining room, the empty China cabinet has been pulled away from the wall and the door behind it is open. Also, the walls in all the downstairs rooms are now bare.

In the living room, there's a buzz of conversation with an anticipatory tone. Up to twenty men mill about, anxious for what's to come. They are dressed in various attire—from street bum, to casual, to jacket and tie. It isn't long before a door opens down the hall, and Wilson strides down toward them with Lou at his side.

A hush immediately sweeps through the room as all eyes are on the doctor as he stops in the middle of the archway between where they are and the dining room.

"Okay, everyone," he says aloud, then gestures toward the open cellar door behind him, "as you know, the day has come. And, as you can see, our remaining stash is no longer here. It's on its way to our new operations center along with," and here he raises his voice in pride, "our soon-to-be biggest acquisition ever."

A pleased murmur emanates from those listening.

"So, we'll be traveling up there to meet it and get ourselves organized. I know you've already established new residences with new identities and have cut ties here.

"Lou, here, has been studying the area and he'll have the street operation in full swing in no time. We know that they're eager to buy, buy, buy and these people have the dough to make us all very wealthy men. When we've exhausted this supply, I don't think there'll be any need for us to work for a good while, or perhaps, ever again."

The others don't hold back their pleasure in hearing this, too.

The doctor's exuberance then turns serious. "However, we may be pulling out not a moment too soon. I had an inkling before and, now, we just received word that there may have been some trouble tonight."

This stirs up grumbling concern.

"Oh, no!"

"What kind of trouble?"

"How serious?"

Wilson shushes them with hand gestures, then says, "It actually could be nothing. Oaf eliminated someone he thought was snooping around. It could have been a Fed. We don't have time to find out."

A groan goes up in the room and someone asks, "If it was a Fed, is the new supply in jeopardy?"

"I doubt it," Wilson says confidently. "The transaction and transport of the new acquisition have been tightly held secrets – even from you – for everyone's own good.

Under Watch at Home

At worst, I believe tonight could just have been a failed attempt by authorities to find out what we've been up to."

"What actually happened?"

"It involves an outside associate we've been doing business with. He's an uptight individual and may have voiced some suspicion in his dealings with us. We currently have him under guard at his house to keep him from doing any other talking. Outside of his house, Oaf spotted someone suspicious sitting in a car and took care of the situation.

"The man we have under guard knew nothing about tonight, prior to tonight, so it's impossible that our plan has been tipped off. I can assure you that this is the case. I was personally with him for part of the evening. Also, gentlemen, I was present to see the initial stage of our plan get underway—quite smoothly if I do say so myself."

Wilson's words and disposition have been overwhelmingly positive, but he knows it's best to instill caution, too.

"So, although our new supply, plus the old, seem safe and on their way, it is conceivable that the Feds may have picked up some of our individual scents. So, making this a clean break out of the area may be crucial. And I know you know what to do. You are all experienced at this sort of thing. Just to reiterate: no cars go with us. When we all leave here tonight, we will go to our respective residences, then when we depart again on foot early in the morning, let's be damn sure we outfox any possible tails as you do every time coming here.

"It's of paramount importance that we totally abandon New York altogether now. Staggering our departures could cost us. It would risk the possibility of one or more of us being apprehended with the extra time they'd have to catch on. You know how integral we are as a team.

The Catch!

"So, if we do our jobs right, we should all be at Grand Central Terminal at approximately 5:45 for a 6 a.m. departure. We'll appear to be nothing more than inconspicuous travelers, going our separate ways. Any Questions?"

Back in Bayonne, the cognac has done its job, relaxing Johnny enough for what he expects to be a peaceful nap, despite Oaf having left the TV on.

However, that isn't to be the case. He restlessly twists and turns from the outset.

At some point during his state of unconsciousness, Wilson shows up in a dream, his face before him, in and out of focus, and moving in and out of distortion. It's an amused countenance, laughing hysterically as these echoed words spill from his lips, "You never would have said *Geezus* with such hopelessness, *you pathetic fool!*"

Then Wilson's voice continues, slowed down and drone-like, "Y o u s a i d *G E E Z U S* w i t h s u c h h o p e l e s s n e s s ... *G E E Z U S* ... h o p e l e s s n e s s ... s u c h a *P A T H E T I C F–O–O–L* a r e y-ou-ou-ou-ou!"

Johnny's body is now covered in perspiration as he sleeps.

Then, later, a new dream invades Johnny's unconscious. It involves Robin, sitting on her bed, her blouse partially unbuttoned as it was when he was last alone with her. Then into the picture enters the uncouth Pete from the Brooklyn house, salivating over her fineness and moving in to satisfy his lust. When Johnny, powerless in his dream, can no longer stand that image, he forces himself to look away to another part of the room. Instead of refuge from that horror, he sees Michael. He's in a corner tightly pinned against a wall by the scarred man, his ripped-apart cheek glistening in the murky illusionary light as he holds a dull and rusty knife to the throat of his good friend.

Now dripping wet in agitated unconsciousness, Johnny suddenly, as if with one forceful act of protest, comes to. Awareness quickly comes to the fore as he raises his back and arms abruptly off the bed into a sitting position.

The awakening is not a silent one. It comes with a loud moan which could have startled a deaf man. Oaf, however, hardly reacts. He just turns his head meekly toward the vicinity of the sound.

Johnny shakes himself to eliminate the residual terror from his dreams, then visually sizes up the situation in the room. Surrounding the bemused-looking Oaf, are about a dozen, scattered, empty beer cans. A couple of hours have passed in which his companion has obviously had a very pleasurable time.

"Looks like you've been partying," he says to the drunken heap before him.

Oaf grins, mirroring his perfectly contented condition. *What a break! He's totally out of it. Gotta wake up fast!*

Johnny gets to his feet. *Don't waste time! Plan as you get ready!*

He goes through the open door to his master bathroom.

Finally showing some reaction to Johnny's wakefulness, Oaf begins to rise unsteadily from the chair he's in and cries out rather mellowly, "Hey-y-y... what's ya up to?"

"I have to see my friends!" Johnny answers brusquely, as he splashes water on his face.

Oaf tries hard to sound gruff as he stumbles across the floor toward the bathroom. "What do ya mean, see your friends? You're stayin' here!"

Johnny steps up to the door opening, wiping his face with a towel. His voice is fiery. "I want to make sure my friends are okay."

Oaf, being thoroughly soused, can't pack any punch into his words. They come out slurred and accompanied by burps. "Why don't you call 'em. You can call 'em, as long as ya watch yur mouth."

Johnny returns the towel to its rack and begins to move past the large mass of flesh in the way. "I'd rather see them in person."

His massive adversary tries to block his path but is too slow and Johnny slips by and over to his closet.

Oaf turns and follows. "Ya can't do that! Got orders to keep ya here 'til morning!"

Johnny opens the door and proceeds to change clothes behind it. "Look at the shape you're in. You think you can keep me here, you badass?" he threatens.

Dressing quickly, he pulls a gold-colored turtleneck knit shirt over a pair of fresh jeans and comes out from behind the door.

Oaf, looking dumbfounded and angry, reaches out to grab him. But, instead, Johnny lurches forward and, with a mighty shove, pushes his surprised attacker off balance. The huge, tottering mass staggers backward, sprawling across Johnny's bed before unceremoniously dropping to the floor.

In a daze, he attempts to get up but gives it a temporary rest as the now revved-up Johnny stands over him.

"I could beat the crap out of you right now," he declares, "but if your boys found out, I suppose it wouldn't be good for me... or my friends."

"Go ahead. See yur friends," Oaf tells him, breathing hard, still on the floor.

"I will, and you'll be coming with me."

"Wha?"

"I'm not going to let you tip anyone off and put me and my friends in jeopardy."

Oaf struggles to his feet, using the bed for support. The effort causes his head to spin and makes him breathe even harder. Nevertheless, he challenges Johnny, "Try makin' me!"

"I don't have to. In case you've forgotten, it's in the best interest of both of us to get to Grand Central together. It is Grand Central, isn't it?"

Oaf relentingly nods.

Johnny goes on, "You'd look pretty sorry to your buddies if I skipped out on you, especially knowing what I know. You could say bye-bye to any cut of the operation due you. And, if I left you here, even if I battered the crap out of you, there's a good chance I'd see repercussions one way or another. However, I'll have to take that chance, if you don't cooperate. So, what'll it be?" he demands, raising his fists.

Oaf has sense enough to know he's in bad shape. "Ya win this time, pal," he concedes and collapses into a sitting position on the bed.

"All right, then. You've got five minutes to pull yourself together. We'll be visiting my friend, Michael, first."

When it's time to go, Oaf, who's still out of it, waits by the front door as Johnny dons a black leather jacket from a nearby closet.

"Hold on a sec," he tells the big man.

The Catch!

Then he retraces his steps down the hall to the den. With a flick of a switch, the heirloom lights up within its showcase. He lingers a moment, the sight of it producing a glimmer of humble satisfaction in his eyes. Then he leaves the room, returns down the hall, and departs the house with his reluctant traveling companion.

Chapter 23

All Through the Night

What an amazing turn of events – Oaf being totally out-of-it – allowing me to do this! And the disturbing dreams—they've helped catapult me out of anything resembling complacency.

Johnny is in his car with Oaf in the middle of the night headed to Michael's Jersey City apartment.

Okay, my confidence and energy levels are both sky-high. Just don't blow it! This can't be a personal endeavor. Remember what the intent is—making sure my special friends, whom I've come to love, are safe and stopping Wilson and his men from poisoning the populace with drugs.

It takes about twelve minutes to arrive in front of Michael's brownstone apartment building in Jersey City. It's in a quiet residential neighborhood with hardly any cars or people around in the middle of the night. He turns off the *Falcon's* ignition. Then he and Oaf get out.

Immediately, their attention is drawn to a slim man staring at them from across the street. He stands inside a bus shelter wearing a dark windbreaker and black jeans.

The way he's shivering is a tip-off that he's been stationed there for some time.

It only takes the man an instant of recognition to come hustling toward them, his hands snugly tucked into his windbreaker's pockets. As he closes in, Johnny detects a nervous twitch in the man's right eye.

"What the hell are you doing here with him?" the man demands of Oaf with a hint of a stutter. The eye twitches more frequently now.

"He wants to make sure his friend is okay," Oaf says, defending himself, speaking very slowly and deliberately to hide how inebriated he is.

The slim man shakes his head and spits on the ground. "If that doesn't beat all! Have you been drinking?"

"Of course not!"

"Well, coming here isn't part of the plan!"

"It beats hangin' around his place all night," Oaf says, careful not to slur.

"I think something's fishy."

Without saying a word, Oaf musters up everything he's got to puff up his thoroughly intoxicated body into its usual menacing pose and glares at the slim man.

It's pretty convincing because the latter backs down. "Go ahead but don't screw this up. Don't let him say anything he shouldn't in there."

"He knows that. Right, mister?"

"Yep. Understood," Johnny confirms.

Moments later, he and Oaf are at the front entrance to the brownstone. Johnny pushes the doorbell for Michael's apartment on the third floor.

It's a sleepy occupant in apartment 3D who embarks from his bed to a kitchen window. From there he sees

Johnny and a huge stranger standing at the main entrance under a porch light down below. Moments later he buzzes them in.

Although the apartment is a walk-up, Johnny notes, as they ascend, the elegance of the all-wood stairwell which is a product of early Twentieth-century Italian architecture.

Glad to see Michael has a decent place to live, considering his ordeal finding one in Manhattan. Could be more modern but it does have class.

The climb is difficult for Oaf, forcing Johnny to stop several times as his companion gets his drunken dizziness under control. When they reach the third floor, Michael is waiting at his door, reasonably awake and totally alert.

"C'mon in," he greets them, not without a look of puzzlement.

Johnny keeps it low-key. "I really can't. I'm in a bit of a hurry."

Michael eyes Oaf, then turns his attention back to Johnny. It takes no time for him to recall his friend complaining about a big, ferocious character who threatened his business a few weeks back. Could this be the guy? The possibility of this makes his pulse quicken. "What's going on?"

"Sorry, Michael. Something's come up—business related. I'll be on the road for a few days."

"Oh?"

"I was already on the way out of town and remembered the concert tomorrow night. Thought I'd better stop by and let you know I can't make it before it slips my mind completely."

The Catch!

Aware that there is no concert, Michael plays along, knowing something is wrong. Putting on a seriously annoyed look, he says, "That's too bad, but where the heck are you going in the middle of the night?"

Johnny takes a chance, quickly declaring, "Connecticut, by train."

Oaf, lacking perkiness, cuts in a little late, "C'mon, Mr. Sloper! We gotta go."

"Yes, do!" Michael says as he continues to play-act "You could have called me in the morning, Johnny."

"Sorry! Leaving now." Johnny says slinking away, then adds emphatically, "Go back and stay in bed!"

On the way back down the stairs, Oaf is seething. "You've gotta watch yur motherfucking tongue!" he warns, so pissed that the words are slurred this time. "Don't worry. You're gonna get yours!"

When they get outside, Oaf puffs himself up again and saunters toward the slim man who meets him halfway in the street. Keeping Johnny in sight, there's a short discussion out of his earshot. A chill goes through Johnny as he wonders if he just put Michael in danger.

"What did you say to that guy?" Johnny demands when they're both back in the *Falcon*.

"I said good night," is the evasive reply. Oaf then reclines his seat and closes his eyes.

"You know my friend Michael has no idea what's going on. He won't be trouble."

"I told ya I told 'im good night."

"Why'd he look ticked off then?"

"Cause I said it pretty nasty. Don't like 'im much."

Hope that's the truth—and I pray Michael got the hint not to leave the apartment.

All Through the Night

After Johnny and Oaf leave, Michael wants to quickly dress and head to Grand Central Terminal, the closest train station for trains going to Connecticut. But then there's the way Johnny told him to go back and stay in bed. It sounded so adamant. He wonders—was it a warning of danger if he should leave the apartment?

So, he stays put but doesn't go back to bed. Not now, anyway. After some hasty consideration, he calls the Jersey City police on his kitchen phone. He explains his suspicion about Oaf, a man whom he supposes was the one who had threatened to destroy Johnny's marina. He keeps the story tight to prevent confusion, leaving out any mention of a Dr. Wilson connection. He ends by mentioning Johnny saying they were traveling to Connecticut by train—supposedly with that same big guy, who seemed unhappy with Johnny revealing that.

The desk sergeant patiently takes it all down and says that police on duty will be warned to keep an eye out for a very big man and a medium-sized one driving around the Jersey City area in a vintage *Falcon* convertible. If seen, they would be stopped and questioned, whereupon Johnny could state the danger he's in if any. Outside of that, he can't be of help. He can't go contacting other police departments in neighboring towns unless he's certain something illegal is happening. Wild goose chases are bad enough, but when it involves other precincts in other municipalities, the backlash of upset can reflect back on him in a very unflattering way.

Michael hangs up the phone, knowing that's no way to leave things. Next, he calls 411 for information and learns there are a couple of trains departing Grand Central for Connecticut before sunrise. It's now 2:15 a.m. But because of Johnny's seeming warning about not leaving the apartment, he stays put on a kitchen chair wondering what to do. About then, in the darkness on the quiet waters of Lower New York Bay, just south of the Verrazano Narrows Bridge, two boats are side by side. One is the *Intercept*. The other is a trawler. Two men stand at the stern of the former as boxes filled with large, plastic garbage bags of cocaine are transported across from the trawler. Similarly, an envelope stuffed with a wad of cash is passed from one man to the other.

In appreciation, after examining the envelope's contents, its receiver says in a distinctive South American accent, "This makes big journey worth it."

The other man points to the cargo transfer going on behind them, and says with a smug grin, "That makes it even more worth it for us."

Meanwhile, Johnny's *Falcon* exits the New Jersey Turnpike and travels east on Route 3 toward the Lincoln Tunnel. The highway curves widely as it begins to spiral downward to where the below-ground-level mouth of the tunnel is. The lit New York City skyline is majestic viewing from this vantage point, but Johnny isn't in an appreciative mood. He looks over at Oaf, instead. He's slumped in his seat, sick as a dog.

After traversing under the Hudson River, it's an easy ride up Tenth Avenue in the dead of night to Robin's West Seventies apartment building. When they arrive, Johnny lets the dozing Oaf know they're there.

Johnny gets out of the car first. Oaf takes much longer. He's burdened with shedding his sleepiness along with a spinning head. Finally, out of the car and on his feet, he pauses, then sheepishly glances diagonally across the street toward the front window of a twenty-four-hour coffee shop. At a table, behind the glass, is a balding man and a discarded copy of an evening tabloid. Almost, as if he has ESP, he takes his attention off what he's been thinking about and peers out. Quickly, the bland expression on his face changes to one of disbelief.

Johnny, having followed the direction of Oaf's glance, observes the look on the man's face and waits. Oaf gives a little wave, but the man just continues to stare without moving.

"C'mon," Johnny beckons Oaf, who looks away shamefully, then begins to wobble slowly alongside him toward Robin's building. Oaf hasn't gone far when Johnny, emotion traced on his face, says, "Hold on a sec." Oaf obeys, and puts on an annoyed demeanor, not saying anything as Johnny stares at the building.

My passion for Robin hasn't diminished. I'm flooded with the feeling of her embrace, so warm and fragrant.

A smile almost breaks out on his face.

So many good moments – stomping around on the beach; walking hand-in-hand in New York; seeing her in a swimsuit, summer dresses, and evening wear – all of them inseparable from the charged sensation of being near her.... Stop with this!

And, quickly, he drops the parade of emotion-filled images.

They just don't figure in with what's going on right now.

"I guess he's been waiting there all night," Johnny finally comments, referring to the bald man in the cafe window.

"Yeah," Oaf responds. "He does nuttin' unless eder you or she does somethin' rash tonight."

Johnny pauses. "You know, on second thought I'd rather not disturb her."

Back in Jersey City, Michael has managed to doze off on the kitchen chair he sits on. His wall clock says 3:15 a.m. when he is jarred awake by his doorbell ringing for the second time tonight.

With blurry eyes, he peers down from his kitchen window at the front entrance of the building. Below, two unfamiliar figures wait for a response.

Michael presses the intercom button by his door. "Who is it?"

Meantime, in Manhattan, Johnny drops his car off at a parking garage on Forty-second Street between Ninth and Tenth Avenues. He and Oaf then head to Grand Central Terminal six and a half long blocks east. It normally isn't a difficult walk, but Johnny is feeling the effects of the long day and night. And, although Oaf is relieved to be out in the open air, moving quickly just isn't in the cards for him. And it doesn't matter. There's still ample time for catching that 6 a.m. train. So slowly, they make their way east to continue their trek across town.

When they get to Eighth Avenue, the next stretch on Forty-second Street ending at Broadway was once considered the pride of the Times Square Theater District, known for its fabulous, ornate auditoriums and first-class musical productions. Names, such as Douglas Fairbanks, Fred Astaire, Fanny Brice, Eddie Cantor, Will Rogers, and the Marx Brothers all played here. However, over the last several decades, the block has receded in importance and its buildings have deteriorated. Now in 1978, it's at the height of its depravity. Legitimate theater owners have moved out and a glut of seedy, pornographic businesses have taken their place. All that remains from that earlier era are the bright neon lights, rendering nighttime to appear bright as day.

Funny—I've been here before, only now I'm seeing it in a new way. The brightness seems to highlight the shamelessness.

Work is going on to restore some of the buildings, yet a disturbing reflection of current society remains. For example, a movie marquee from a resident porno theater boasts to those on the still busy sidewalk of its latest feature *Cindy Loves Coke and Cain*.

That's jarring, especially knowing Wilson's criminal activity is a major contributor to the damaging drug culture running rampant.

Nearby is another adult establishment, offering live peep shows and simulated sex acts. Its marquee flashes *XXX*, which alternates with the neon outline of a naked woman. Yet there's more, and it comes in the form of real people parading on the street at this hour.

One is a drugged-out individual wearing a headdress with a cut-off shirt. His sizeable belly is exposed to the chilly, night air. He repeatedly walks a few paces, then stops, twirling his body and waving his arms with the apparent intent of entertaining anyone who notices.

Another man, older with a straggly beard and tattered clothing, stands on a fruit crate, warning about the end of the world. Most walk by as if he isn't there; some stop to listen or ridicule him.

The poor guy's been at it for years. Hope he manages to get off that crate someday and secure some sort of normal life for himself.

Then there's the more common homeless, some walking aimlessly around, begging for money, others sacked out in doorways under cardboard boxes or huddled against buildings wrapped in rags.

Also about, is a big, nonchalant, black man who strides among everyone announcing out loud, as if to nobody, the names of drugs he's apparently selling.

And, sadly, smiling wearily, is a heavily made-up girl, no older than fifteen or sixteen, looking for a chance to ply her wares of seduction.

Occasionally, these different varieties of human diversification interact, seeming to find solace in some kind of street connectedness.

Johnny observes all of this. *I can't just block them out! They're human beings. Someone, rather everyone, should feel a sense of duty to somehow eradicate this—allow these people to feel whole, whatever it takes.*

Johnny then notices a well-dressed young couple in their twenties strolling hand-in-hand and laughing riotously at the chaos that surrounds them.

They think this pathetic scene is a joke? How can they not be saddened and feel the need for all this to change?... Come think of it, I used to be pretty ambivalent about this myself.

The young man finishes a cigarette at one point and nonchalantly tosses it to the ground, while his female companion continues to giggle as if it's a sign of the pair's superiority.

But Johnny can only observe this rude behavior and keep moving with Oaf. *My priority needs to be on how to turn the tables on Wilson's gang.*

Of course, loud music from boom boxes and traffic sounds, even at this hour, underscore all the visuals.

And to think, I used to groove to the energy here. The decay is eating away at decency.

When they get past the bright lights and wild goings-on and reach the corner of Fifth Avenue, Oaf's brow seems to be fevered. His pace can't get any slower. Around the corner, south of the avenue, are the long, wide steps, leading up to the front entrance to the main branch of the New York City Public Library. Oaf looks over at them and asks, "Wha time ya got?"

"A little after four."

"Need a break," he says, already staggering in the direction of the stairs.

Johnny doesn't object. "Sure, I can use a rest."

It's been a long, weary night, so much churning inside me. Being subject to Wilson and his gang, with no regard for the harm their drugs are doing, and seeing what's reflected in many of the faces on Forty-second Street, is disheartening. There's also the feeling of being held in check by the threat of harm to my friends. Yet, I know I can't go down the road of hopelessness.

He watches as Oaf sprawls out across one of the lower steps. Continuing over to the stairs, as well, Johnny sits down about twenty feet away. Then, just as he's about to lean back and close his eyes in contemplation, he hears a scurrying sound not far away. He looks over and sees a squirrel, which probably wandered over from nearby Bryant Park. It instantly brings back a memory.

It's the 1950s and he sees his three-year-old self, startling a squirrel as he rushes down a hill of rough terrain with tears in his eyes. He had been lost after being led to an abandoned house in the woods by some older boys, then deserted, a despairing situation for anyone that age. Instead of staying put, he found his way out of the woods to the hill, down which he can now visualize himself treading. At the bottom is a busy highway. When he reaches it, the memory takes a rewarding upswing. For a car has stopped alongside the road and two kind middle-aged gentlemen get out and approach him.

The men take him to the nearest police station. There, he remembers sitting on a counter answering questions the best he could. Soon he's in the front seat of a patrol car, fascinated by the big two-way radio and other police paraphernalia inside. All the attention has calmed him down, especially knowing he's being taken home. Then, when the car turns onto a familiar street, he sees his mother as she waits on a corner. As the vehicle gets closer, he can make out the joy on her face as she realizes it's him inside.

It was a look of joy from a state of pure Love. At that moment she had been synonymous with It.

It's a rewarding realization to have come to in the midst of his current dilemma, the feeling, adding warmth to his bones at a time when the chill could easily have brought on the shivers.

That warmth is still with him when he begins to hear retching sounds. It's Oaf. He's gotten up and is throwing up the night's consumption right there on the steps. When he's done, he plops down away from the mess he's made and falls asleep immediately, snoring loudly.

Johnny grimaces, then looks away with detachment, able to hold onto the pleasant feeling he has. Soon, his weariness brings on sleep as well.

All Through the Night

And sleep he does—for almost an hour. Then, out of the blue, while in the cocoon-like comfort of slumber, comes this sharp pain to his side, accompanied by a force that knocks him several feet across the steps. Oaf has just kicked him with all he had.

What the—! I should have known reality would win out.

Several moments go by.

Wait! Don't go there! It's only my wind knocked out. I'm breathing again, but my side...

Johnny places a hand on the painful spot where he was kicked. He then dares to look up in the direction of the malevolent force's origin and sees Oaf standing over him all pumped up. He looks down at the steps, an easier sight to take, focusing his attention instead on the flow of oxygen in and out of his lungs. After a while, he looks up a second time.

Oaf has been waiting for him to regain his senses. Now satisfied, he relaxes the tension in his body and says matter-of-factly, "I feel better now."

Johnny continues to stare at him with a bit of trepidation. Oaf has made his point. Johnny will no longer have any control over him.

Oaf then asks what time it is. Slowly, Johnny arches himself up on all fours and manages to pull back the sleeve of his leather jacket, the pain in his side excruciating.

"What time is it?" Oaf demands again, impatient with Johnny's less-than-speedy responsiveness, tensing up as if he's ready to kick him again.

Johnny has one of the newfangled glow-in-the-dark, digital wristwatches and is able to read its screen in the dark. "It's just after five-thirty," he says, moaning as he speaks.

The Catch!

"Five-thirty! Get up. We need to get there early."

Johnny forces his weight back on his knees, every effort bringing intense pain to his injured rib cage. Then he rises to his feet, not knowing if another blow is coming now that Oaf is back to being himself. But a subsequent, powerful thrust of a limb is not forthcoming despite the eagerness to do so in Oaf's eyes.

Instead, Johnny's adversary says, "I'd smash ya. I'd obliterate ya, scum. Make pulp outta ya, right here." Leaning closer, his jaw inches from Johnny's face, he adds, "Nobody'd ever know you'd once been human."

Then, reluctantly abandoning his offensive front, he moves away, adding, "Unfortunately, I gotta to get ya to the train in one piece."

With this new reprieve, Johnny's already moving into another space, eons from the problems of the world. The kick has helped transition him there.

"C'mon," Oaf urges him now, a dozen feet ahead. "Let's get goin'."

Johnny obeys, the persistent ache in his side making the going tough. However, he's soon up to speed, keeping pace. And, in no time, he's totally disregarding his discomfort.

Because of the changes in his life, the sudden attack and accompanying hate-filled words have not resulted in any type of reciprocal interior reaction. It's actually helped him to withdraw to that Spot that he's come to realize is his Well of Replenishment, a Place synonymous with his authentic Love Nature.

And, in that state, he's able to create a distance from the tangible world, yet, ironically, appreciate it, taking in the beautiful architecture here on the east side of town. The structures before him, including the library, the Chrysler, American Standard, and W.R. Grace buildings—are all exquisite. *Great examples of man at his inspired best!*

The grandeur of their presence brings another memory to mind. It's the time, as a troubled adolescent when he entered an empty church on a weekday afternoon. *What was bothering me, I don't remember, only that I was in a repentant frame of mind. Then, the weight of whatever it was got less as I became awestruck by the church's spacious interior and felt the Presence of a Higher Power encompass me. I wasn't even particularly religious then, yet it made an impression. I forgot about that until now.*

But now is a different time, and the remembrance is powerful enough to bring on another resonating one. It's the sound from the catch—the Aurora Singers performing it one more time in his head!

I can see the conductor and the singers in vivid detail, the charged rush of imagined sound a boon to my walking, the high notes vibrating right through my bones as if I'm right there at Carnegie Hall. And the rhythmic movements of the conductor's arms, so effortless, yet intense, seem to correspond with how my body is moving, the blood coursing through my veins in sync with them.

And, as the last bars play out in Johnny's conscious mind, he and Oaf pass through the doors into Grand Central Terminal.

Chapter 24

The Catch!

It almost feels like this may end well.
Now that the singing has ended in Johnny's head, it's the hallowed tones within Grand Central Terminal that echo in his ears. Most emanate from vendors getting their stands ready for business this early Saturday morning.

Johnny follows Oaf through the generous, high ceilinged, waiting area—ears sensitive, eyes alert, and legs charged. He looks around and takes in the feel of the historic structure, its solidness and obvious durability meeting with appreciation.

They continue on through a more confined area, past some vendors and a subway entrance, to a short, downward-sloping ramp, leading to the main concourse. It opens up to a 125-foot vaulted ceiling over a space 375 feet long by 120 feet wide. The first person in sight is a starry-eyed, young soldier, standing next to a stuffed duffel bag. As they pass, the soldier yawns and Johnny takes notice of the innocence of youth mirrored on his face.

"We're gonna the tickets now," Oaf says, cutting the subtle stillness.

Johnny says nothing and continues to follow him to a short row of people waiting in line. It's the only ticket booth open at that hour. And it's there that he sees his first familiar face. Pete, the gruff-looking man from the Brooklyn house, is second from the end. Dressed slovenly in beat-up jeans and a tattered, brown corduroy jacket, he fidgets in place, looking irritable.

Not wanting to draw attention, Johnny gazes past him at the surrounding viewable area. It's obvious that there can't be more than thirty or so people filling the huge space. *I wonder how many of these are Wilson's men?*

A few minutes later, Oaf pays for the tickets, and as they leave the ticket line, Johnny spots an opening in a side, stone wall that has the word, POLICE, imprinted above it.

Some feeling of security… only, I don't see any cops—anywhere! What would they know of a gang of cocaine hoodlums departing New York, anyway?

While he's taking note of this, he easily spots another familiar face. It comes with a scar. The scarred man is leaning against a wall, smoking a cigarette, inconspicuously checking out the scenario. *He must be wondering if the gang is all here.*

"O'er here," Oaf directs Johnny. And, without hesitation, he follows him over to a wall. Once there, they both lean their tired backs against it, a common practice for those getting ready to board their trains. There isn't seating available outside of the waiting room.

Feeling like he has the upper hand now, Oaf gives Johnny a surly grin and reiterates what the well-built, Asian man said earlier, "Ya got it nice. Coupla comfortable days ta take it easy, then ya get to go home."

Like that's really going to happen. It doesn't make sense. They know I could be big trouble down the road.

Instead of commenting on whether he feels doomed or not, he places a hand on his aching side and says, "I don't think I'll be comfortable until I totally recover from your kick."

"Probably shoulda kicked you again, ya piece of shit!" Oaf says under his breath.

Johnny ignores the insult and stays alert to everything going on around them.

How do I find a way out of this mess? Gotta keep watching for an opening!

Sticking to that plan, it takes only moments to spot the rest of Wilson's men he's familiar with. At the information booth, stationed in the center of the space is Lou, who browses a pamphlet, one of many accessible there. He's dressed similar to when he last saw him in Brooklyn—wearing a cardigan sweater over an open, white-shirt and wrinkle-free slacks. The scarred man's companion, Jack, at the diner, stands out, too. He's in the open, wearing a drab suit, munching on a bagel in one hand and a coffee in the other. The composed man, who accompanied Oaf during a visit outside Johnny's home, is reading a tabloid, also leaning against a wall. He still has his smoker's cough and Johnny can hear it among the other sounds echoing about. His previous guard, the Asian man, is also accounted for. At the moment, he's at an ATM getting cash. Then, of course, there's Wilson, himself, looking very much the part of a respectable traveler, dapper in his full-length, trench coat, standing alone in the middle of the floor reading an early edition of the Wall Street Journal.

The Catch!

That accounts for everyone I'm aware of. Many of the others, loitering around, must be part of the gang, too.

Barely able to contain his pent-up energy, Johnny's body is antsy under his clothes. Oaf picks up on it and studies him bewildered for a few seconds.

A minute, or so, later, an announcement comes over a loudspeaker. A New Haven-bound train is arriving on Track 23.

"Okay. Time to go," Oaf announces. "Track 23."

Track 23 is across the concourse floor, clearly marked above the archway that leads to it. Johnny can see others begin to make their way to it as Oaf takes a few steps, but Johnny hesitates. *I still need a break of some kind. But what?*

"C'mon!"

Johnny begins walking, hanging his head in thought at first. *This is it. No other choice, damn it!*

About fifteen feet later, walking in Oaf's shadow, an unexpected impulse prompts him to raise his head in mid-stride and glance over his shoulder. There, just entering the main concourse, is a slim figure dressed in black. He immediately looks familiar. Then the man's right eye twitches and Johnny instantly recalls him stationed in the bus shelter across from Michael's apartment building.

Of course! The two watching Michael and Robin would also be leaving the city. This could change everything! Is the other one here? He must be. Gotta be!

Seeing this new possibility, he slows his pace considerably and scans the terminal floor—one way, then the other, and back again. His scan stops on a questionable man wearing a baseball cap, his head turned away from him.

"C'mon! Don't have all day," Oaf blurts out. His impatience has amplified the volume of his voice, making it audible to everyone around.

This stirs the curiosity of the baseball cap-wearing man who looks in their direction. It takes a second, but visualizing him with a bald head brings certainty.

The guy outside Robin's apartment! God, I hope both she and Michael are okay! No matter, now there's nothing to stop me from doing something.

Meanwhile, Oaf hasn't been ignorant of how much his voice carried. He knows he has to control the damage and not create a scene, especially with Wilson present. So, he slows down his own pace, enabling him to sidle up to Johnny. He gets in his face so close… *God, his puke breath is unbearable!...* that Johnny involuntarily jerks his head back as Oaf whispers with exasperation, "All right. Take yur time, ya slimeball. Just keep heading to Track 23."

Johnny isn't listening, though. He's turned inward, instead. *Now it's only me at risk. Will there be a more opportune moment, or… No! Can't wait!*

Suddenly on the blank screen of his mind, he imagines Michael right in front of him, shouting, "When are you going to be the Man you really are?!"

In another flash, he sees the leader of the Aurora Singers conducting right in front of him—only, he's not conducting his singers. They're silent as the maestro turns toward Johnny, signaling him to act now!

The impact of the images is like a current of electricity passing through him. It's time to let go and surrender to Something Greater. Then, without a lessening of tension, he feels an infusion of calm, his mind letting go of its grip. There's no longer any indecision. That's when he raises

The Catch!

his head, his whole physical being an expression of that renewed vitality.

They are now within yards of the archway to Track 23. That's when a faint, distinct sound can be heard. It's the swoosh of air brakes as a train comes to a halt on the other side of the archway.

Likewise, Johnny stops in his tracks, his left foot hitting the ground in front of him. And, instead of continuing forward, he's amazed to feel his weight shift back the other way, even though he's willed it. Next, as if watching from some far-off place, he observes his body pivot voluntarily ninety degrees. And, before he can think about what he's doing, he starts to walk briskly toward the Lexington Avenue side of the terminal.

Oaf is appalled. In a panic, he moves quickly after him. In ten paces he's breathing down his neck.

"Whacha doing?" he demands, his voice anxiety-stricken just above a whisper.

"I'm hungry," Johnny says, not knowing what else to say and looking ahead.

Oaf holds back his fury. "Too late fa that. Yuv gotta get on the train now!"

But Johnny keeps walking without saying anything.

By now they aren't the only legs moving with urgency in the great terminal. A whole series of them gravitate in the same direction.

I have no idea where I'm going. Just follow the feeling!

When he reaches a food stand just off the concourse in a corridor leading to Lexington Avenue, he stops and looks around. He can see a discreet semicircle forming around him.

Everything feels so surreal as if an accelerated buzz of impulses is passing through my brain without words.

Suddenly I know—I've gotta stay and face what's challenging me. No running away.

Literally breathing down his neck is Oaf. *I can see him, smell his putrid breath and hear him, yet it's as if he isn't there.*

In total disregard, Johnny turns his back on him and lopes back out to the middle of the concourse floor.

Oaf starts out after him, but Wilson rushes over wild-eyed and intercepts him. "What's going on?!" he demands furiously.

"He's gone crazy!" Oaf wails.

Once again, legs move in concert with Johnny's. The men, who move on them, form another semicircle around the spot where he stops—halfway between the information booth, located dead center in the cavernous room, and the archways to the tracks. It's now deadly quiet, most of the occupants in the terminal now aware of the odd happening.

Johnny just stands there, his back to the archways, and watches Wilson and Oaf catch up with the others, bunched mostly two deep in the human semicircle before him. Then in the few seconds that follow, he surveys the scene.

As his eyes dart from one grouping to another, images from overnight begin to fill his screen of vision. All that was wrong on Forty-second Street brings forth the compassion that's laid dormant for so long in his heart. The drunk, the doped, the destitute, the arrogant – all products of greed, lust, laziness, and the craving for personal power and superiority – all the result of not knowing or ignoring that there's more to Man than just earthly engagement. It's something that Johnny has come to know to be true. Due to his new perspective on life, he can feel the trueness of it pulsating vibrationally from his heart.

It's now clear to him as he finishes his sweeping view of the scene that the improprieties in the world, when seen, can't just be ignored. At the least, he has to deny that they are acceptable to man's True Nature.

It's obvious that outside the terminal, night has become dawn. The sun has risen and New York City is suddenly kissed by its radiant rays. And, as if a switch has been turned on inside the terminal, light streams down on its inhabitants from the huge windows above the floor.

Reassured by the unexpected bath of brightness, Johnny calmly sets his shoulders and tilts back his head. He's ready to do the only thing that comes to him. With his posturing looking very much like that of the family heirloom, he opens his mouth, and with all the unearthly Energy available to him, shouts out into the ethers, "No-o-o-o-o-o-o-o-o-o-o-o-o-o...." It's the denouncement of what all these men stand for. It's the denouncement of his own past life of limits. And it comes with the feeling of freedom of uttering something that resonates with the heart. "...o-o-o-o-o-o-o-o-o-o-o-o-o-o-o!

It's a stunning moment. Everyone in the terminal is frozen. The sound has a quality they've never heard. It catches them off guard, shocking every atom in their bodies.

And when he's finished sounding it, its echo continues. It bounces off the constellations of the zodiac high above. It reverberates through the archways and down the tracks. It sweeps through the waiting area. It rattles the

The Catch!

condiments at the food stands. And, most of all, it stills the assembly of minds before him to the point of numbing all thought.

Everyone stands without moving while the last vestiges of the resounding echo are heard. All, that is, except Johnny, who poises himself to sprint by thrusting his upper body over his feet. Then, with legs churning to build speed, he bolts straight for Dr. Wilson in the middle of the semi-circle.

When the resounding ends, all that can be heard is the impact of Johnny's strides as he hurtles through the space that separates him from the others.

As if in a daze, Wilson slowly recovers from the shock of Johnny's act. He'd lost all sense of perspective as the waves of sound cut irritatingly through his form. He's not sure of anything, other than that the source of that irritation is coming straight at him with a head of steam. His knee-jerk reaction is to reach for the cold, steel object inside the breast pocket of his coat. Placed for ease of use in an emergency, it's in his hand in a second flat and comes out from under cover.

Despite being in the middle of pumping his arms and legs hard, Johnny can see what's happening. *Don't stop! Just keep going, regardless of...!*

Then another figure comes into sight. It's the scarred man, right next to Wilson. Unbelievably, he's reaching in to force the arm with the gun upward. Johnny is just a fraction of a second away as a shot goes off into the air, missing everything. Then, he crashes his shoulder into Wilson like a freight train, slamming him backward with such force that he and Oaf, right behind him, go sprawling to the floor.

Johnny's momentum takes him into the open, free of the semi-circle. *I can't believe what just happened!*

Are there more guns? Am I still in danger?

He keeps on scampering, rounding past the information booth, not knowing what else to do.

From behind him, the scarred man shouts, "F.B.I.!" He stands with his pistol pointed at the two men on the ground.

"F.B.I.!"

"F.B.I.!"

"F.B.I.!"

A series of federal agents reveal themselves with guns drawn among the broken semi-circle. Meanwhile, a stream of New York City cops come rushing out of the opening under the POLICE sign, helping the Feds corral everyone in the center of the terminal floor.

In the confusion and excitement, Johnny's not sure of anything.

Was that 'F.B.I.' being shouted?

To be safe, he continues, jogging now, across the main concourse toward the incline to the waiting area. Suddenly aware of the pain in his side, he groans loudly.

Then reaching for his sore ribs, he never sees the young soldier's duffel bag. As he trips on it, he catches a glimpse of its no-longer-sleepy owner, pulling the bag away too late.

Johnny's impetus then sends him lurching forward off-balance, forcing him to look ahead as he struggles to stay on his feet. In the distance, are the main doors of the terminal that open out to Forty-second Street. Rays of light blind him as they shine through their panes of glass

The Catch!

and make his gold turtleneck glow beneath his unbuttoned leather jacket.

Then, suddenly, something he sees peripherally makes him feel vulnerable. For, out of the shadows, a figure emerges. It's moving swiftly towards him, collision a certain fact.

And, in that unnerving moment, his body goes cold, numb. There is nothing he can do to prevent the impact.

But when the two bodies meet, it's like a caress, arms reaching under his and chests bumping, softening the impact, and slowing Johnny's forward uncontrolled momentum which takes both of them gently down to their knees.

And that's when shouted words become distinguishable. "Johnny, it's Michael! Michael! Are you okay?"

Heat races back into Johnny's body as recognition of his friend registers with him.

The two of them scramble to their feet, Michael making an effort to help him up, then stepping back to view him better.

Johnny is still a bit shaken and looks as if he's ready to bolt again. At the same time, he flails an arm at Michael, his fingertips dragging across his shoulder, as if to prove to himself that his friend is really there.

Out of breath, he says, "It's you. I don't believe it."

Michael is out of breath, too, but he's not at all concerned and his voice verifies it. "Everything's all right! The F.B.I. has everything under control!"

Johnny is dumbfounded. He stands there all ears, slightly bent over, a hand on his sore side, and still tensed for anything.

Michael puts up both hands to calm him and speaks rapidly. "Take it easy. Everything's really all right. The F.B.I is here in force."

"Wha-"

"They caught the men on the *Intercept* in the middle of a drug transaction. They didn't think you were involved but had to be sure. I told them you couldn't be and what you just did should prove you've been innocent."

"You're not kidding me?"

"No. They've been on to Dr. Wilson and his men for a while. They were just waiting to catch them all in the act. Tonight, they were watching when Wilson and his men came to your marina. Then, later, the ones not on the *Intercept* broke away from their tails and the agent watching your house was murdered. They were stumped, but they stopped by my apartment as a last resort a couple of hours after your visit. You had told me you were taking a train up to Connecticut, so they came here and so did I."

Johnny pauses a moment as he lets it all sink in, then steps up, despite his pain, and hugs Michael.

"Unbelievable!"

When they part, they both look back and see the scarred man jogging up the incline holding a gun. The young soldier still stands nearby watching everything with amazement.

Michael sees Johnny cringe in fear and says, "Don't worry! He's an agent, a good guy."

"What? He is?"

"Yes, an F.B.I. agent."

When the scarred man gets to them, he stops and looks at both of them with respect. He huffs and puffs from his

The Catch!

exertions, but between breaths, he turns to Johnny with extra awe and holds up his badge.

"Lorenzetti, F.B.I.... It looks like you're an honest man after all. We had that feeling from the start, but you never can tell. Sorry to have to lie to you the other night. Part of the job."

"I get it, but can hardly believe it," Johnny says.

"I know. It's been a crazy night, but you're free and clear, Mr. Sloper. We'll have to debrief you, but you look like you're in pain."

"A bit. Was kicked in the ribs by the big guy escorting me here. A few may be broken."

Lorenzetti looks at Michael. "Can you take him somewhere to get checked out right away?"

"Definitely!"

"Good." Lorenzetti hands Michael a business card. "Call me after he's seen a doctor. We'll set up a time when all of you can be debriefed, including your female friend."

Then, after taking another deep breath, Lorenzetti looks back at Johnny and adds, "Good thing you gave that train information to your friend here. That was a major break for us."

"If I remember correctly," Johnny says, "what you did was an amazing break for me—coming to my rescue back there!"

"Just doing my job," Lorenzetti says, dismissively. "But you and your friend here," he continues with a voice that takes on extra reverence, "made it easy for us to round up these badasses. This has to be the most awesome moment of my career."

Almost looking embarrassed for being so frank, Lorenzetti gives them a little nod of approval, then quickly

The Catch!

diverts his eyes before saying, "Wilson is no doctor, by the way. His name isn't even Wilson. It's Jeffrey Taylor. He's been in the drug game for quite some time. We finally have the goods on him."

With that Lorenzetti turns on his heels and jogs back to where the captors are all being handcuffed and led away.

They watch him go for a moment, then Michael turns to Johnny as they begin to leave.

"Okay, we're taking you to the nearest hospital."

"We?"

"Robin is waiting outside making sure my car doesn't get towed."

"Really?"

"Really! She still wants to be your friend, you know," Michael says, winking. "You never know what could develop. Capeesh?"

Johnny wags his head in disbelief. "Talk about having special friends. You guys...!"

Just then, the doors to the terminal swing open, and a horde of reporters come storming by them, TV cameras and all.

Johnny watches, fascinated. Michael abruptly tugs on his sleeve. "Let's get out of here."

Johnny yields to his friend's better judgment. "Of course!" Then, together, they leave through the same doors.

Outside, Robin stands next to Michael's car, looking majestic in Johnny's eyes.

It's a beautiful day. Sunlight pours down on the three of them.

Epilogue

THE BAYONNE DAILY NEWS – Sunday, July 27, 1980
<u>Sports Around Town</u> by Tom Burbeck

I caught up with Johnny Sloper and his lovely wife, Robin, yesterday. Johnny is the owner of Johnny's Bayonne Marina, one of the many highlights on our waterfront, and the sponsor of the Hudson County Softball League's newest team, The Motley Mariners. Johnny is also their player/manager.

Tom Burbeck: I'd like to start by saying congratulations on recently getting hitched, Johnny!

Johnny Sloper: It took a long time.

TB: Until the right woman came along, I assume?

JS: Absolutely!

TB: What took so long?

JS: I first had to find out what I am as a man, then be set in being that. During that period, I came to realize that having a mate doesn't make you complete. It's best to be certain that you're already complete within yourself before taking on a committed relationship.

TB: Hmm, not your run-of-the-mill response. Do you agree, Robin?

Robin Sloper: I do. Johnny came to realize what it truly means to live life as Love, something far greater than

The Catch!

ordinary romantic love. We both feel that's essential. How can you wholly love someone else when there's no intention for Love to be your total life experience?

TB: Well, there must be some truth to that. You do seem to be the perfect couple! Now, Johnny, regarding your new team, why did you name them the Motley Mariners?

JS: I like the fact that we're a terrific mix of guys—ethnically, age-wise, and talent-wise. Most of us originally played in Sunday pick-up games at Bayonne Park. Our thing is to have fun playing. If we lose, we still get satisfaction just going at it. Of course, the intent is to win, and we've won our share, considering the talent on the other teams.

TB: Speaking of talent, Bobby Reiss is leading the league in hitting with a .542 average.

JS: You bet! Rabbit, what we call him because of his speed, is a terrific outfielder, too. By the way, that young whippersnapper is the reason I only play occasionally now. He's constantly teasing me about my eroding skills. (Johnny laughs) And, you know, at 41, I think he's right!

TB: That's funny! Tell me about some of your other players.

JS: Sure. The biggest surprise is Steve Zukoski. We call him Sir Steve. He's always been our pitcher, but after losing a ton of weight and working out, he's become our star slugger, too. Then there's my good, banker friend, Fred Cohen. Once an outfielder, he's become a steady presence at third base when he's not loaning me money to finance marina projects. And, of course, there's Michael Jones, a very close friend of Robin and mine, and an exemplary human being! He's right up there with Rabbit in hitting – second in the league – and outfield play.

Epilogue

TB: And who are the others here, listening in while we sit on the deck of your beautiful home?

JS: My Uncle Gene, young Ralph Cheney – my main man at the marina – and my sister, Jane.

Uncle Gene is a recently retired Navy Captain and has been one of the greatest influences in my life. He set me up in business when I was down and out. A year ago, he decided to move back up here from his naval base in North Carolina. Together we built this house with separate living quarters for him and us [meaning Robin and himself] and we've become a close-knit family.

Ralph Cheney—I couldn't ask for a better employee. Despite his youth, he knows the marina business inside and out, having worked for me since he was sixteen. I made him our permanent manager a year ago. Our confidence in him gives Robin and me more free time to pursue our shared interests away from the marina.

And Jane, my sis, has always been a great support to me—in good times and bad. She lives nearby and is a teacher in town whom everybody loves and respects.

TB: Okay, last question—what do you think you need to do to win your division?

JS: Winning is great, but, as I've alluded to, I'd rather place an emphasis on how the guys play. Good sportsmanship is key. I just encourage the players to stay disciplined and do their best.

FOOTNOTE: I was going to edit out Johnny and Robin's comments above about their marriage. After all, this is a sports column. But then I spent some more time with them and what they said had more meaning for me, and perhaps for you, too, the readers of this column. They gave me a tour of their wonderful house and the highlight

The Catch!

was reading an inscription on a breathtaking figurine that they have on display in their library. It gave me a better idea of why these two are what they are beyond the world of sports. Johnny said he had to find out *what he was,* rather than *who he was.* After reading the following, I feel I was able to understand where both of them are coming from, an excellent message for all. With their permission, here it is:

"Catch the Glory!
Catch the Sound!
Stand tall and catch the Pitch,
Know the Love Unbound.
Then be the Pitch
And sound the Pitch.
Be the answer to the Call.
To be Love Unconditional
The Catch is All!

ACKNOWLEDGEMENTS

The Catch! has its origin going back to 1980, writing it by hand on a New Jersey beach. It started out as a first-person, past-tense narrative, but I only got so far with it, not knowing where the story should go. So, I put it aside. Then, after philosopher Kenneth G. Mills became my mentor and spiritual guide, I found a purpose for bringing it to life and the rest of the story began to develop in my head. However, my writing skills weren't where they needed to be and I again put *The Catch!* aside. Then I started writing screenplays, eight in all before I realized it was time to go back to work on *The Catch!* Dr. Mills had once said after reading excerpts that it would be published, which proved to be a great incentive for going back to it. I thank him foremost for not only that but also for all that I gleaned under his mentorship.

Next, Erin McMullan, a talented Canadian editor who helped me improve all my screenplays, suggested the idea of using inner monologue for Johnny in the manuscript. Knowing what he was thinking and feeling throughout allows the reader greater insight into his character. For that and for giving me her general overview of the story, I thank her profusely.

Then there are my friends, the readers, who gave me feedback as I went through draft after draft. John Hoover actually made notes on each of the twenty-four chapters and was very helpful. Stuart Diamond also gave me lots of advice after reading an entire draft. Gregory Serdahl lifted my spirits with his praise after reading just one key chapter. Other readers – Katrine Geneau, John Arciuch, Mary Joy Leaper, Terry Stevens, Lynn Small, and Bruce Philp – all contributed something of value. I appreciate and thank them all because it's a lot to ask of anyone to read a fledgling novelist's first novel.

CPSIA information can be obtained
at www.ICGtesting.com
Printed in the USA
BVHW071813200123
656717BV00007B/383

9 781662 866692